$2.50

P9-CMQ-890

PENGUIN CRIME FICTION

VENETIAN MASK

Mickey Friedman, a former reporter and columnist for the *San Francisco Examiner*, is the author of three previous novels. Her latest novel, *Magic Mirror*, has just been published by Viking. She lives in New York City.

VENETIAN MASK

MICKEY FRIEDMAN

PENGUIN BOOKS

PENGUIN BOOKS

Published by the Penguin Group
Viking Penguin Inc., 40 West 23rd Street,
New York, New York 10010, U.S.A.
Penguin Books Ltd, 27 Wrights Lane,
London W8 5TZ, England
Penguin Books Australia Ltd, Ringwood,
Victoria, Australia
Penguin Books Canada Ltd, 2801 John Street,
Markham, Ontario, Canada L3R 1B4
Penguin Books (N.Z.) Ltd, 182–190 Wairau Road,
Auckland 10, New Zealand

Penguin Books Ltd, Registered Offices:
Harmondsworth, Middlesex, England

First published in the United States of America by
Charles Scribner's Sons 1987
Published in Penguin Books 1988

This is a work of fiction. Names, characters, places, and
incidents either are the product of the author's imagination
or are used fictitiously. Any resemblance to actual
events or persons, living or dead, is entirely coincidental.

LIBRARY OF CONGRESS CATALOGING IN PUBLICATION DATA
Friedman, Mickey.
Venetian mask / Mickey Friedman.
p.   cm.
ISBN 0 14 01.0971 4
I. Title.
[PS3556.R53V4 1988]
813'.54—dc19   87-37466

Printed in the United States of America by
Offset Paperback Mfrs., Inc., Dallas, Pennsylvania
Set in Times Roman

TO JAMES OLIVER BROWN

Les masques sont silencieux
Et la musique est si lointaine
Qu' elle semble venir des cieux
Oui je veux vous aimer mais vous aimer à peine
Et mon mal est delicieux

From "Marie," by Guillaume Apollinaire

(The masks are silent
And the music is so far away
That it seems to come from the heavens
Yes I want to love you but to love you just a little
And my pain is delicious)

PART ONE

PROLOGUE

IN VENICE, at Carnival, a veil writhes and unfolds in the wind. A mask peers out of a dark upstairs window. Voices singing madrigals drift over the next *campo*. All this can happen, even today.

In the six-months-long Carnival of Venice's dissolute eighteenth century, black domino cloaks, tricorn hats, and white masks concealed the unalterable: sex, age, station. The disguised figure could be: a debauched nobleman on his way to the gaming tables, a beautiful nun from a Murano convent hurrying to meet her lover, a servant delivering a clandestine message. Babies wore masks in the arms of their masked mothers. All were equal in anonymity. Recognition of reality was betrayal.

Carnival has been resuscitated in recent years, propped up in the interest of luring tourists during Venice's damp and chilly February, with its frequent shrouding fogs, its almost certain rains, its entirely possible snows, its ever-more-likely *acqua alta*, the high tide that covers the Piazza San Marco with a sheet of frigid water from the encroaching Adriatic. During the ten days before the beginning of

Lent the streets of Venice are choked with people, many in costume but many others drably, if sensibly, dressed in down jackets, with cameras slung around their necks. The Piazza echoes, not with the strains of the Venetian *furlana*, but with rock music loud enough to rattle the domes of the Basilica. Wine bottles smash on the ancient paving stones. At lunch counters harassed waiters wearing paper hats serve pizza after pizza.

Venice sinks, its beauty peels away in the poisoned air, and its Carnival is reduced as are all its glories. Yet in Venice, at Carnival, even today the wind catches a veil. Figures wearing red robes glide across the choppy, gray-green Basin of San Marco in a gondola. A Renaissance noblewoman, her skirt hem edged with pearls, shrugs out of her cloak. Such moments are dilations, entrances to a Venice of the imagination.

Venice has at times been a starting point—as it was for Marco Polo—but it has more often been a destination. Many Venetian stories begin elsewhere.

As does this one.

SALLY ALONE

THE COLD OF THE STONE parapet seeped through Sally's coat as she leaned staring at the surging waters of the Seine. A barge pushed laboriously past, then a glass-sided sightseeing boat, its top deck damp and empty, a few bundled-up tourists huddled inside. The sky was lowering, almost as dark as the water, and the wind rattled past the shuttered stalls of the dealers in old books and prints that lined the quay. It chilled her face until the bones ached. She gazed at the leafless trees, the towers of Notre-Dame, the stone facades of this city she hated so much.

By now, Brian would have called Jean-Pierre. She imagined Brian in the hallway where the phone was, sitting on the backs of his heels and leaning against the wall the way he did. Would he be laughing with relief, his earlobes pink, or would he be serious, concerned? *I don't know how she took it, Jean-Pierre. She just walked out. I'm really worried about what she might do*. And Jean-Pierre would be worried, too. Except maybe they were speaking French, the way Brian liked to, with Jean-Pierre correcting every other word. The thought made her sick.

The wind whipped tears into the corners of her eyes, but she wasn't crying. She pulled her knit hat farther down over her ears. In Tallahassee, it was eight in the morning now, the day just starting. Pale sun lay on the white buildings around the capitol, sifted through Spanish moss, warmed the red brick and ivy of the state university. It was cold in Tallahassee in January, but never cold like this. In Tallahassee, it's only eight in the morning and this hasn't happened yet. In Tallahassee, it wouldn't happen at all.

I don't know what she might do, Jean-Pierre. What am I going to do? Sally's feet were so numb she could hardly feel the sidewalk under them. She turned away from Notre-Dame and continued along the Seine. When they'd come here last fall, Brian had taken her on this same walk. His voice hoarse with excitement, he had read from his green Michelin guide to Paris—facts, figures, bits of history she immediately forgot. She was passing the Conciergerie now. Up ahead was the Pont-Neuf, with its statue of some king on a horse.

What was so great about this stuff, that it was worth skipping lunch and trying to talk to people who couldn't understand you and stepping in dog shit for? She'd finally gotten him to stop for a sandwich, or what they called a sandwich here—a huge hunk of bread split in two, and one thin slice of ham in the middle. No mayonnaise or mustard, much less lettuce or tomato. She'd been looking out the café window afterward, and Brian asked her what she was thinking. When she'd said, "I'm watching the dogs go to the bathroom," his face closed as if she had insulted him personally.

He was going to law school. That was the understanding when they got married. The word "Sorbonne" had never been mentioned before the wedding. He had sent off applications, gotten accepted. She had her brand-new degree, her elementary education credential. Then he saw a notice on a bulletin board on the way to class, or overheard some conversation, and from then on it was the Sorbonne and nothing else.

At the Pont-Neuf, she crossed to the statue. Henri IV. That's who it was. She stood directly in back of the horse's hindquarters and stared at its muscular bronze rump. I'm looking at myself. A horse's ass. Because if I had any sense at all, I would've seen this coming, somehow.

A real horse's ass. Yet she had never understood or foreseen anything Brian did, so why should she have foreseen this? She had been amazed that he asked her out for the first time. He was so handsome and she, she knew very well, was nothing special. She had been amazed when he wanted to marry her. She had been amazed when he decided to come to France. Why shouldn't she be amazed now?

The only thing is, I wish he hadn't brought me so far away from home.

She bent her head against the wind and continued down the quay.

BRIAN AND
JEAN-PIERRE

JEAN-PIERRE'S THROAT pulsed as he watched Brian thread his way through the smoky, crowded café. Brian was slim, with loose golden-brown ringlets that fell over his forehead. Apollo, Jean-Pierre thought. Michelangelo's David. And then cursed himself for thinking of Brian in clichés. Brian is Brian. Brian is Brian, and that's enough. Jean-Pierre was dark, with brushy black hair and a pouting underlip. He had often thought that when he and Brian were together they looked almost like Typical French Student and Typical American Student.

Brian couldn't possibly be anything but American. Jean-Pierre had seen it in that first blinding moment in the courtyard of the Sorbonne, had known even before Brian stopped him and asked, in halting, absurdly accented French, the way to one of the lecture halls. Jean-Pierre's lips curled a little now, as he watched Brian's rangy American walk.

Brian stood beside Jean-Pierre. When Jean-Pierre felt Brian's hand squeeze his shoulder, he swallowed and looked down at his empty coffee cup. *"Bonjour,"* he said.

"Bonjour." Brian slid into a chair next to Jean-Pierre, pressed his palms together, and rested his face against their edges. "God," he said.

The Café du Coin was on the Boulevard St. Michel, in the Latin Quarter. It was brightly lit, loud with scores of discussions. Waiters rushed by with trays, slopping beer or coffee on the tabletops when they slammed down glasses or cups. Jean-Pierre had introduced Brian and Sally to the group here, at a table across the room from where he and Brian were sitting now. Bringing Brian into the group had given Jean-Pierre an excuse to see him regularly.

The first encounter had not gone well. Jean-Pierre had tried to explain in advance to Brian about Tom and Tom's significance, but Brian hadn't seemed impressed. When it became obvious that Brian knew next to nothing about the student revolt in Paris in May of 1968, Tom had raised his eyebrows at Jean-Pierre. Jean-Pierre flushed and saw Francine and Rolf exchange smiles.

Even worse had been Sally—pale, freckled, brown-haired, wearing jeans and a strange, shapeless sweater with a motif of geese in flight. Jean-Pierre remembered his dismay when he met Brian's wife. Not only because she was too plain-looking for Brian, but because when Jean-Pierre first saw Brian in the Sorbonne courtyard, he had felt—everything. Everything he felt now.

Brian was slumped in his chair, his gaze unfocused.

"It was bad?" asked Jean-Pierre.

"It wasn't fabulous." Brian shook his head. "I don't understand her. Anything about her. How her head works, anything."

Jean-Pierre tried to suppress his jealousy. He didn't want Brian to worry about understanding Sally. Brian's knee was near his side. Jean-Pierre patted it, he hoped consolingly, and felt his own muscles weaken at the touch. "It will be all right," he said.

"Yeah," Brian said. "I could use a coffee."

When he finished his espresso, Brian looked at Jean-

Pierre for the first time since he sat down. The pupils of his eyes were huge. "I did it," he said.

"Yes." Jean-Pierre sat forward.

"I had to. It wasn't fair. It wasn't possible."

"Of course." Jean-Pierre's face was burning. "You've just begun to explore what you are. It's the beginning of a voyage of discovery. It's exciting—a miracle, really." He loved to explain these things to Brian.

"That's right." Jean-Pierre's square, short-fingered hand lay on the table. Brian picked it up and brushed his lips over Jean-Pierre's knuckles.

Jean-Pierre couldn't speak for a moment. Then he burst out, "Brian, I'm so impatient to be with you always!"

Brian sighed, and Jean-Pierre felt immediate, bitter regret for his words. "I've still got some kind of responsibility to Sally," Brian said.

"Of course, of course. You mustn't worry at all—"

"I can't just dump her here in Paris. She has to figure out what she's going to do." Brian's jaw was set, almost pugnacious.

"Naturally, naturally." Jean-Pierre nodded vigorously. "What did she say?"

"Nothing. She just got up and left."

"Nothing? Surely she—"

"Not a word."

Jean-Pierre was baffled. Sally was very strange. Then he thought, Sally might run away back to the States. Today. Or she might kill herself. He was surprised and ashamed at how much these ideas appealed to him.

"You never liked Sally," Brian said, and cut off with a gesture Jean-Pierre's protest. "But there's a lot to Sally. She's a good person, a really good person. She thinks about things, too. Don't imagine she doesn't think about things."

Jean-Pierre forbore to mention how Brian had often raged against Sally—her obtuseness and insensitivity and even, he seemed to remember, her stupidity.

"Sally doesn't deserve to be hurt," Brian said. His face was morose.

"Certainly not." Jean-Pierre's tone was a little more brisk than he had intended.

After a moment, Brian looked around. "You haven't seen any of the others?"

"They were going to be at Tom's. I'm sure they're very curious by now."

Brian smiled. His eyelids drooped. "They'll have to be curious a little longer," he said.

"Why is that?" said Jean-Pierre, and held his breath.

Brian's smile widened. "There's something we have to do first."

Jean-Pierre closed his eyes until the first wave of joy subsided. "All right," he said, and wound his scarf around his neck before going out into the cold afternoon with Brian.

AT TOM'S

MAYBE BRIAN chickened out," said Tom. His raucous laughter filled the room.

Francine didn't glance up from Jean-Paul Sartre's *Being and Nothingness*. Rolf smirked as he lit another cigarette, but said nothing. Only Olga, Tom's wife, called from the kitchen, "What's so funny?"

Tom stopped laughing. He didn't like to include Olga in the group's business. Usually she wasn't around, because she was at her research job at the Pasteur Institute. Today, of all days, she was home with the flu. She put her head around the door. Her short gray hair stuck out wildly where she'd been lying on it in bed. "Did you say something?" she asked.

Tom shook his head. "No. Nothing."

She glanced at the others. "I'm making tea. Does anybody want some?" When nobody replied, she disappeared into the kitchen again.

Tom poured himself more wine. In his forties, he was twenty years older than the other group members, his disciples. At first, when the fervor was fresh and his book was just out, disciples had been easy to get. Tom sometimes wondered, more frequently as time went on, what different turn his life might have taken if he hadn't been at the Sorbonne when the French student revolt broke out in May 1968. He could've been home in the States, he could've been in Vietnam, but he'd been at the Sorbonne. He'd known nothing about French politics, but he'd jumped in with both feet because he was young, and it had been exciting to dig cobblestones out of the streets and lob them at the *gendarmes,* and stay up all night in strategy meetings where he couldn't understand half of what was being said.

Tom would never forget the electricity, the intoxication. Luckily he'd had the good sense to keep a diary. The published version had made a nice splash in both the United States and France. Even today, when the French put together a solemn May '68 retrospective on television, complete with the pontifical bullshitting they did so well, Tom and his book, *From the Barricades,* were always mentioned, although these days Tom wasn't often asked to participate.

May '68 was a long time ago now. Tom hadn't gotten seriously into anything since. At first it hadn't mattered, because there had been plenty of people around who were willing to hang out in the cafés and talk. Hanging out in cafés talking was what Tom liked to do, and it finally occurred to him that it might be the basis for a career. He would take some of the people he hung out with and study them. That's how the group had begun. Tom would have liked to have chosen them on the basis of particular traits, but by the time he'd gotten the idea nearly everybody had drifted away. After a lot of changes, he'd ended up with Jean-Pierre, Francine, and Rolf. Olga had her laboratory; they were his, although they didn't know it. Tom kept meticulous notes. He would watch them, experiment with them. When the time was right, he would produce a work —he was uncertain of the form it would take—to rival, even eclipse, *From the Barricades*.

Tom watched Francine as she shifted her position on the couch, her eyes still on her book. Her heavy breasts, unfettered under her sweatshirt, moved and resettled. Her thighs strained at the red corduroy of her trousers. Tom hoped to try some experiments with Francine when the time was right.

The room was stuffy, overheated. Books and newspapers overflowed the brick-and-board shelves and covered every surface. The apartment, in a modern concrete box near the Tour Montparnasse, was barely big enough for Tom and Olga and their teenage son, Stefan. Tom really had no place to do his work.

Rolf had been glancing at yesterday's issue of *Libération*. He put it down and stretched his thin arms over his head. "I'm off," he said.

"No!" Tom whirled toward Rolf too violently. "We agreed to wait," he said, striving for a reasonable tone.

"We *have* waited," said Rolf. He stood up, blond and wraithlike in the cold light from the window.

None of them knew much about Rolf. They deduced that he had spent some years in the States, because he occasionally referred to New York, Boston, Denver, or other places. He never said anything about where he had been before that. His English was perfect idiomatic American, spoken with a slight, indefinable accent. Tom had met him at the little bistro where Rolf worked as a waiter and had solicited him for the group because he thought Rolf had an interesting outlaw quality. Tom sometimes referred to Rolf as the Man of Mystery. If they were having a discussion and Rolf was silent, Tom would turn to him and ask, "What does the Man of Mystery have to say?"

Tom said, "Come on, Rolf—" and Olga walked in carrying a teapot and mug on a tray. She was wearing a blue quilted bathrobe with a tattered tissue protruding from one pocket.

"I'm going back to bed," she said. "I ache all over. Every muscle. Sweetheart"—she turned to Tom—"if

14

you're going out, pick up some oranges, would you?"

Tom scratched deeply and ferociously in his beard, which was black with gray. "Oranges. Right," he said in a neutral tone.

As Olga left, Rolf picked up his brown leather aviator jacket and started to put it on. Tom wanted to grab the jacket away from him. Instead, he said, "Rolf, listen. This is important. It's something we were going to see through together, all of us. I mean, we saw it start, we saw it grow—"

"And when the time comes, we'll probably see it end," said Rolf. He was arranging a yellow wool scarf around his neck, crossing it meticulously in an X over his chest.

"Maybe so. But that doesn't make it less important." Anger throbbed behind Tom's eyes. He hadn't wanted Brian in the group at all, much less Sally. Those two had been Jean-Pierre's doing, but to reject them would have been to lose Jean-Pierre. With so much time and energy invested, Tom had had to make the best of it.

Rolf zipped his jacket. "What are you going to do when they arrive? Sing 'Here Comes the Bride'?"

Francine closed *Being and Nothingness*, marking her place with her finger. "Don't act like an idiot, Rolf," she said, her French-accented voice husky. "You understand very well what Tom is talking about." She shook back her dark, frizzy hair. She had brown eyes, a faint mustache over her top lip.

Rolf smiled slowly, coldly. "I understand what he's talking about, and I've waited half the afternoon, and that's long enough."

Francine put her book down and stood up. She walked to Rolf, slipped her arms around his waist, pushed her pelvis against his. "Oh, Rolf. Don't go, Rolf," she said in a playful entreaty.

Rolf's face flushed. He put his arms around her and bent to make gobbling noises against her neck. She shrieked with laughter, and the two of them took a few staggering

15

steps and collapsed on the couch, where they rolled, giggling, in breathless mock battle.

Tom took his glass and moved to the window, looking out over the leafless trees, the curving gray mansard roofs, the billboards advertising Renault, Coca-Cola, Credit Lyonnais. He shivered. Francine's screams were subsiding into softer cries. The doorbell rang.

MADAME BERTRAND

SALLY HAD GONE back to the apartment, finally, because she couldn't think of anywhere else to go. The weeks that followed passed in numbing cold. She put on layers of clothes and took long, aimless walks, or lay on the couch listening to the yapping of Bijou, the excitable fluffy white dog that belonged to Madame Bertrand, the concierge.

Sally believed Madame Bertrand knew what had happened. Whenever Madame Bertrand pulled her lace curtain back to peer at Sally as she crossed the courtyard, Bijou barking frenziedly inside, Sally thought she detected scorn in the way she dropped the curtain and turned heavily away, back to the big black-and-white television set she watched all day.

It seemed to Sally that her own body was disgusting. When she bathed in the deep, claw-footed tub, she averted her eyes from her small breasts with their anemic-looking nipples, her skinny, bluish-white flanks, her unappetizing light-brown triangle of pubic hair. No wonder Brian had fallen in love with a man. Although, really, she couldn't convince herself that Jean-Pierre's stocky body would look that much better than hers.

Brian continued to live with her, although he spent much of his time with Jean-Pierre. His attitude toward her varied from extravagant concern to exasperation. When he was exasperated, he spoke in distinct, measured tones.

"What I'm asking you, Sally, is what you think you might want to do."

Gazing at the knuckle of her right thumb, she said, "I don't know."

She felt him lean toward her. "Well, what do you *want?* Can you tell me what you *want?*"

She knew the answer to that one. Raising her eyes to his, she said, "I wouldn't mind having a friend."

His face contorted with pain, and as she looked down again, she felt a flicker of satisfaction.

He wanted her to keep seeing the group, asked her constantly to participate in whatever they were doing. Sally didn't know why, unless he felt guilty at leaving her by herself so much. It certainly wasn't because she liked the group, or they liked her. They didn't even seem to like each other very much, although they were together constantly. Sally supposed they were together because of Tom, who used to be famous, although Sally was uncertain what he had been famous for.

"There was a big student uprising, and a general strike and everything. Tom was right in the middle of it, and he wrote a book," Brian had told her. Sally knew he was parroting Jean-Pierre.

"Did they overthrow the government?" Sally asked.

"Well, no. I mean, I don't think so."

Sally had resisted the temptation to say, "Then who cares?" but Brian must have seen it in her face, because his jaw tightened and he turned away.

On the few occasions when Sally consented to join the group, it was horrible. Francine, when she addressed Sally at all, was condescending. Tom made elaborate attempts to bring her into the conversation. Rolf stared at her with an intensity she didn't understand. Jean-Pierre, completely tongue-tied, jumped to pay for her Coke, her *croque-monsieur,* her ticket to the movies. Sally said almost nothing. She sat watching Brian, thinking how much she hated him.

Mostly, Sally was alone. She walked along the gravel paths of the Luxembourg Garden, under the leafless trees, past the ice-crusted ornamental pool, the gray-gold stone Luxembourg Palace, and deserted tennis courts. Even on the coldest days, a group or two of old men in black berets would be there, bent over a checkerboard.

The other people who were always there were mothers who brought their toddlers to play. The red-cheeked children were bundled until they could hardly bend in their snowsuits, brown high-topped shoes and knit balaclava helmets, miniature scarves knotted around their invisible necks. Sally sat on a green metal chair and watched them as they stumbled around in the gravelly sand. One day, a tiny, pink-suited figure put a steadying mitten on Sally's knee and then, startled blue eyes saying she didn't know Sally, withdrew the mitten fast, tumbled to the ground and crawled rapidly away.

Brushing at the grit the mitten had left on her knee, Sally started to cry. She cried all the way back to the apartment building, where she stood in the courtyard, head bent and nose running, without the will to go in and face the roaches in the kitchen, the rock-hard end of yesterday's *baguette,* the emptiness.

Bijou's muffled barking sounded suddenly louder, and glancing at Madame Bertrand's apartment, Sally saw that the door was open. Madame Bertrand stood on the threshold with Bijou, his black eyes bright, in his usual paroxysm at her feet.

Embarrassed, Sally wiped her eyes and started to move, but Madame Bertrand beckoned to her. When Sally approached, with Bijou's yaps reaching a crescendo, Madame

Bertrand stood back and ushered her into the apartment.

Madame Bertrand had swollen ankles and wore a loose dress and backless black felt carpet slippers. She didn't speak English, Sally knew. She motioned to Sally to sit down in an armchair in front of the television. Images slid across the screen—black figures on a white background. Sally sat. The chair was still warm from Madame Bertrand's body.

Madame Bertrand moved slowly to a cabinet, and Sally heard the glass clinking. Bijou, now silent, settled beside Sally's chair. The French commentary on the television babbled on. The program was some sort of ice-skating exhibition.

Madame Bertrand handed Sally a glass containing two inches of golden liquid that smelled like fermented apples, then lowered herself to the edge of a straight-backed chair and turned her attention to the television. Sally sipped, and blinked as the brandy slid down her throat.

Feeling awkward, continuing to sip, she watched the flickering screen. Bijou gave a faint, whistling snore. A man and woman glided onto the ice together and began to skate to fast, brassy music. They spun and jumped. He lifted her over his head and she touched the ice again smoothly, flawlessly. Then the music slowed and they drifted far apart across the ice, not looking at each other, but making the same gestures, spinning at exactly the same rate with one leg extended.

They would have to know each other so well, Sally thought. They would have to know each other so well. The tears started again, and left warm tracks down her cheeks as she and Madame Bertrand watched the couple on the screen.

TOM EXPLAINS

ONE DAY TOM came over to see Sally, to have a talk with her. He was sick of Sally and privately wished she would get the hell back to whatever part of the American boon-docks she had come from and take Brian with her. From the beginning Brian and Francine hadn't liked one another, and that had skewed the group. Sally hadn't done anything disruptive, but just sat there like a blob. Worst of all, neither of them understood, the way Jean-Pierre, Francine, and Rolf understood, how important May 1968 had been.

Tom had offered to talk to Sally some time ago, but Brian had forbidden it. Now, several weeks after his confession to Sally, Brian admitted he was at his wits' end, completely fed up. The group sat around and planned what Tom should say.

"She's got to understand that it's not *her*," Brian said.

Francine snorted. "You're being absurd. Can't you *act?* Sartre would say—"

Brian ignored her. The sleeves of his plaid wool shirt were rolled up, and the café light picked out the golden hairs on his arms. "It wasn't Sally at all. It was Jean-

Pierre," he said. He turned to Jean-Pierre, sitting beside him.

Jean-Pierre was very serious. "That's so," he said. "We would have fallen in love no matter what she was like."

Rolf drained his beer. "What she really needs is for someone to show her a good time in bed," he said.

Brian reddened, and he said, "I resent—" at the same time Tom said, "Well, I'm not volunteering for *that*."

Brian stood up abruptly and said to Tom, "Tell her whatever you want to. I don't give a shit." He grabbed his jacket and stalked out with Jean-Pierre trailing in his wake.

Rolf grinned. "Something I said?"

"Honest to God, Rolf," Tom said, but his irritation faded. He didn't need their advice. He knew what he wanted to tell Sally.

When he got there, though, he found that talking to Sally wasn't as easy as he'd imagined. It was like talking to a lump of dough. Her light brown eyes hardly changed expression, no matter what he said.

"You're hurt, yes," he said, being as agreeable as possible. "But try to look at it from Brian's point of view. He didn't intend or want to hurt you. There are times in life, Sally, when hurt is inevitable. You just grit your teeth and take it. And you know what? It strengthens you in the end."

He thought he saw Sally swallow a yawn. He used his annoyance to increase his intensity. "Brian has to work out his destiny," he said. "It's his duty to be what he is. Anything else is a sham and a lie."

Sally didn't seem to be listening. She was staring past Tom's shoulder so fixedly that he glanced back to see what was so interesting. His gaze fell on a little clock on a table behind him, and he realized she must have been straining to see the time. As he turned toward her again, Sally sneezed several times in succession.

Tom steadied himself and offered her his crumpled handkerchief. When he started to talk again, he was drowned out by the honking of her blowing her nose. When she had finished, and energetically wiped the tip of her nose, he took a breath. He looked at Sally. He slowly expelled the breath and stood up. "I hope you'll think about this conversation," he said.

"Okay." She proffered his soggy handkerchief, which he delicately replaced in his pocket.

By the time he reached the street, he felt better. He had made some good points. He guessed he had given her quite a bit to think about.

THE BEGINNING
OF THE GAME

THE GAME was first mentioned on a freezing midnight. The table at the Café du Coin was littered with empty beer glasses, foam drying on their sides, and greasy plates that once held *croques-monsieur*. Outside, wind pulled at the folded awning with a tearing sound.

Conversation was awkward because Francine and Brian had quarreled an hour or so earlier. The two of them fought frequently, but this incident had been even sharper than usual. Tom was afraid Brian would drive Francine away. Tom was uneasy about her, in any case, because he had gotten her into the group under false pretenses. He'd been on a panel at a poorly attended seminar. Francine approached him afterward and asked if he'd met Jean-Paul Sartre during the student revolt. Tom hadn't known then that Sartre was Francine's hero, but there had been an interesting hunger in her eyes, so he'd said yes.

Her look had changed from hungry to ravenous, and Tom had since had to do some fancy footwork to keep up the fiction that he and Sartre had been slightly acquainted.

So far, he had gotten away with it.

Then Brian had come along and started twitting Francine about Sartre all the time. The latest disagreement had been the worst yet. After some preliminary fencing Francine had gotten furious and said, "Naturally, an American schoolboy couldn't be expected to understand Sartre. It's too intellectually demanding."

Brian, lounging back, countered, "Come off it, Francine. Where Sartre is concerned, you don't know your ass from first base."

At the sight of Francine's suddenly pale, still face, Tom had been certain that she was going to walk out and, goddammit, he'd have to start over again with somebody else. To his surprise, she didn't leave, but retreated into forbidding silence. Now, a tendril of hair wrapped around her finger, she was reading *Being and Nothingness*. Tom was trying to talk with Brian and Jean-Pierre, both of whom were yawning. Tom's voice was hoarse, but the close call had unnerved him, and he was anxious that the group not break up for the night. "Try looking at it from this angle, then—" he was saying, when a figure with a warty, bright green rubber head and staring, bloodshot eyes appeared at the table.

"Prepare to meet thy doom," said the figure in a threatening voice.

Tom gave a start when he looked up and saw the weird face, and Brian and Jean-Pierre started to laugh. Francine glanced up from her book. "You don't have to put on a mask to convince us you're a monster, Rolf," she said.

"Grf, grf, grf." Rolf capered about menacingly and bumped into a passing waiter. Brian and Jean-Pierre howled with mirth, pounding their fists on the table.

Tom recovered himself. "God, your appearance has improved. Did you get a haircut, or what?" he said to Rolf.

Rolf peeled off the mask and tossed it onto the table, then dropped into a chair. His bony face was flushed. "I found it in a garbage can on my way here from work. It kept my face warm." He called to the waiter, "Jacky! *Un esprèss'!*"

Brian wiped tears from his eyes. Still chuckling, he said to Tom, "You looked like you thought you *were* about to meet your doom."

Tom was defensive. "Jeez, Brian. *You* glance up unexpectedly and see something like that and see how *you* react."

"I did. And I knew right away it was Rolf."

Tom scratched his beard, his fingers moving rapidly through the thick, wiry hair, as Francine said, "Of course you knew it was Rolf. We know Rolf, so we knew it was Rolf."

Equilibrium restored, the reanimated conversation swirled through several rounds of espresso. Could one person know—really know—another? Jean-Pierre and Brian said yes. If you were close to another person, as they were close to each other, you could without question know that person completely, even to the most secret depths. Rolf said that, on the contrary, if the self existed at all, it was completely unknowable to others. Francine spoke of Being-in-itself and Being-for-itself. Tom nodded at everything as if he knew the answer, but refused to take sides. The bulging eyes of the mask stared up through the smoke at the ceiling of the Café du Coin.

It was probably the presence of the mask that suggested the idea of going to Carnival. They would go to Venice, dress in costume, and test their knowledge of one another. As the notion took shape, Tom's blood surged. Here, after all these years, was a chance to find the focus he had needed.

Everyone except Brian had heard of the Venice Carnival, but no one had actually been to it.

"Carnival comes just before Lent. You dress in disguise and have fun and say good-bye to the pleasures of the flesh," Jean-Pierre explained to Brian.

"You say good-bye by indulging them like crazy," said Rolf.

"You mean it's like Mardi Gras in New Orleans, or the Carnival in Rio. Not a traveling amusement park with rides and things," Brian said.

"Mardi Gras! Exactly." Jean-Pierre nodded encouragingly.

Once Brian understood, he became enthusiastic. As the discussion progressed, he began to insist, without much support from the others, that Sally be indulged.

"Of course she has to be there," Brian said. His voice was loud, almost strident. "Don't you see it may be our only chance to find out what she's thinking."

Tom saw pain on Jean-Pierre's face. He watched Jean-Pierre brace himself in his chair, as if preparing for a blow.

After a while, when the discussion began to wind down, Tom wrote out the rules of the game:

"One. We will go to Venice for the end of Carnival, traveling separately and staying in separate places, except for Sally and Brian." ("If I don't go with her, she certainly won't agree to come," Brian explained to Jean-Pierre.)

"Two. Each of us, in the coming weeks, will secretly assemble a costume. The costume must cover face and body, with all outstanding physical features disguised. Through our costumes, each of us will try to represent his own, most private concept of his inner self. This can be conveyed in any way that seems right to the wearer. It is forbidden, however, to dress in your regular clothes and say your everyday appearance is your true self.

"Three. At an appointed time—probably the day before Carnival ends, when Venice is sure to be crowded with thousands of masked revelers—each of us will put on his costume and remain within a hundred yards of the foot of the Campanile in the Piazza San Marco for half an hour.

"Four. We will try to identify one another.

"Five. We will discover, through this means, whether we know each other well enough to recognize how each of us

27

would describe his own true self."

"Et voilà." Tom put his pen down with a flourish. The others bent over the notebook to check the text.

After a few minutes, Francine sat back. "Suppose we recognize someone, or think we do. What then?"

"Let's see." Tom thought. "We ought to have a system of challenges. Say, Francine, you wanted to dress as—as an Earth Mother—"

Francine's lip curled with obvious scorn, and Tom said hastily, "It's just an example. Anyway, in that case, you'd wear a long robe or something, maybe a headdress with fruit, and flowers twisted in your hair—"

"And everybody thinks she's Chiquita Banana," said Rolf.

Tom went on, "So then the person would challenge you. He'd have to name what you're dressed as and say something like, 'Earth Mother, are you Francine?' Or, you know, Ceres, or something in the ballpark—"

"But then that person is giving away *his* disguise," Brian objected.

Brian was right. They lapsed into silence until Jean-Pierre suggested an alternative. They would circulate, observe, note their guesses on paper. At the end of the half hour they would meet, unmasked, at a prearranged place. When they arrived, they would show their papers immediately. This was to prevent cheating, although, of course, no one would cheat, since that would cancel the point of what they were doing.

Everyone agreed, and Tom scribbled down the procedure. Then he said, "That's important. No winners and losers. It's an experiment, not a contest."

"Another thing," said Francine. "Speculation and jokes about what costume a person might choose are forbidden. Starting now."

All were in accord on her stipulation, but it left them nothing interesting to talk about. The gathering broke up soon afterward.

28

SALLY'S DISGUISE

No," SALLY SAID. She was lying on the couch staring at a wavery brown water stain on the wall. She had looked at the stain so much she had begun to see an outline of the state of Florida. She could pick out pretty much where Tallahassee was. In Tallahassee, in the springtime, you saw the redbud first—deep pink blossoms delicately furring branches that had seemed bare the day before. Then dogwood. She remembered walking with Brian under the dogwood trees in the evening, looking up at the streetlights through masses of white-petaled flowers. After dogwood, azaleas—

". . . difference if I said it meant a lot to me?" Brian was saying.

Rain pelted the window. A shutter was banging somewhere with a desperate, angry sound. Sally's head was so heavy she could hardly turn it to look at Brian. "I don't want to," she said. She wondered how many times she'd have to tell him.

"Sally—" Brian lowered his face into his hands. His fingers were long and well shaped, the veins in his hands not ropy or prominent, but smooth, delicate blue. "I don't know how this happened," he said, his voice muffled and cracking.

Sally had never seen Brian cry, and she didn't want to. Flutters in her stomach came together and congealed in a ball of anxiety. She couldn't think of anything to say. She didn't want to go to Venice, to dress up in a costume representing her true self, whatever that meant, and play a game with Brian's friends.

Brian raised his head and there *were* tears in his eyes, quivering and about to overflow. One spilled. He brushed it away with a knuckle and said, "It's the last thing I'll ever ask of you."

What if he broke down and sobbed? She thought she would go crazy. She stared at him. The other tear spilled. He wiped it away, then pressed his fingertips to his eyes and drew a deep, quivering breath.

"All right," she said, and was immediately overwhelmed by self-loathing.

Brian rushed to Sally, bent over her, and gave her an awkward hug. As he released her inert body, he said, "You're a wonderful person."

Maybe she could go to Venice costumed as a Wonderful Person. Brian went on talking, trying to get her to be enthusiastic. His eyes were dry now, and she began to wonder if he'd manipulated her, crying to get his way.

After he left, she continued to lie on the couch. The rain drummed, the shutter banged with repetitive fury. In the dim, musty-smelling entrance hall of her grandmother's house on Brevard Street, next to the elaborately carved hall tree with its misted mirror, hung a faded print. As a little girl, she would stand on the seat of the hall tree and look at it. It showed two columns topped with statues, and in the background an elaborate building with arches along its sides. Standing near the columns were people dressed in weird costume—long capes, white masks, and three-cornered hats. At the bottom of the picture were the words "In Old Venice."

In Old Venice. She drifted, dozed. A particularly heavy gust of wind threw what sounded like a bucketful of rain against the window. She sat up, wide awake. She had figured out her disguise. She would go as a corpse.

JEAN-PIERRE
IN THE RAIN

JEAN-PIERRE'S UMBRELLA was worse than useless. Not only was it not keeping him dry; he had to fight to prevent it from turning inside out. Clutching it with both hands, one gripping the base of the spokes, he stared up at the light in Sally and Brian's apartment across the courtyard. Water curled down behind his ears, dropped off the end of his nose. His shoes and trousers were sodden.

He wasn't sure why he had followed Brian. He had known well enough that Brian was going back to his own apartment to talk to Sally about Carnival. Why did he wait until he heard the tiny metal cage of the elevator descend and then, trembling with haste, fumble himself into his raincoat, pick up his umbrella, and rush down the stairs in time to see Brian turning into the street?

Brian, hunched inside his hooded yellow plastic poncho, had never once looked around, never noticed Jean-Pierre following at all. That bothered Jean-Pierre, because he felt that surely, surely, if Brian were following *him* so closely, he would feel Brian's presence. That's why he wasn't worried about their experiment in Venice. No matter how heavily disguised Brian was, Jean-Pierre would feel his presence.

But what if Brian didn't feel Jean-Pierre's presence? How ridiculous they would look, the great lovers whose perfect harmony could be duped, misled by a cheap costume! Jean-Pierre flushed. It couldn't happen. He and Brian would know one another. Yet here was Jean-Pierre, only a few yards from Brian's bright yellow back, and Brian obviously felt nothing and had no idea.

Brian had been talking with Sally a long time. Wind tugged at Jean-Pierre's umbrella, and he redoubled his hold and turned the top toward the blast. No doubt Sally, with the stubbornness her listless attitude masked, was refusing to go to Venice. Jean-Pierre hoped Brian wouldn't convince her. He wouldn't try very hard, surely? Squinting through the rain, Jean-Pierre caught his breath. Brian had crossed in front of the window and bent over. Jean-Pierre saw just the top of Sally's head as Brian embraced her.

The pain and nausea that swept over Jean-Pierre made his grip loosen on the umbrella, which immediately turned inside out. Cursing, his eyes stinging, he let go of the abominable thing and watched it fly down the street like a crazed, crippled bird and lodge itself at the base of a chestnut tree.

His knees weak with shock, he leaned against the stone post at the entrance to the courtyard and raised his eyes again to the window. No one was visible.

Brian had touched Sally. He had crossed the room specifically for that purpose. Had he actually kissed her? The thought made Jean-Pierre dizzy. He didn't think Brian had kissed her. The whole thing hadn't lasted long. A few seconds, at most.

Yet, they could be kissing now. Lying together on the faded green couch in their shabby apartment, tasting each other, their hands exploring. They could be laughing, clinging, pressing close to one another, completely unaware that Jean-Pierre was out there in the rain, completely unaware that he existed at all.

Standing with his eyes fixed on the window, Jean-Pierre knew he couldn't bear this pain. He had to know. He would knock on the door. If they were naked, embarrassed, so be it. If Brian felt shame to see Jean-Pierre, to realize the hurt he had caused, so be it. Jean-Pierre was readying himself to march across the courtyard when Brian walked out of the building.

Jean-Pierre was horrified. Brian mustn't see him. He turned in the direction opposite to the one he thought Brian would take and sprinted down the street, his footfalls creating huge splashes of water. When he reached the corner, he risked a quick glimpse back. Yes, there was Brian's receding back, unmistakable in the poncho. Breathing heavily, Jean-Pierre clung to the metal pole that supported the streetlight. Brian was probably going back to Jean-Pierre's apartment. Jean-Pierre would say nothing about what he had seen. In fact, what had he seen? He wasn't sure. He had to think about it, to think about everything.

Jean-Pierre's raincoat was soaked, and his clothes felt clammy underneath. Brian would be surprised not to find him at home. Jean-Pierre would stop for a quick coffee, buy a newspaper. He would tell Brian he went out for a coffee and the newspaper, and his umbrella was destroyed, so he got soaked. They would laugh together at Jean-Pierre's bedraggled appearance. Weakly, Jean-Pierre started off in search of a café.

TOM SPECULATES

TOM POURED HIMSELF another cup of coffee and stared out at the rain. God, Paris in January. He'd been through—he figured it up—twenty goddamn Januaries in this town, and every year it seemed to get worse. He knew when he and Olga were first married there had been clear, sunny winters. He remembered distinctly walking through the Tuileries with Olga on a clear, bright day, with Stefan in a stroller. No leaves on the trees, and Olga was wearing a red wool scarf she used to have, so it was winter, all right. Stefan in red, too. Hat and mittens. But the point was, the sun was shining. Bright. He shoved the spread-out newspapers aside and sat down at the table.

The apartment still smelled like garlic from last night's spaghetti sauce. He didn't know why that depressed him, but it did. That, and the rain, and the crumpled newspaper beside his hand, and—

He should work. He had an afternoon clear, for once. The thought made him tired. He'd drag out his notes, get organized, and then about the time he got going, Olga would be home from work, so pleased that he was going at it again, and Stefan wouldn't believe a word of it, would look at him with something Tom had begun to identify as contempt.

It was a bitter irony that Tom, author of *From the Barricades,* should have a son like Stefan. At the age of fifteen, all Stefan cared about, literally all, was getting a good score on his *baccalauréat* exams in a couple of years so he could be accepted in one of the *Grandes Ecoles,* the top schools. Other people's children had ideas, protested, argued, wore strange clothes, and cut their hair in funny ways. Not Stefan. Tom would have loved to argue ideas with Stefan, but Stefan never had the time. Stefan was—well, in Tom's day you would've called Stefan a grind. Stefan was a grind, and a French grind at that, despite the fact that his parents were American. Stefan spoke French better than he spoke English, played soccer when he played anything at all, and wouldn't know a football if one hit him in the head.

Tom sighed. At least he had the group, and the trip to Venice. He had a focus now, as he'd had in '68. He would observe, make notes, and at last write up his conclusions about—

His conclusions about—

He didn't have to draw formal conclusions. He could write his observations, as he had in *From the Barricades*.

But to write observations, you have to have something to observe. Something has to *happen,* so you can observe it.

The game. The game would be revealing. Tom had no doubt he'd be able to identify the others. He smiled at the thought of their amazement. They were sitting around a table in some Venetian trattoria, laughing, unmasked. Rolf, the Man of Mystery, was in a black cape and black slouch hat. The conventional Jean-Pierre was a conventional Pierrot, the sad clown, with a black-and-white satin clown costume, a skullcap, a fat tear painted on his cheek. Brian was a Renaissance prince, ambiguously beautiful, in green velvet bound with gold braid. Sally—Sally was a barefoot hick, wearing overalls, a straw between her teeth. As for

Francine—well, he couldn't help thinking of Francine as an Earth Mother, even though she hadn't liked the idea. He saw her full, luxuriant body in a semitransparent white shift, garlanded about with leaves and flowers and fruit. Her hair was dressed elaborately with berries and blossoms. He focused on every aspect of her costume. She'd be wearing nothing underneath, so you'd see the outline of her thighs, the slightest tightness in her nipples.

He shifted his position in the chair. She'd been scornful of the idea. Better think of something else for her.

And for himself? The obvious thing, the first that had leapt to mind, was Socrates. He wondered if it were too obvious. Socrates the teacher, leading his disciples to wisdom step by step. Socrates, willing to die for his beliefs. Socrates, with his unsympathetic, nagging wife—although, Tom had to admit, Olga wasn't unsympathetic, really, and she didn't nag. Tom didn't have much in common with her anymore, that was all. Anyway, Socrates— the only thing was, Socrates was gay. If Tom himself dressed as Socrates, would it be taken as a declaration on that level as well? Because understanding as he was of Brian and Jean-Pierre, he would never—he didn't have the slightest interest, ever.

Except maybe with Brian. Just once, out of curiosity.

He shook his head and rubbed his hands across his face. Then he drank off his coffee, got up, and poured himself another cup.

That was the problem when you had somebody around who was as handsome as Brian. You forgot sometimes that he was an ignorant, snot-nosed kid. The group had been completely off balance since the romance between Brian and Jean-Pierre started, and this was no time for the group to be off balance.

Tom should work, but he felt a little shaky. If he went to the Café du Coin, somebody might be there, even though the weather was so rotten. He went to find his jacket and umbrella.

AFTERNOON AT
THE BISTRO

ROLF PICKED UP the plateful of picked-over bones from in front of the florid man in the gray suit. The bistro had been only half-full for lunch because of the weather. It had hardly been worth it for Louis, the owner, to call Rolf to substitute for the regular lunch waiter, who was sick. As far as Rolf was concerned, it was as good a way as any to spend a rainy day.

The florid man was smoking a cigar. The smell had reached every corner of the small dining room, and smoke hung unmoving above the tables. A young couple with a camera and a green Michelin guide gave the florid man dirty looks in between bites of *canard aux olives*, the day's special. The man was oblivious. Rolf grinned to himself. Americans. Californians, maybe. He addressed himself mentally to the woman: *You might get away with that anti-smoking crap in California, but this is France, baby.*

The woman turned her head and looked dolorously out the window, then made a remark to her husband. Cursing the weather. *Why the hell were you stupid enough to come to Paris in January, anyway? It ain't the Bahamas, you know.*

She looked a little like Sally, but prettier. Brown hair, freckles, across the nose, but where Sally's hair hung past her shoulders with no particular style, this lady had a very chic cut. Sally was so plain, so provincial. She reminded him—she really reminded him a lot—

Rolf raised his eyebrows in an inquiring expression and approached the gray-suited man. *"Dessert? Café?"*

"Un esprèss'," the man grunted, slobbering on his cigar.

In the kitchen, picking up the espresso, Rolf noticed that his hands were sweating. He'd had to leave America because of women like Sally. There were a lot of them there, those trusting, unsuspecting sorts of women. He had gotten angry sometimes that they were so stupid.

The United States was very large, fortunately, and a young man of twenty, twenty-one, could go wherever he pleased. He could live in university towns, work at jobs like this one, find roommates to share some bug-infested garret, find women.

The cup rattled in its saucer as he set it in front of the man.

It hadn't been good, after a while, not good at all, and Rolf had thought it best to come back to Europe, where things would be different. How odd that things were not very different at all. He was working as a waiter, hanging out with students, and—Sally was a lot like the others.

The American couple had finished eating. As Rolf picked up the plates the husband was saying, "I'm going to have an asthma attack if we stay here five more minutes." To Rolf, he said, *"L'addition, s'il vous plaît."* Rolf nodded and glanced at the woman. She looked nervous. Probably wondering if her husband had pronounced everything right when he asked for the check. *Dump this asthmatic jerk and come with me, baby. I'll give you a visit to Paris you'll never forget.* He saw her naked, writhing, gasping.

Somebody like Francine you could approach with all sorts of ideas and hell, not only did she go along with you, she contributed a few wrinkles of her own. When neither of them had anything better to do, Rolf and Francine got together and had a pleasant enough time. Yet the edge wasn't there. The edge that came from adding in shock and outrage and, to be honest about it, fear. It was tricky, though, because if a woman's fear excited him, it was likely also to spark his rage. A situation like that was difficult to balance, and that's why he'd come back to Europe.

The Americans were already struggling into their raincoats, and the husband was glancing impatiently at Rolf. Rolf deliberately turned his back and, in leisurely fashion, began to add up their bill. The Venice trip would be diverting. He was thinking of going as the Devil. An attractive Devil, carrying a pitchfork that branched into penises. He was sure he'd have no trouble recognizing the others. Francine would be a whore in black net stockings; Brian, a naughty little boy in blue satin knickers and a starched white Peter Pan collar; Jean-Pierre, a big dog slavishly drooling over Brian; Tom, some witless, has-been revolutionary waving a tattered banner and shouting an outmoded slogan.

Tom was ridiculous. Rolf had been interested at first, because he'd heard of Tom, and had even read Tom's book. Now, he thought he should have checked out of Tom's stupid entourage long ago. He didn't know why he hadn't.

Sure he knew. He'd stayed because of Sally. When he first saw her, he got a jolt that made his mouth go dry. Which was all the more reason to get out. After Venice, he would for sure.

Sally's costume? Against his will, he saw Sally wearing a schoolgirl's plaid skirt and a prim white blouse with a ruffle around the collar. He saw her eyes start to open very wide.

"I don't know what you have to do to get a check around here," he heard the American man saying in a loud voice.

Rolf finished adding the numbers, folded the paper and put it on a saucer. Blandly, he placed the saucer at the American man's elbow. The woman was talking in a low, agitated tone. Rolf heard her say, ". . . don't do things exactly the way we do at home, that's no reason to—" before he moved off.

It was midafternoon. The remaining diners chatted desultorily over empty coffee cups, the dregs of the wine. The florid man stubbed out his cigar, and the American pulled a credit card from his wallet. Rolf wandered to the window. It was still raining.

FRANCINE'S
HANDIWORK

FRANCINE, her tongue clamped between her teeth, spread paste-soaked newspaper over the roundish blob of papier-mâché in front of her. In this weather, it would take a long time to dry. She brushed hair from her forehead and sat back to study her work, looking from the blob to the photograph in the book beside her. The shape, the roundness, was good. She hadn't gotten the nose right, though. And speaking of noses, she hadn't solved the problem of how she was going to breathe.

She'd worry about that later. First, get the shape.

Finally, she thought she had it. Especially the profile. Sophie, the sixteen-year-old daughter of the family from whom Francine rented a top-floor maid's room, was hanging around, bored because of the rain. Francine pointed to her handiwork and asked, "Who does that look like?"

Sophie studied it gravely. "I don't know."

"Come, Sophie. Look at it."

Sophie picked at her underlip and said, at last, "I don't know. Really, it looks like a goblin."

"Sophie!" Francine picked up one of the small Indian-print

42

pillows from her bed and hurled it at Sophie who shrieked with laughter and screamed, "A goblin! A goblin!"

"You're an idiot!" Francine yelled, ducking the pillow that sailed back at her. "Don't they teach you anything at your silly school?"

"Not about goblins," Sophie gasped, and laughed hysterically until Francine had to laugh, too. They were still giggling when Sophie's mother called her. Sophie's mother preferred that Sophie not spent a great deal of time with Francine.

After Sophie left, Francine looked closely at her creation. It would be painted, of course, but it seemed to her obvious, despite Sophie, that this could be nothing but the head of Jean-Paul Sartre.

She had already bought a man's suit and tie at the flea-market at the Porte de Ouen. She'd pad herself with pillows to achieve the correct body shape, carry a cigarette, and—there it was. Sartre, the symbol of her true self.

Francine had known immediately that she would go to Carnival as Sartre. Since first reading *Being and Nothingness* she had felt a mystical connection with him. When others had said *Being and Nothingness* was dense or difficult, Francine had not agreed at all. Francine had felt that Sartre was speaking directly to her.

Francine discovered Sartre when she came to Paris from the provinces to go to school. She had been confused, directionless, until she found him, or his spirit found her. It maddened Francine that Tom was so evasive about what Sartre had been like in person. Tom confined himself to the blandest generalities, when Francine wanted to know how the philosopher had smelled, the timbre of his voice, the texture of the skin on the back of his hand. Tom claimed to have forgotten. She would find a way, somehow, to force him to remember.

Brian had laughed at her. He had said that when it came to Sartre, she didn't know her ass from first base, whatever "first base" might be. Remembering it made Francine tremble with fury and panic. Brian would not take Sartre away from her. Her throat began to close at the thought of Sartre snatched away, sullied by unfeeling, unthinking, beautiful Brian.

No. Let Brian laugh. Francine and Sartre could laugh, too. She saw Sartre's eyes, goggly behind his glasses, light up with mirth. He reached out to Francine and chuckled. *My clever, wonderful child.*

Francine smiled. To dress as Sartre, re-create herself in his physical image, was an idea that greatly excited her. Obviously, there was a parodic element in it, but she knew Sartre would understand that she meant it as an homage. Because she did, in all sincerity.

She gazed at the profile, listening to the rain drumming on the roof. Having the papier-mâché head here was almost, in an eerie way, like having Sartre himself with her. She watched him dreamily, wishing he would speak, would share his wisdom with her and only her.

When the head was finished, she'd find a large box to pack it in to take it to Venice. In Venice, she would be Sartre.

The others, she was sure, would not have costumes so perfectly matched to their inner lives. They would be completely transparent. Tom would be a dithering, frightened old woman; Rolf a sleazy thug in tight pants, picking his teeth with a knife. Jean-Pierre would be a fussy little priest, with a picture of Brian around his neck instead of a cross. Brian would be a shallow, stupid Narcissus, entranced by himself and his own image. Sally—Francine yawned, then chuckled. Sally was like the pool Brian—or Narcissus—looked at himself in. He tried and tried to get an admirable image from her, but she wouldn't show him one. That's why he couldn't give her up. But how could Sally ever construct a costume to represent a pool?

Francine turned her attention back to her head of Sartre. She could hardly wait for it to dry so she could paint it. After that, she and Sartre would be one.

EMBARKATION

SALLY CLUTCHED her boarding pass. Brian sat gloomily beside her in his molded-plastic chair, a large box tied with string at his feet. The two of them were the only people in the departure lounge who weren't chattering happily. The conversations around them, she guessed, were about how excited everyone was to be going to Carnival. Many of their fellow passengers carried hat boxes and bundles that probably contained pieces of their costumes. A man on Sally's other side had a Cavalier's hat with a curling plume, and the woman he was with wore a black lace dress under her white fur coat, and roses in her hair.

Sally had gotten a little excited, herself, when she was putting together her outfit, but that had passed, and now she dreaded the whole thing again. Brian didn't seem to be anticipating it as eagerly as he had been earlier, either. Something was wrong, Sally knew, but she didn't know what. Brian had gotten jumpy and sober, and over the past weeks she had watched pale blue circles deepen under his eyes.

She thought he was bothered by the letters. He had received four of them, in little white envelopes with no return address, with Brian's name and address written on the front in a hand she didn't recognize. Sally always got the mail, because Brian was home so rarely. She put the first letter under the clock for him, and when he returned and opened it, she heard him draw in his breath. She didn't ask what it was because she was sure he wouldn't tell her. The other three he hadn't opened in her presence.

In the meantime, plans for the Venice trip had continued. She and Brian rigorously kept their costumes secret from one another, designating certain closets and drawers off-limits. Sally had no idea, not the slightest, what costume Brian might choose. When she tried to imagine, she couldn't picture anything. As for the others, she didn't care. She was going to play the game, parade around at the foot of the Campanile, whatever that was, from two until two-thirty tomorrow afternoon. After that, everything was going to be different, because the one thing she knew was that she couldn't go on like this.

French words came out of the loudspeaker, and people began gathering their possessions and standing up, so Sally guessed the flight had been called. They were lucky to have gotten a cheap fare and avoided the long train ride. The announcement was repeated in English, and she and Brian, not looking at each other, picked up their things and joined the crowd pressing toward the woman checking boarding passes.

It hadn't been as easy as Sally thought to figure out a corpse disguise. You could do Death, all right—skull, scythe, black hooded cape—but Corpse was harder. The only article of clothing she could associate with a corpse was a shroud. Or maybe a winding-sheet, a term she had run into in her literature classes. Sally wasn't sure what a winding-sheet looked like, or whether it was really a sheet at all. She took a bed sheet and tried winding it around herself in various ways, but it didn't look like anything but a Roman toga.

Then she thought of bandages. She could wrap herself like a mummy. That was closer, but her experiments with a roll of gauze left her convinced of the impossibility of any one person being able to wrap himself up all over.

By now, she was deeply interested—more interested than she'd been in anything for a long time. She finally solved the problem when she found, in the fabric section of a department store, a kind of white cheesecloth that looked like medical gauze. She bought several meters.

She also bought a white leotard and tights—she'd wear her thermal underwear beneath—and white satin ballet slippers. She went home and put these on and then wrapped her body in the gauze. She swathed her arms, swirled it around her head, let it fall over her face. Then she went to the mirror.

It was horrifying. The gauze fell away from her body in loops, the ends looking tattered, as if the winding-sheet were loosening. The effect could be more Ghost than Corpse, but it was dreadful either way. Her heart began to thud with fear, as if she really were looking at her dead self. She clasped her trembling hands in front of her, and that was even worse—like a lost, supplicating half-rotten dead girl. Her eyes stung. She hoped Brian would be terrified when he saw what he had done.

She made one mitigating adjustment. She bought, in a store that sold religious articles, a little circlet of white silk blossoms intended for a young girl to wear to her first communion. With that on her head, at least she'd look as though someone had cared enough about her death to send a few flowers.

The only thing lacking was a mask, and everybody said the best place to buy a mask was Venice.

She and Brian settled into their seats on the plane. All her absorption in her disguise had dissipated. When she

47

thought of it now, it seemed ridiculous, as did this whole trip. A bunch of kids playing Halloween games. She stared glumly out the window at the overcast sky. At least, by tomorrow afternoon it would be over.

PART TWO

INTERLUDE

ON A DAMP, FOGGY MORNING toward the end of Carnival, everyone wants to come to Venice. At the Piazzale Roma, buses from the airport disgorge full loads of passengers, and the parking garages are filled to capacity. A crowd waits at the vaporetto stop for the next boat. It is not a roistering, jostling crowd. Clowns stand subdued, studying the toes of their ridiculously oversize shoes, and a young boy in a devil's red cape and horns clings to his mother's hand. A thin man wearing a brown leather jacket, a backpack propped at his feet, smokes and watches a group of chattering teenage girls wearing crowns of flowers woven with multicolored ribbons.

Here at the Piazzale Roma, nothing has begun. The autostrada is still a recent memory. Mestre, the industrial district, with its factories wafting corrosive smoke, crouches too near. To reach the desired Venice, one must travel by water, make the slow journey along the undulating length of the Grand Canal.

The merrymakers shuffle aboard, and the vaporetto begins the journey. It stops at the railway station to pick up other voyagers and, engines drumming against the muffling fog, proceeds along the Canal, past Venice's grand houses, narrow palazzos with arched windows, peeling facades, and white stone balconies. In the subdued light the Canal is such a dark green it might as well be black, and the palazzos, in sunshine deep red, dusky pink, pale ochre, are washed into a monochrome that is, all the same, eerily beautiful. When the water rises and recedes in the vaporetto's wake, it is possible to see that the foundations of these houses are covered with slimy-looking vegetation.

The boat continues at a stately pace. It reaches the Rialto Bridge and, several stops later, the Accademia Bridge. At each stop there is the shock of impact with the floating landing stage, the rope expertly looped, the barrier slid back, the tickets taken. Passengers strain forward, trying to see ahead, wondering if they will ever reach San Marco.

They do, of course. The boat slides past the massive gray domes of the Church of Santa Maria della Salute, then past the gold ball that holds the weathervane atop the Customs House, and suddenly, almost too much to take in at once, there is the Molo, with its columns holding statues of Saint Theodore and the lion of Saint Mark, the pink-patterned marble Palace of the Doges, the Byzantine domes of the Basilica, a line of moored gondolas, the towering red-brick Campanile. Across the water, floating surreally, is the Palladian Church of San Giorgio Maggiore. Cold, damp, obscured by fog and unreasonable expectations, Venice is waiting.

UNEXPECTED
MEETING

HIS JACKET COLLAR turned up against the night wind, Tom emerged from a warren of dark, winding streets into the square in front of La Fenice, Venice's opera house. The steps of the Fenice were crowded with revelers, and the square was full of light, much of it provided by a television crew. A creature with the beaked and feathered head of a bird, wearing a cape covered with fluttering strips of iridescent material, whirled and swooped for the cameras, casting a huge and menacing shadow on the blank gray wall of the church of San Fantin. Two women in the powdered white wigs, satin knickers, and buckled shoes of the eighteenth-century dandy strolled arm in arm. From somewhere came the sound of a drum, and voices raised in argument or raucous song. Gray-and-white cats slunk through the confetti strewn over the paving stones.

Tom took his list from his pocket. Rolf, normally the wild card, had been the easiest. Tom had called—actually, he'd had Olga call, telling her he was playing a joke—the bistro where Rolf worked to ask if anyone knew where Rolf was staying in Venice. Genial Louis, the owner of the bistro, had been delighted to tell Olga that Rolf would be on the Giudecca, at the home of Louis's cousin. Tom had the address noted down, but he hadn't been over there yet. Francine had been easy, too. She had been to Venice before, he had remembered her saying. Going back through his notes, he found the name of the *pensione* where she'd stayed previously. A phone call confirmed that she was there again. Jean-Pierre had been more difficult, but after ten or fifteen calls to hotels, Tom discovered that he was registered at a little hotel near the Salute church. Sally and Brian, he'd found by the same method, were at a place called Albergo Rondini, not far from here. He was on his way now to have a look at it.

A group of twenty or so clowns, all dressed identically in baggy striped satin and red fright wigs, spilled into the square and jostled Tom into a corner near a *taverna*. He put his list away, wondering why he was doing this. It was strictly against the rules, and what good would it do anyway to lurk and spy? He told himself it was research. His work, after all, was more important than arbitrary rules. Also, though, he had to admit that if he didn't show up well tomorrow, it would be a blow from which his ego would never recover. He truly believed he'd recognize them all, but he wanted an edge, a small edge, in the unlikely event anything went wrong. He'd get dressed early in the morning and check around some more. No guarantee that he'd see anything special or recognize anybody, and when you thought about it, there was nothing wrong—

He turned his head slightly and saw Brian.

Brian was sitting at a table in the *taverna*. His face was flushed, and he was talking, very seriously, to someone wearing a Harlequin costume. The Harlequin was sitting with his back to Tom. His black, Napoleon-style hat bobbed as he nodded at Brian. His suit was the traditional pattern of multicolored diamonds, but the colors were muted. A smooth baton of light-colored wood was stuck in his belt. Glasses of red wine stood in front of Brian and the

Harlequin, and a nearly empty carafe was on the table between them.

Tom moved back into the shadows. He felt as if Brian's appearance had somehow laid bare his machinations. At the same time, he was curious about this Harlequin to whom Brian was speaking with such intensity. The *taverna* was packed, and people inside moved back and forth across the window, blocking Tom's view and then clearing it again. Brian was leaning forward, gripping the Harlequin's shoulder. He looked as if he might be crying. The Harlequin leaned toward Brian and rested his gloved hand on Brian's arm. Tom pressed closer to the glass, but a headdress of blue chiffon spangled with gold stars moved between him and Brian. Through a starry blue haze he saw Brian lean back. The Harlequin poured more wine into Brian's glass.

If Tom went into the *taverna,* even jammed with people as it was, Brian would surely see him. They weren't supposed to meet until after the experiment tomorrow. Tom continued to watch. The Harlequin gestured, and the waiter brought another carafe of wine to the table. Brian talked, his face the face of a distressed child. Brian had never talked to Tom like that. Feeling cheated and dissatisfied, Tom turned away.

IN THE PIAZZA

A LITTLE GIRL in a pink bonnet, pink hoop skirt, and starched white petticoats, a perfectly round pink spot painted on each cheek, stood in the uncertain sunlight of the Piazza San Marco feeding pigeons. Birds flapped around her, fighting for the few grains of seed she flung from her chubby fist. A pigeon fluttered up and landed on her bonnet.

"*Bellissima*," someone breathed, and cameras whirred and clicked as the fifty or so people surrounding the child pressed closer.

Not far away, a turbaned pasha and his harem swept by. Under the graceful stone arches that lined the portico of the Procuratie Nuove, an alchemist wearing a symbol-covered silver cloak, wisps of white beard sprouting from his silver mask, posed for a cowboy with a camera.

The Piazza was thronged, from the portals of the Basilica, where the huge red-and-gold standard of St. Mark curled and uncurled in the wind, to the temporary bandstand at the opposite end. Under the arcades bordering the Piazza on either side, young people sat with their backs to shuttered shop fronts and passed around bottles of cheap wine. There was an occasional sound of breaking glass.

Sally huddled at the foot of the Campanile, the soaring red-brick bell tower that stood near the Basilica, a gold angel balanced on its pointed green spire. She felt colder than the coldest corpse. Her thermal underwer might as well have been as thin as the gauze that hung limply from her body. The chill of the Piazza's pavement invaded her feet through the flimsy soles of her ballet slippers. The only warm part of her was her face, which was actually perspiring in the stale air under her mask. She had bought the mask late yesterday afternoon. A blank white oval, completely featureless except for the cut-out eyes, it added the right macabre final touch to her costume, but she couldn't help wishing now that it had breathing holes.

The weather today was cold, but at least there was a little sun, which was better than yesterday's fog. Yesterday she had thought Venice was the weirdest, gloomiest place she'd ever seen. As they'd ridden the vaporetto along the Grand Canal, Brian had told her that the houses she was looking at were called palazzos, which was Italian for palaces. Maybe so, but she had never thought of a palace as being quite so shabby. Some of them seemed well maintained, but many looked as if they were ready to crumble into the water.

Another thing about Venice was, it was almost impossible to get around in. More than half the time the streets dead-ended, completely unexpectedly, at a canal. There might be a bridge down the way, but that meant turning back and taking a chance on reaching it by the next alleylike passage. Sally had made quite a few false starts, even with a map, before she got to the Campo San Maurizio, where the man at the hotel had told her the mask market was. On that walk she had discovered, too, that the major streets were so crowded they were almost impassable, but take a couple of turns off the beaten track and suddenly you were all alone, with a dark little canal in front of you and, in a niche on the wall, a painted plaster statue of the Virgin Mary with a plastic flower stuck into the rusted-out screen in front of it.

Sally halfheartedly studied the multitudes, costumed and not costumed, milling around her in the Piazza. She would certainly never be able to identify anyone, even if she were warm enough to try. Her nose itched. If she sneezed inside this mask it would be a disaster. To take her mind off it, she surveyed the crowd more closely. Two cats danced with a mouse. Off to one side stood a gnomelike figure in a baggy suit and tie with the oversized papier-mâché head of a man wearing glasses. Sally had no idea at all what *that* might be. She saw several Pierrots in loose white satin with black neck ruffs and skullcaps. One of them was about two years old, clinging to his father's pants leg.

She hugged her elbows for warmth. Eighteenth-century Venetians in black capes, tricorn hats and white masks paraded near her, and she saw a Harlequin or two. Then her eye fell on a dreadful-looking woman. The mouth of the woman's mask was contorted in an anguished expression and the eyes were staring and wide. As a headdress, she wore a tangle of black rubber snakes, very real looking, their red glass eyes catching the light. Struck by the figure's hideous aspect, Sally couldn't remember for a moment the name of Medusa the Gorgon, the character from Greek mythology who had snakes on her head instead of hair. Medusa, Sally recalled, was so horrible looking that anyone who even glanced at her was turned to stone.

Sally realized the Medusa was Brian.

She had no doubt it was Brian wearing a headdress made of snakes, a flowing dark blue robe, and a mask with a terrifying, grimacing face. She watched him stalk through the crowd. The snake headdress must have been in the hat box he'd carried on the plane. The infant Pierrot caught sight of Brian-Medusa, and she saw his small mouth form an O as he drew closer to his father.

Brian swept around the side of the Campanile, and Sally followed. "Medusa!" someone called, and Brian stopped to pose for the importuning photographers. He raised his arms so his robe billowed in the cold wind. He flung his head back. The snakes bobbed and danced. The small Pierrot wailed, and his father picked him up.

Sally wrung her hands. Brian, who was so beautiful, had chosen to represent himself as a being whose looks turned people to stone. She didn't understand why. Brian knew he wasn't ugly.

Maybe it didn't have to do with being ugly. Maybe it had to do with people looking at you, and because of how you looked, they changed. She would ask him. She thought she could ask him, after last night.

Because Brian had come in very late, and he had made love to her. She had been awakened by the weight of his body on her bed, the smell of the wine he had drunk. He had muttered, "I'm afraid, I'm afraid," and pulled her to him. She didn't know why she hadn't been affronted when she'd realized what he wanted, hadn't pushed him away in disgust. She had been, she guessed, too sleepy and altogether too lonely.

It was the last time, though. When he withdrew from her body, that was the final separation. She lay beside him, listening to his purring snores, bidding him good-bye.

Brian was standing between the Campanile and the Basilica. Behind him, doing a wide, right-angled extension to the Piazza, stood the columns she had seen in her grandmother's print. For a moment, Sally had the impression that the scene was frozen, except for Brian. The gawkers and merrymakers seemed in suspended animation, and only the rippling sleeves of Brian's robe, the bobbing snakes on his head, moved at all.

Then he dropped his arms and strode purposefully away from the Campanile. He was crossing in front of the Basilica, walking toward the Clock Tower that marked the entrance to the crowded shopping street, the Merceria.

Sally was confused. The rules had stated that they were to stay in the vicinity of the Campanile for the full half hour. The time wasn't nearly up. She saw Brian's head-dress moving as he pushed through the crowd. She followed him.

HARLEQUIN

A HARLEQUIN SAT ON the marble railing of the elegant six-teenth-century Loggetta at the foot of the Campanile, dan-gling his feet. This Harlequin was essentially identical to several others in the vicinity, or so it would seem at first glance. A close look would reveal subtle differences.

The costumes of the others were sleazy and cheap, with garish diamond-shaped patches of red, green, yellow, and blue. His was made of lozenges of patterned Fortuny silk in pale colors, and his wide collar was handmade Venetian lace. Their two-cornered black hats were cardboard or plastic; his was sturdy wool and a bit faded, as if it had been worn in commedia dell'arte performances long ago. Other Harlequins did not carry the *batocchio* that was the character's trademark, but the Harlequin at the Loggetta had the baton of smooth, light-colored wood stuck through his belt. They wore various sorts of masks; he wore the traditional black mask of the Harlequin, ugly and sensual at once, with beetling brows, a wrinkled forehead, a wen over the eye.

The Harlequin seemed relaxed. He lifted one foot to the

railing and rested his hand, in its tight, cream-colored kid glove, on his bent knee. He moved gracefully and without haste. Yet his attention was fastened closely on the Medusa moving through the crowd in front of the Basilica.

The Medusa wasn't making easy progress. Now, at the height of Carnival, people were surging into the Piazza, and the Medusa was moving against the flow. The Harlequin was motionless, intent. A laughing young man reached up and tugged at the Harlequin's ankle. Immediately, the Harlequin flung his hands in the air mimicking surprise, rocked back and forth pretending to be on the verge of falling, recovered himself and elaborately resumed his former position. The people near him laughed and applauded.

The Harlequin saw that the Medusa was approaching the Clock Tower, with its elaborate gilded face and the mechanical Moors who struck the hour with their hammers. Soon the Medusa would be lost from sight.

The Harlequin sat up straight. He launched himself from the railing and landed neatly on the ground. He looked around, began to move, and his slim, slight figure was lost in the crowd.

RIO DELLA
MADONNA

CATCHING UP with Brian was hopeless, but Sally had no trouble keeping his headdress in view. She pushed forward intently, dodging her way along. Her attention fastened on Brian, she ran full tilt into a figure wearing a flowing black hooded cloak and holding a staff. The figure turned toward her, and deep within the hood, where its face should have been, she saw an expressionless white oval, a circlet of flowers askew on a gauze-draped head. She screamed, the sound muffled and lost in her mask.

She was looking in a mirror—a mirror the black-cloaked figure wore over its face like a mask. At the end of the staff was another mirror, oval, in a black frame. For an instant the black hood hovered close to her, its rippling edges reflected in the glass, surrounding her image. She stared at her own blank visage, at her white-gloved hand raised to where her mouth should be, then moved away.

She searched wildly for Brian. Her ears pounded with the din of the crowd and someone's shrill laughter and, she wasn't sure why, with fear.

At last she reached the Clock Tower and the Merceria.

The crush was even worse in the narrow shop-lined street, and she could only inch along. Brian was quite far ahead of her, but she could see his headdress and an occasional glint of red when a snake's eye caught the sun.

When she saw him turn into a side street, she pushed feverishly ahead, terrified that she would lose him. She reached the place where he'd turned. The street was much less crowded, but he was nowhere in sight.

Sally rushed on and glimpsed Brian's back down a passage. He was turning a corner. When she reached the end of the passage, she saw him among a group of revelers crossing a wrought-iron bridge over a small canal. He hesitated, looking down at something in his hand. A Pierrot brushed past her, the floating black net ruff around his neck catching and pulling at her gauze. He glanced back, and she saw the sparkle of a bright tear embedded in the cheek of his mask. When she looked toward the bridge again, Brian was gone.

Crossing the bridge, she discovered three possible directions Brian could have taken. The streets were almost deserted now, although she could still hear raised voices, occasional laughter.

She chose to explore a tiny lane, and came quickly upon a group of masked children playing in a cul-de-sac. Turning back, she took the next alternative. As she hurried along, a polar bear and an ape rounded a corner, singing, their arms draped over one another's shoulders. They blocked her way and danced a shambling dance around her, singing raucously in Italian.

When the song was over they shouted, "Ciao!" and reeled away, making low, mock-gallant bows, nearly colliding at the corner with a person in a silver, symbol-covered robe and a bearded mask who pushed hurriedly past them.

Disconsolate, she wandered aimlessly. She couldn't find Brian, and now she herself was lost in the twisting streets and dead ends.

Eventually, she emerged at the edge of a narrow canal. The sun was brighter than it had been all day. Down the way on the opposite side, just past a little arched bridge of white stone, a black hooded figure crouched at the canal's edge, reaching toward a bundle in the water.

Sally didn't think she'd made a noise, but the figure looked up, and when it did, a blinding light flashed from its face. Sally cried out, her voice choked in her mask. The figure hesitated, then moved, and the light flashed again. It stood, whirled, and ran.

Sally blinked away the dark spots that hovered in her eyes. She saw the floating bundle, and light glittering on the pavement where the hooded figure had crouched. As Sally crossed the bridge she saw that the light was reflected from fragments of a broken mirror. Beside it lay a black staff with an empty mirror frame on the end.

She looked more closely at the dark bundle in the water —a mass of black snakes, a billowing blue robe.

Brian threw away his costume, she thought, even as she began to run across the bridge, but by the time she was kneeling where the black figure had knelt, she could see that the cloth hadn't collapsed as wet cloth would. She could see the outline of Brian's knuckles and fingernails inside the soaked white glove.

"Brian?" she whispered, her rush of breath loud and hoarse.

She reached for his hand. Pushed halfway into his glove was a square of folded paper. She removed it and felt for a pulse, but there wasn't one. She shuddered, her arm jerked all by itself, and Brian's hand fell back in the water, lazy ripples spreading from it.

She pulled at Brian's shoulder, trying to turn him over. He was heavy. The snakes, dime-store black rubber with red glass eyes, seemed malevolent witnesses to her dread. She managed to lift his head out of the water. His mask had loosened so that he seemed to be staring over the top of it, his own unblinking eyes above the mask's empty eyeholes

65

and distorted mouth. His face was a grayish color. When she tried to tilt his head forward, dark pink water flowed from beneath the mask.

She gave a gurgling cry and let him go, knowing he was dead. She felt scalded and frozen at once. She huddled on the stones, immobilized.

At last she noticed the square of wet paper was on the pavement beside her. Numbly, she unfolded it. The black ink was running, but she could still read the message:

The game is over. Come see me now.

Under the words was a crudely drawn map. A rectangle was labeled, "Piazza S. Marco." An arrow indicated another black line, over which was written, "Rio della Madonna." Sally tried to concentrate on what the paper might mean, but the image came and went leaving little trace in her mind.

She was still kneeling, staring at the paper, when she heard a light, swift sound of running feet. She wadded the paper and pushed it into her glove. A Harlequin dashed from a side street and took half a dozen steps before skidding to a halt. Motionless, he stared at the floating Medusa. The Harlequin wore a black two-cornered hat and had a round piece of wood stuck through his belt. He looked like the Harlequin in a sun-bleached print hanging in a stall on the Quai St. Michel.

Slowly, and, it seemed, warily, the Harlequin approached Sally. She felt anaesthetized, disconnected. She wasn't sure she could speak or move, but when he was close enough she gestured toward the canal. "It's Brian. He's dead," she said. She saw the Harlequin's eyes blink, but she couldn't tell if he'd heard. *"Brian. My husband."* This time her voice was too loud, ear-splitting, terrifying.

The Harlequin knelt beside her and, as she had, felt Brian's pulse. When she saw him reaching for Brian's shoulder, she looked away. She couldn't stand to see

66

Brian's dead eyes again. She heard the Harlequin's indrawn breath and a faint plashing sound, and felt her head begin to swim. Then the Harlequin took her hand and pulled her to her feet.

The Harlequin's strange black mask covered only the upper part of his face. She could see his lips, which were very pale, and she watched them form the words, "Come with me." He had an accent—Italian, she thought. His tone was meditative. She continued to watch his lips, waiting for him to say more, until she felt a tug and remembered that he was still holding her hand.

She looked back at Brian. The snakes winked at her with hateful red eyes. The Harlequin dragged her forward. She stumbled. They ran.

THE MIRROR
DISMANTLED

ROLF HAD TO GET out of Venice. He'd rigged his mirror-face so he could see out one side, but his field of vision was very narrow, and he had to twist his entire body to look around him. The sun, so bright earlier, had disappeared, and when he moved, cold wind snatched at his cloak.

He whirled in a complete circle, trying to see if anyone was watching. He was back near San Marco, standing on the Riva degli Schiavoni, the wide walkway by the water. In front of him, tied-up gondolas rode the increasingly choppy waves. At his back, laughing crowds surged by, choking the stone bridges along the Riva.

He'd left the staff, forgotten it when the loony-looking figure in the tattered bride outfit surprised him. How stupid could he be? But even though the loony bride had seen him, she wouldn't know, nobody would know, that it was Rolf behind the mirror, so nobody would know the forgotten staff was his. If he could get out of his costume without being seen, and get the hell out of Venice, he'd be all right. He wouldn't go back to Paris either. Not right away.

Passersby buffeted him. Some of them might remember his costume. His strong impulse was to tear it off here and now. He couldn't, though, because everyone was looking at him—the lounging gondoliers, the chubby woman in a brown coat dodging through the throng with her shopping bag, the—God almighty, the idiot with his camera up to his eye about to take Rolf's picture. Rolf turned his back on the photographer, pushed his way into the crowd and shuffled with the rest, step by slow step, over the bridge next to the Doges' Palace. Naturally, even in this mob, the goddamn gawkers had to stop and look down the canal at the Bridge of Sighs. Rolf willed himself to be calm. The crush would clear once he was over the bridge.

It did, and he felt freer, lighter. He flexed his hands. Now to get out of this fucking outfit. He wished he hadn't done such a good job of modifying the around-the-neck shaving mirror he wore and attaching it to his hood. Stupid games, and now look what had happened.

He had thought he was so smart, with his mirror disguise. He'd finally decided on the mirror instead of the Devil because he didn't believe in any true self. People reflected each other. What one person saw in another was his own image, nothing deeper or more profound than that.

What am I thinking about this for? I must be crazy. He had reached an out-of-the-way street where curved lines of laundry, strung between upper stories, flapped over his head. In a sheltered corner, he unfastened his cloak, unhooked the mirror, and lifted it from around his neck. He wadded cloak and mirror into a loose ball.

First, he felt the shock of chilly air; then the vast, overwhelming relief of being able to see all around him. His chest filled and expanded, and he expelled the air in a long, whistling sigh.

Okay. Okay. Now he was just a guy in jeans and a sweater holding a crumpled black bundle. He put it on the ground and stamped on it, over and over again. The faint crunch of the mirror breaking was satisfying, as was the violent, repetitive motion of his leg. Sweating, he picked it up and went to look for a garbage can.

The one he found was overflowing, surrounded by additional bags stuffed with trash. He picked up one of them. It contained the remains of a meal—the end of a loaf of bread, cheese rinds, shriveled brown apple cores, an empty plastic mineral water bottle. He dumped it all on the ground, shoved his cloak inside, wadded the bag tightly, and managed to force it into the overfilled can. He walked away without looking back.

Next, he had to get over to the Giudecca, where he was staying with his boss's cousin, get his stuff, and get out. He'd have to go back to the Riva to catch the vaporetto.

When he reached the stop, he'd just missed a boat. He bought his ticket and sat on a bench inside the wooden waiting platform, leaned his head back, and felt the platform move slowly up and down with the swelling and subsiding water.

Rolf's head was drumming. He had managed to forget the poem for a while, but now, before he could clamp down, the verses came into his mind again:

> *The woman whose visage turns others to stone*
> *Changes trusting friends into people alone.*
>
> *The woman who has snakes for hair*
> *Changes faithful lovers to men in despair.*
>
> *There's no way to guess what the woman will do.*
> *Who can predict what she'll change about you?*

The poem had been delivered that morning. The first he'd known of it was when one of the kids shuffled upstairs and handed him the envelope with his name typed on it.

As soon as he'd read it, he'd known it was about Sally. *Changes trusting friends*—because of her, the group had lost all coherence. And as for changing faithful lovers to men in despair, the situation was obviously rocky between Brian and Jean-Pierre these days, and who was to blame for that but Sally?

What bothered Rolf most, though, was the last verse: *Who can predict what she'll change about you?* The person who had sent the poem to Rolf knew something. Now that Sally was dead, the person who had sent the poem could be dangerous to Rolf. Rolf pictured Brian, Tom, Jean-Pierre, Francine, trying to guess behind which face lurked knowledge of his secret.

Sally the Medusa was dead, floating in the canal near the little bridge. Rolf hadn't thought she'd be so strong, or react so fast. Nothing had happened the way he'd wanted.

Rolf was shaking convulsively. He had to get the hell out of town. People drifted onto the platform. A balloon popped. Confetti drifted through the air. Finally, the boat arrived.

IN THE HOUSE
OF THE HARLEQUIN

SALLY BLINKED at the rice-shaped pieces of pasta swimming in the bowl in front of her. The Harlequin sat on the table, his feet resting on a chair and his chin in his hand, watching her. All around them people came and went, stacking cartons, putting down armloads of lilies or radishes. Pots banged, glass clinked, cleavers made decisive thuds, and everyone spoke Italian at top volume.

"Take off your gloves, so you can eat," the Harlequin said.

She glanced dazedly at her gloved hands lying in her lap. They looked like helpless, sick white animals. They were so sick they couldn't even move.

"Come," said the Harlequin. He took one of her hands, tugged at the fingers of her glove, and peeled the glove off. When he repeated the process with her other hand, a damp wad of paper fell out of her glove and rolled across her lap onto the floor. Sally didn't remember seeing it before.

The Harlequin hopped down and picked up the paper. He smoothed it carefully and studied it, his lips pursed. Although Sally thought she was watching him every minute, she didn't see how he made the paper disappear.

"What happened to Brian?" she asked. Her tongue felt thick. A doctor had been here a little while ago, or at least a man in a doctor's costume, and he had given her a pill.

"I thought you could tell *me*," the Harlequin said.

Sally took a breath. The explanation seemed too complex for her abilities. "There was a mirror-man."

"Ah. And his mirror broke."

"The staff. That one broke." Sally was doing better than she had expected. "His face was—" She lost the drift. "Where's that paper?" she asked.

"Don't think about paper. Eat your soup. Think about mirrors."

Sally stared into the bowl. Steam curled up and enveloped her. "His face was a mirror. He had a black cloak and hood, and his face was a mirror." She looked up, triumphant at having managed the story so well. Abruptly, her eyes stung. "Brian's dead," she said. "We have to call the police."

"Yes," the Harlequin said. He rocked back and forth from heel to toe. Her white mask and circlet of flowers lay on the table, but he was still in full costume. Behind his mask, his eyes were unreadable. He picked up the spoon lying next to her soup bowl and handed it to her. "Please eat. A few small bites."

She spooned some of the soup into her mouth and swallowed it. She wasn't sure where she was or why she had left Brian and rushed with the Harlequin through the streets of Venice until they reached this place.

They had come down a lane to a wrought-iron gate that stood ajar and passed through the gate into a small, bleak wintry garden. She remembered walls covered with stringy ivy, a carved wellhead of dirty-streaked white stone, a shed with a red-tile roof, a haphazard stack of empty red clay pots.

Then they were in a long, low room lined with upright benches, the floor an uneven checkerboard of dark red and

73

white stone. A small boat lay in a far corner, and a couple of oars were propped against the wall. The Harlequin had conversed in Italian with a man in a light blue smock. Sally smelled dampness and saw water—a canal, maybe even the Grand Canal—through the arched windows at the end of the room.

They had climbed stairs and crossed several rooms that looked fancy enough to be in the movies before they reached the kitchen, where they now sat at an old, well-scrubbed-looking trestle table.

"Another small bite," said the Harlequin, but she couldn't. She knew that if she weren't so woozy she would be dreadfully afraid.

She mustered her strength and said, "Who are you?"

"First, I am someone who wishes you well," he said, holding up at index finger with a theatrical air.

"Yeah, but—"

"You may call me Michele."

She squinted at him. "I thought you were Italian."

"Well—I am Venetian."

"Then how did you get a name like Kelly?"

He frowned, then said, "I see. You have misunderstood. My name is Michele. It's like Michael in English, only pronounced Michele."

It sounded like Me Kelly, Sally thought. She said, "Me Kelly." She started to giggle. "Me Tarzan, you Jane." The giggles came faster, and the spoon fell out of her hand.

"No, no, no." The Harlequin took her shoulder and shook her gently. "This won't do, Sally. I can't have you laughing at me in my own house. You're being very impolite."

He was right. Sally choked back her laughter. Her mother would be embarrassed that Sally had been so hopelessly rude. As tears of shame welled in her eyes she wondered when she had told the Harlequin *her* name.

She dabbed at her nose with a piece of the gauze that was still wrapped around her body. "I'm tired," she said.

She looked at the worn surface of the table. She could put her head down there, although that probably wouldn't be very polite, either.

She decided to do it anyway, but once she started, her head dropped more rapidly than she'd planned. Someone caught her, though, before it hit anything.

JEAN-PIERRE'S
DISCOVERY

JEAN-PIERRE'S MOUTH had a bitter, metallic taste that was unpleasant to swallow. The pillow beneath his face was soggy with sweat, tears, saliva. A part of his brain that hadn't realized his life was over sent a memory: of a pillow cover slick and disgusting with the fluids of despair; of his fists clenched, his tooth marks on a knuckle; of this horrible taste in his mouth. He had been—ten years old? Eleven? And his dog, Hercule, had been killed by a car. Jean-Pierre saw the brown eyes, the panting, furry face of Hercule, and his tears poured again.

He was still wearing his white satin Pierrot costume. The elaborate ruff, layers and layers of floating black net, was crumpled around his head. His black skullcap and mask with its melancholy face and glittering tear had been flung into a corner.

Jean-Pierre had chosen to represent himself as Pierrot because the figure of Pierrot was so banal. Pierrot, the sad clown, the deceived, the unrequited lover, was everywhere —on sentimental cards silly people sent each other, in advertisements, on scented letter paper intended for schoolgirls. Jean-Pierre's love for Brian had reduced Jean-Pierre to that banality. His love had scalded out whatever individuality and volition he had and left the dross. It had destroyed Jean-Pierre and left the debased Pierrot.

Over the past days, as Jean-Pierre watched Brian drift away from him, he had seen himself consumed. He had said nothing. What could he say? He was at the mercy of the slight indentation at the corner of Brian's mouth, the line of Brian's backbone, Brian's hair when the light caught it. Aching, he had watched Brian drift and change. Yet there had been a pretense of normalcy, moments when Brian's finger would trace the line of Jean-Pierre's cheek, when Brian's body would respond to Jean-Pierre's touch. At those times Jean-Pierre was gloriously happy, almost able to convince himself that the shadows under Brian's eyes weren't deepening, that Brian day by day wasn't more sober and distracted.

The tears continued to roll from Jean-Pierre's eyes. He lay still, inert, letting them flow.

Brian's decision to dress as Medusa had been a slap at Jean-Pierre, Jean-Pierre knew. It was a deliberate attempt to wound, to hit at Jean-Pierre's obsession with Brian's beauty. He had known Brian's disguise beforehand because, finally, they had told each other what their costumes would be. Brian hadn't wanted to cheat, but Jean-Pierre begged until he gave in. As the time drew near, the thought that they might not recognize each other had become agony for Jean-Pierre. Actually, Jean-Pierre hadn't been afraid that he himself wouldn't recognize Brian, but that Brian wouldn't recognize him.

"If I don't recognize you, that would be the point of the game, wouldn't it?" Brian asked. His eyes were wide, guileless.

"Not really." Jean-Pierre searched for a way to explain, to justify. "We know we're secure in our love. Unshakable." He watched Brian narrowly, no longer sure his words were true.

77

"Unshakable." Jean-Pierre heard irony in Brian's tone as he repeated the word.

Jean-Pierre went on, "It isn't our love that's in question. This game is just an outward sign, something silly and basically unimportant—"

"If it's unimportant, then why—"

"The opinions of others don't count, of course they don't. If the opinions of others counted, we would never have been together at all." Jean-Pierre felt dizzy at the thought of the others sneering and exchanging significant looks when he and Brian failed to pierce each other's disguise. "I would simply like to show, to prove publicly—" He stopped, and looked helplessly at Brian.

After a silence Brian said, "All right."

Jean-Pierre was flooded with shame. "Not if it makes you uncomfortable," he hastened to say.

Brian's expression didn't change. "I said all right."

It had been dreadful. Brian went on, without a flicker of preparation or ceremony. "You want me to say first? I'm going to dress as Medusa the Gorgon."

Jean-Pierre was stunned. He made Brian repeat himself, to make sure he'd understood. He stared at Brian in horror and cried, "But why?"

Brian shook his head. "We said we'd tell each other *what*. We didn't say we'd tell *why*."

Stung, Jean-Pierre fell silent. Brian said nothing else, but rubbed his eyes wearily with his long fingers. Jean-Pierre stole glances at him. Medusa! He had assumed Brian would dress as a medieval knight errant or a supple young Greek athlete—something admirable and heroic. Instead, Brian would be costumed as a monster. Jean-Pierre knew, with desolate certainty, that no matter how much he loved Brian, he would never have been able to recognize him as Medusa.

After some moments of hesitation Jean-Pierre said, "I shall be Pierrot."

"Okay." Brian didn't ask why, gave Jean-Pierre no opportunity to explain that Pierrot represented the debasement of his own true self.

Then, Jean-Pierre had feared desperately that everything was lost. He castigated himself constantly for forcing Brian to cheat at the game. He tried to apologize, but Brian said it didn't matter, and something in his tone made Jean-Pierre feel completely cut off.

This morning, Jean-Pierre had received the poem. The concierge who gave it to him at breakfast time had no idea when it had been delivered, or by whom. It didn't matter. Only Brian could have sent it, for only Brian knew where Jean-Pierre was staying. The clumsy, silly poem told Jean-Pierre what he had dreaded and known—that it was over. Yes, trusting friends had become people alone, and faithful lovers were transformed into men in despair. The last line had been the most cruel: *Who can predict what she'll change about you?* The gratuitous malice of it made Jean-Pierre cringe as if he were hearing a constant, whining, high-pitched noise.

Heavy footfalls and laughter came from the hallway outside Jean-Pierre's room. Jean-Pierre pushed himself up from the pillow, turned over, and sat hugging his knees. His tears had not abated. His eyes were so swollen he could hardly see.

How could Brian have been so cruel? Abruptly, Jean-Pierre thought of Sally. Perhaps the poem hadn't been Brian's idea. Sally had always been in the background, spoiling things, coming between Brian and Jean-Pierre. She might have said something to Brian about a poem. She might have convinced Brian, against his better judgment, to go along with the idea.

Jean-Pierre had believed that love was the most destructive emotion. He discovered, as he sat weeping, that other passions can be even more dangerous than love.

THE AMAZON

THE FIRST GRAPPA MADE Francine's eyes water, but the second went down more easily. She rested the glass on the long table, noticing how much steadier her hand had become. She loosened her tie.

The head of Sartre she had constructed so laboriously was disintegrating in the dank canal where she had thrown it during her flight. She couldn't keep it and risk having been seen following Brian. She made a fervent mental apology to Sartre, knowing he understood, as he understood everything. Violence and death were not unknown concepts to him. The thought, and the grappa, made her feel more calm. She had to make a plan. In a few minutes, it would be easier.

The little *taverna* was hung with bright garlands of twisted paper. Gaudy, cheap masks adorned the walls. A few patrons were singing, swaying back and forth, their arms around each other. Francine had left the padding from her suit in the bathroom. With her belt cinched all the way in she could still wear her trousers.

She wanted another grappa. As she looked around for

the waiter, the couple sitting next to her, a man and woman in space suits, got up and left. Their place was taken immediately by someone else, whom Francine didn't notice until the person spoke to her in Italian.

It appeared to be a woman, her face half-hidden by a fierce-looking helmet mask that swept up in wings at the sides of her head. Bleached-blond hair fell to her shoulders. She was wearing a bronze-colored breastplate with conical protuberances at bosom level. The breastplate ended in a short skirt that suggested the dress of a Roman centurion. Between the bottom of the skirt and the tops of her thigh-high black leather boots was an expanse of six inches or so of deeply tanned flesh. She wore studded leather gauntlets around her wrists and carried a coiled whip in one hand.

The eyes that stared at Francine through the eyeholes of the ferocious mask betrayed frank interest. The woman spoke again.

"Non parlo l'italiano," said Francine.

The woman hesitated, then said, "You speak English?"

"Yes."

"I am asking if I may buy you a drink."

Francine looked at the woman again. She thought in a situation like this Sartre would probably have said yes. At least it would provide a distraction until she could decide what to do next. "Grappa," she said.

The woman waved her coiled whip at the waiter and ordered two grappas. She turned back to Francine. "You are from?"

"Paris."

"Ah, Paris." The woman shrugged away Paris with a slight movement of one broad shoulder.

Francine had never doubted that Paris was the most desirable place on earth to live. "And you?" she asked, nettled.

"Here and there," the woman said. "Often here. In winter I sometimes stay in Switzerland for the skiing. In summer my friends and I go to Crete. But I always return to Venice."

The drinks arrived, and Francine quickly swallowed half of hers. Just in time, because her stomach had begun to quake again. As the liquor slid down and she could forget, she began to disapprove of this wealthy, suntanned Amazon.

The Amazon was leaning close to Francine. The metallic point of one of her breasts dug into Francine's arm. "Your disguise is amusing," she said.

Francine looked down at her worn brown suit with its too-long legs and sleeves, the beige tie with green dots. "Thank you."

"May I ask you what it is supposed to represent?" The woman's breath disturbed the hair next to Francine's ear.

Francine would not discuss Jean-Paul Sartre with this person. A thought came to her. "I'm disguised as my father," she said.

Francine's father, who ran a thriving butcher shop in Poitiers, would never have dreamed of wearing a suit and tie as threadbare and unfashionable as the ones she had on. Still, what she had said was true in the spiritual sense. Intellectually, spiritually, Sartre was her father.

The Amazon's eyes regarded Francine with even more interest than before. Her tongue flickered out and wet her lips. "Intriguing," she said. After a moment she asked, "Are you in love with him? Your father, I mean?"

Francine finished her drink. She was feeling hot and more than a little dizzy. She unbuttoned her collar. "Yes," she said. She nodded vigorously several times. "I am. I am, really."

The woman reached under Francine's hair and put her hand on the back of Francine's neck. She pulled Francine's head down to rest against the hard, uncomfortable breastplate. "And did he do things to you? Touch you? Make you feel delicious pleasure and guilt and fear all at once?" she asked.

82

Francine imagined Sartre doing those things to her. "I want him to," she whispered.

"Yes," the woman said. Her voice hissed off into a sigh.

Francine's eyes closed. Sartre jumped on the insides of her eyelids. He gabbled,

> *The woman whose visage turns others to stone*
> *Changes trusting friends into people alone.*

Francine shivered and sat up.

The Amazon looked at her curiously. "Are you all right?"

The woman who has snakes for hair—Francine wished she hadn't had so much to drink so fast. "I'm fine."

"I don't want to hurt you," the Amazon said. She held up the whip. "This is only for show. A little joke."

"I see." Francine felt slightly ill.

"You're so charming, dressed as your father. I don't suppose he's here, is he? Dressed as you, perhaps? What fun the three of us could have together!" The Amazon had a greedy look in her eyes.

"He isn't here." Francine thought of the head of Sartre, drowned by now.

The Amazon's hand was on Francine's back. She said, "There is a masked ball tonight—an important party. Would you like to go?"

Questions were going to be asked, and Francine wanted to avoid them. "All right," she said. The Amazon smiled and put money down to pay for the drinks.

TOM AND THE TIGER

IN THE LOBBY of the Hotel Danieli a satyr bowed balletically, his bare torso gleaming under a garland of leaves. After a ripple of applause he strutted among the onlookers, the shaggy brown hair that covered the lower half of his body flouncing at each step. In the background, almost drowned by murmured conversations, a piano tinkled through "The Girl That I Marry."

As the satyr was lost amid champagne-sipping bystanders, a woman in a white robe and an elaborate headdress of crystal beads took his place at the foot of the staircase. Beads swung next to her cheeks, cascaded to her shoulders, caught the light as she curtseyed to enthusiastic applause. Someone cried *"Stupenda!"* as she began her circuit of the room.

Rain Goddess, Tom thought. Sitting in a leather chair on the edge of the crowd, he watched her pass. Even now, he couldn't prevent himself from guessing what costumes represented.

In his fevered wanderings Tom had finally stumbled into the Danieli to get out of the cold and came upon this costume fashion show. He himself was still wearing his robe covered with alchemic symbols. He had drawn the figures on the silver cloth himself, using up an entire afternoon. Vibrating, he stared at the sickle moon for silver, the slashed pyramid for air, the trapezoid for salt. Everything was wide open now. He was back on the edge, where he'd been in '68.

He had dressed as the alchemist: the seeker, experimenter, transformer. The members of the group, he reasoned, were his *materia prima,* the raw material for experimentation. Venice was to be his crucible and Carnival his sacred flame. He wanted to watch his materials meld and glow and change. He wanted to see them become, at last, the *lapis philosophorum,* the philosopher's stone, capable of transforming dross into gold.

Capable of transforming the dross of his life into gold.

He was back on the edge, and it was up to him to do something with it. Images crowded his mind: Brian with the Harlequin; the scene at Brian's hotel last night; the floating Medusa, the woman whose visage—

The woman whose visage turns others to stone
Changes trusting friends into people alone.

Tom's mind was skyrocketing out of control. He had to calm down, figure out what to do.

He thought of Olga. She'd been with him in '68, right beside him, caught up in it, too. Funny how she had changed—gotten a job, settled down to an ordinary, uninteresting life. If you wanted to be harsh about it, you could say she'd betrayed her ideals, which was something Tom was determined never to do. He had a chance, now, to prove that his way had been best, after all.

A flurry of exclamations brought Tom's attention back to the staircase. Spotlighted at the top were two figures in gold eye masks, dressed identically in turbans and robes of patterned gold and wine-red. As they descended, their flowing sleeves swept the staircase, their trains slithered behind them. Only because of the courtly way the hand of one lightly supported the hand of the other did Tom think they were male and female.

Tom knew, watching them, that they didn't have to worry about dross or betrayed ideals. Their impurities were gone, burned away in some refining fire.

The couple reached the bottom of the stairs and sank simultaneously into deep obeisances to the crowd. They rose and circled the room. As they passed him, Tom heard the whisper of their robes against the carpet.

He got up abruptly and pushed his way to the bank of telephones he had seen in a hallway. He had a pocketful of *gettoni* because of all the calls he'd made tracking the group. He pushed one in the slot, got the operator, and gave the number, reversing the charges.

Olga sounded surprised and happy to hear from him, but once he had her on the phone, he couldn't think of anything to say.

"How's Stefan?" he asked, his voice sounding thin and high in his ears.

"Fine. He's studying. Stefan!" she called. "It's your father."

"He doesn't have to—" Tom began, but there was a shuffling sound as she passed the phone to Stefan.

"Hello," Stefan said.

"Hi," said Tom. "Just wanted to say hi from Carnival." He waited for a response, and when none came, he went on, "It's really fantastic here. You wouldn't believe some of the costumes." He racked his brain to think of a costume that would interest Stefan, but couldn't. "What are you doing?" he finished lamely.

"Studying."

"Yeah? Studying what?"

"History."

"Great. Well, listen. I wish you were here to see what Carnival is like. Fantastic!"

"Here's Mom."

The shuffling sounds came again, and then Olga said, "So you're having a good time?"

"Oh, yeah. It's—intriguing." Tom thought of something. "Let me ask you a question, Olga."

"What?"

"Suppose you were going to dress up in a costume that would represent your idea of your true self. What would you dress as?"

Olga laughed. "My true self? I guess it would have to be a middle-aged researcher at the Pasteur Institute who lives in Montparnasse with her husband and son."

"No, that's no fair. You know what I mean."

He could almost see her pursing her lips, thinking, could almost feel her sorting through responses in search of one that would please him. Finally, she said, "I think I would dress as a tiger."

He was so surprised he could hardly speak. "A tiger?"

"It's what came into my head. It's the idea of being a hunter. I pursue things, you know, in my work. I mean, I track down answers. It sounds silly—" she gave a little laugh, but he could tell she was serious—"I think of the tiger as silent, and tenacious, and independent—"

And merciless, ferocious.

"It's silly, I know," she went on. "If I had more time to think about it, I'd come up with something better."

"No. That's very interesting."

"And you? What would your costume be?"

He was blinking rapidly. "I don't know. I hadn't really thought about it."

She started to say something else, but he interrupted. "I'd better go. Just wanted to check in," and they said good-bye.

He left his hand on the receiver, resting against it, thinking of Olga, the fierce, lithe tiger, padding intently through the jungle. He had lived with a tiger, and he had never known it.

BRIAN

BRIAN WAS HELD, surrounded, supported by the cold, foul water of the canal. His troublesome beauty had dissolved at the moment of his death. People who drowned felt pain, but now he felt nothing. He stared into the dark water and saw nothing. His mouth and nose were filled with water, and he tasted nothing, smelled nothing. He was flotsam on the Adriatic tide.

Brian should not be dead. He should hear reverberating footsteps, a voice saying his name. Brian had loved, or believed he had. He had been loved, or so his lovers believed. Now that he was drowned and lost, none of it counted.

He was heavy and cold. Death was the coldest, heaviest thing he had ever tried to carry. If his lips could move, if he were not strangled by salt water, Brian would scream out, *No matter how afraid you are of death, you aren't afraid enough*.

If there were other voices, other footsteps, Brian didn't hear them. He shouldn't be dead, but he was. The only thing left was a rage so acrid and hot that it could boil every canal in Venice, blacken every statue, mosaic, cupola.

In Venice, a juggler tossed glittering balls high in the air in front of an open-mouthed crowd. Stray cats crouched under a bench in the Giardinetti, eating leftover pasta from a paper plate. A chubby-legged baby in a high chair threw a spoon across a kitchen. The canal where Brian had floated was empty. Ripples moved along it, stirred by the wind.

THE SCOUNDRELS' BALL

IT WAS RAINING in Tallahassee: a warm, gray, tropical rain. Water slid from the broad leaves of the magnolia tree, drenched its almost luminous white blossoms. A little girl huddled under the sheltering yellow-flowered cape jasmine bush. Inside the house, her grandmother's house, people were talking loudly, laughing. Music was playing. She heard breaking glass.

Her grandmother's china! Her grandmother had a plate the girl loved—gold-rimmed, painted with pansies. They had broken it. Despairing, the little girl stretched out on the ground.

Sally woke herself, groaning. She lay still for a moment, then sat up. She was swept by sadness that she wasn't in Tallahassee after all.

The talking, laughter, and music that had invaded her dream were real, and not far away. She was in a dark room, a soft bed. Light seeped around the door frame, and by the faint illumination she made out a large dressing table with a three-part mirror, a fireplace, heavy curtains, rectangular dark patches—paintings—on the walls.

She was in the house of the Harlequin, Michele. Brian was dead, and Sally had left him floating in a canal, abandoned him and run away with the Harlequin. The thought was so odd that in thinking it she felt only a vague amazement—the kind of amazement she might feel at being quoted an unlikely but irrefutable statistic.

She was still wearing her leotard and tights, but her gauze wrapping and gloves were gone. Yes, the Harlequin had removed her gloves, and a wad of paper had fallen out of one of them. It had been, she now remembered, a map and a message. *The game is over. Come see me now.* She didn't recognize the writing.

Sally had never felt so disoriented and cut off. She huddled in bed with her fists pressed against her eyes.

After a while she felt able to move. She slipped from the high bed and wandered through the room. A door led to a large closet, and in the darkness she caught a faint, sweet scent, magnolia perhaps, coming from the clothes.

Another door led to a bathroom. She found a switch and winced as the light glared abruptly on white ceramic tile and chrome fixtures. She used the toilet and then, washing her hands and splashing water on her face, stared at her reflection in the mirror. She was so pale that even her freckles looked bleached.

Back in the bedroom she felt under the bed for her ballet slippers, but didn't find them. There was a silver-backed hairbrush on the dressing table. She pulled it through her hair a few times.

The door wasn't locked. It opened on a dimly lit hallway with striped silk walls. She turned to the left, toward the music, and in a few minutes emerged into a dining room.

Illuminated by a chandelier made of huge glass flowers was a long table covered with the remains of a buffet. It was littered with plates containing stubbed-out cigarettes, half-filled and forgotten flutes of champagne, crumpled, lipstick-stained napkins. Gelatins were losing their shapes, sauces dripped from the edges of bowls to the tablecloth. A large gray cat stood in the middle of the wreckage, licking something from a platter. When he saw Sally, he started, jumped down, and dashed away.

Cautiously, she moved past the table. At one end of the room were floor-to-ceiling windows covered with gathered and scalloped curtains of white gauze. She pulled one back and looked out. Below, the Grand Canal shimmered darkly. A deserted vaporetto stop glowed with a bluish light. A motorboat droned by, and she caught a brief glimpse of its shadowy occupants. It must be very late.

The music and noise were coming from the next room. Sally moved toward the half-closed door and peered through it.

She saw a long, narrow room full of smoke and people in costume. They lounged on sofas and chairs or stood talking. At the far end, a group of musicians were playing a number with a strong, sensuous beat, and many people were dancing. Two men in pinch-waisted suits and fedoras tangoed together. A tall blond woman wearing a copper-colored breastplate, a coiled whip in one hand and a glass of champagne in the other, swayed alone in the middle of the floor.

The Harlequin was dancing with a tiny, white-haired woman dressed in cream-colored lace, with a red mask over her eyes. She and the Harlequin danced beautifully, with grace and abandon.

Then the Harlequin missed a step, and Sally realized he had missed it because he had seen her. He recovered, spinning the lace-clad woman to a perfect finale. He bent and brushed his lips over his partner's knuckles and moved through the room toward Sally.

"So you've awakened," he said as he slipped through the door into the dining room.

"Yes."

"Welcome to the Scoundrels' Ball. Although, frankly, I doubt if you are qualified to attend. Only those who can prove they are scoundrels are allowed. You can imagine how much gossip I hear from people vying for an invitation."

Sally wondered what the white-haired woman in the lace dress had done to qualify. She wondered if the Harlequin had forgotten about Brian.

He hadn't, because his next words were, "I'm very sorry about your husband's death."

"Well, I—"

"These festivities tonight are inappropriate, but it was too late to cancel them. I apologize."

"It's okay, but—"

"You are very understanding."

He took her elbow firmly and guided her back through the dining room and down the hall. She went with him meekly, but when they were once again in the bedroom she said, "Listen. I have to go."

"You must not. That you must not do."

"I have to. Brian—"

"The authorities have been notified about Brian's tragedy, and they know exactly where you are." He leaned toward a ceramic clock on the mantel. "It is a little past four in the morning. You can do nothing now. Isn't that true?"

The Harlequin sat down on the bench in front of the dressing table. He toyed with the silver-backed brush. Sally looked at his infinite reflections in the tripartite mirror.

"What happened to Brian?" she asked.

"The police, as I say, have been notified. They want to speak with you tomorrow morning. At that time, they may be able to tell you."

Sally clasped her hands together tightly. "He was afraid," she said.

"Yes."

The Harlequin didn't sound surprised. Sally couldn't tell what he was thinking. "Why don't you take off your mask?" she asked.

He nodded. "I intend to, and gladly, but it isn't time yet. In fact"—he stood up and walked to the closet—"I have to ask further forbearance from you. I want you to put on a mask yourself. Not the one you wore before, but another." He went into the closet and she heard his muffled voice saying, "I asked Maria—ah, here it is."

He emerged carrying a hanger with a dress on it. The bodice of the dress was black, the sleeves voluminous and white, caught in at the wrists. The skirt was a mass of white ruffles edged in black. He tossed it on the bed and said, "There was more. Let me see." After another brief foray into the closet he emerged with a fringed red shawl and a black gaucho-style hat and dropped them next to the dress.

"Antonia dressed as a señorita last year. You and she are quite close in size. I think these will fit," he said. "Your foot is broader than Antonia's, but Maria has shoes she thinks will do well enough. It's only for a short time, after all. She'll bring you the shoes and a mask."

Sally stared at him. "You want me to dress up in those clothes?"

"I do. At dawn, which will be fairly soon now, we will go to Torcello, an island across the lagoon, for breakfast. I want you to come."

"Why?"

"Surely you realize there is danger. I want to keep an eye on you."

After a long pause Sally said, "Who's Antonia?"

"My wife."

"She doesn't mind that I'm using her room?"

"She rarely uses it herself. She spends most of her time in Milan."

Sally didn't speak. He said, "I'll have Maria bring flowers for your hair, also." He slipped out the door and was gone.

THE SEÑORITA

I'VE GONE NUTS, thought Sally. She was sitting at the dressing table, wearing the señorita costume. She had showered, washed her hair with Antonia's shampoo, dried it with Antonia's hand-held dryer. Antonia must have duplicates of all her possessions at her place in Milan. Sally was wearing Antonia's beige silk underwear and her stockings. A number of Antonia's hairpins, from an onyx box on the dressing table, were securing the hair Sally had twisted into a knot on the top of her head. Only the cracked patent leather pumps belonging to Maria, the housekeeper, weren't Antonia's.

Sally had opened the dressing table drawer and found Antonia's makeup—a jumble of lipsticks, lip pencils, eye-liners, eye shadows, blushers, gleamers, foundations, powders, sponges, camel hair brushes. Reasoning that señoritas were supposed to have dark eyes and rosy cheeks, she had experimented. Now, she stared in the mirror at a woman with black-lined eyes, bronze eyelids, scarlet cheeks and lips. Her own mother wouldn't recognize her.

Let me explain, Mama, she said to her mother, who was

sitting at the kitchen table with her shoes off, grading papers. Brian fell in love with a man—yes, I said a man —practically as soon as we got to Paris. Somehow we ended up in Venice, wearing costumes. And, Mama, Brian is dead. What happened? I don't know. The problem is, I've been sort of taken prisoner by a Harlequin. He says there's danger, so he wants me to dress in a señorita costume and go off in a boat to breakfast with a lot of people who are drunk as skunks.

Sally waited. Her mother put down her red pen and, after a moment, said, *My Lord, Sally!*

That was all.

My Lord. There was a rising babble of voices in the hall outside. Sally tucked behind her ear the peach-colored rosebuds Maria had brought and fastened them with some of Antonia's bobby pins, then put the black hat over her topknot and secured the cord under her chin. Last, she tied on her gold eye mask trimmed in black, chin-length lace.

She was a señorita. A beautiful, mysterious señorita. She clasped her hands in the soft ruffles of her lap. It's me, Mama.

A soft knock sounded at the door, and the Harlequin peered in. "Very good, very good," he said. "Come with me. Don't forget your shawl. It will be cold on the water."

She wrapped herself in the bright red wool and followed him out the door into the hall, which was jammed with his masked and costumed guests. As Sally emerged, a woman with transparent green wings screamed, "Antonia! *Cara!*" and lunged toward her. Michele held up an arresting hand, shook his head, and spoke in Italian. The woman put her hands to her mouth, laughed shrilly, said, "'Scuse me, please," to Sally, and fell back into the crowd.

Michele bent to Sally's ear. "I have said you are a friend from America, here for Carnival. No one will ask more."

The crowd was moving down the hall. Although they had obviously been up all night, nobody seemed tired. They chattered animatedly, smoked, laughed. Sally joined the flow, Michele close behind her.

As they went down the staircase, Sally returned to a thought that had occurred to her while she was dressing. The Harlequin said there was danger. He could be right, but how did she know the danger didn't come from him? She didn't know who he was or whether she could trust him, and on the whole, she thought she'd better try to get away.

She might be able to sneak off when they got downstairs. He could hardly drag her back forcibly in front of all these people. She wiggled her toes. Maria's shoes were a little loose, but she could run all right. She would run— well, she'd run to the nearest police station. What was police in Italian? *Polizia*. So she'd find a place that said *Polizia* and go in and tell them—provided they spoke English, of course—she'd tell them—

They emerged into the ground-floor room with the benches and the marble-checkered floor. The doors onto the Canal were flung wide, letting in a dank, watery smell and the morning chill. Water slapped against the outside walls, eddied around the crooked wooden mooring poles in front of the house.

People were climbing into motorboats at the front steps. Someone called "Michele!" and the Harlequin's attention was taken by a man in a vampire costume.

Now was the time. She could probably get out the other door, the one that opened on the garden. She took a step backward, keeping her eyes on Michele and on the people gathering to get in the boats. She'd take a few more slow steps, then turn around and go for it. Michele was slapping the vampire on the arm in a gesture of camaraderie.

When she was about to turn, she saw Francine.

She was positive it was Francine, dressed in a rumpled man's suit and tie. Francine's frizzy black hair was unmistakable, as was the slouch with which, arms crossed, she rested one shoulder against the wall. She was wearing a simple black eye mask that left the lower half of her face uncovered, so there really was no doubt. As soon as Sally recognized her, someone in the crowd beckoned to Francine and she moved toward the open door. Sally watched the top of Francine's head disappear as she got into a boat. A moment later the boat sped away.

Sally stood still, wondering what Francine was doing here, whether she was connected to the Harlequin, whether she knew something about what had happened to Brian.

"Sally! We'll get the next one." The Harlequin was beside her, his hand on her arm. She went with him through the doors into the keen morning air and down the moss-slippery steps to the waiting boat.

TORCELLO

SALLY STOOD UNDER an arbor covered with gnarled, leaf-less vines. Trestle tables had been pushed to one side of the red-tiled space, and chairs were stacked near them. Bordering the arbor was a brownish lawn edged by empty flower beds. A square brick tower stood in the distance.

"Torcello was thriving before Venice existed," Michele had told her as the boats slid down a weedy canal past quiet fields and a few tumbledown houses. "A cathedral stood here when the Most Serene Republic of Venice wasn't even dreamed of. And now—" He gestured at the bucolic scene, and she watched a flock of birds rise out of the tall, mist-covered grass and fly away.

A cold wind played through the arbor, making the loose vines sway and the ruffles on Sally's skirt tremble. From behind her the smell of coffee drifted from the lobby of the inn, and through a window she could see a blaze in the fireplace of the large, rustic, low-ceilinged room. Firelight played on exposed beams, silver coffeepots, and trays piled with pastries. Only a few people lingered, as she did, outside in the chill, and those wandered aimlessly, not talking, their long capes, the plumes on their hats, the ruffs around their necks, seeming to droop. Conversation from inside was subdued. The half-hour boat ride in the silvery predawn light, leaving Venice behind like a floating city in a fairy tale, had sobered everyone. The mood had shifted with the location, and it was obvious the Scoundrels' Ball would soon be over.

Sally could see Francine inside, sitting on a couch drinking coffee and eating a roll. Next to Francine, toying with a bunch of purple grapes, was the blond woman Sally had seen in the ballroom—the Amazon in the metal breastplate. As Sally watched, the Amazon picked a grape and offered it to Francine. When Francine nodded, the Amazon pushed the grape into Francine's mouth. Sally thought she let her fingertips linger on Francine's lips.

When Francine finished the grape, she got up and moved toward the table where the coffee was. Sally opened the door and went inside.

Francine was pouring coffee and hot milk. Sally went to the table and picked up a cup. She turned to Francine and said, "Hello."

Francine looked straight at her. Sally saw acknowledgment, but no recognition, in her bloodshot eyes. "Hello."

Sally held out her cup. "May I have some, too?"

"Of course." As Francine took the cup and poured, Sally was overwhelmed by a sense of power. Francine didn't know her. Francine had no idea that behind this mask, dressed in this beautiful dress, was Sally. Sally knew who Francine was, but Francine didn't know who Sally was. For once, Sally was in the driver's seat.

Sally dropped her voice as low as possible and made an effort not to speak with a Southern accent. "Are you a friend of Michele's?" she asked as she took her cup from Francine.

"Count Zanon? We're slightly acquainted," Francine said.

Sally was floored. *Count?* Her eyes swiveled, and she saw Michele in a corner surrounded, as usual, by a group of people. The Harlequin was a member of the nobility? She was impressed.

"You're a friend of his?" Francine was asking.

"Yes." Sally maneuvered her cup under the lace of her mask and sipped. She had here, she realized, an opportunity to find out what Francine was up to, whether she knew anything about Brian. "What brought you to Carnival?" she asked, watching Francine closely.

Francine hesitated, then said, "I came with friends."

Sally glanced around. "The others are here, too?"

"No." Francine sagged a little. "Finally we—we got separated."

"You don't know where they are?" Sally strained to keep her voice husky and unaccented.

Francine seemed to regard Sally more warily. "Not exactly."

Sally sensed she was pushing too hard, but she was eager to know what Francine would say. "But how could—"

The Amazon appeared at Francine's side and put a proprietary hand on Francine's arm. Before the Amazon could speak, there was a sound of spoons tinkling against glass and a general shushing. Sally turned to see that Michele had climbed onto a bench and was waiting for everyone's attention. Before the room was totally quiet, someone called out "Bravo!" and there was vigorous applause.

As the clapping continued, the Harlequin stepped from the bench to a tabletop, and from there leapt and caught hold of one of the exposed ceiling beams. Amid rising applause and laughter, he hoisted himself onto the beam and straddled it. He mimicked riding a horse, then pretended to have gotten a splinter in his backside. After removing the splinter in elaborate pantomime, he pretended to impale his finger with it instead.

Finally, he stretched out along the beam, put his hat over his eyes, and lay motionless. Faint snoring sounds mingled with the titters of the crowd. A limp hand slid from his chest and dangled in the air, followed by the leg on the other side. The crowd began chanting in unison, and Sally heard the Amazon whisper to Francine, "They are calling him to wake up."

Michele's other hand fell and dangled, then his other leg. The chant grew louder, more rhythmic. Sally realized that her clasped hands were pressed to her chest, and she was laughing with everyone else.

Eventually, the Harlequin stirred. His head moved, tentatively at first, then quickly. His hat fell off as, to the shouts of the crowd, he rolled off the beam, catching himself at the last minute, his legs flailing in simulated panic. The crowd screamed as he clambered back onto the beam. He steadied himself and rose to his feet, then bowed to the plaudits of his frenzied audience. Sally heard Francine, beside her, calling, "Bravo!"

When the noise had subsided, he made a short speech in Italian. There was more applause at the end and a general stir in the room. The Amazon said to Francine and Sally, "You have not understood? He has said that dawn has come, the sun is up, and it is time to take off our masks."

UNMASKING

SALLY'S HAND went to her throat. She'd be exposed in front of Francine. Francine would know that Sally was here at a party, dressed as a señorita, instead of—

She needn't have worried. The Amazon seemed to want nothing more than to remove Francine from Sally's company. The Amazon nodded curtly to Sally as she ushered Francine away amid the exclamations and chatter as everyone unmasked. Watching Francine and the Amazon go, Sally remembered her liberal use of Antonia's cosmetics. From a distance there was a good chance Francine wouldn't recognize her even without her mask.

Michele had lowered himself from the beam and was standing on the tabletop. Sally watched him loosen the Harlequin mask. The heavy-featured, sensual black face came off in his hands and she saw him for the first time.

She was dismayed. Having become so accustomed to Michele's mask, she had somehow expected his face to look much like it. Unmasked, he looked pallid, diminished, tired. He was, she guessed, somewhere in his forties. His face was thin and slightly sagging, his nose narrow, his eyes brown and not especially large. His straight, light brown hair was neatly barbered. It was impossible to believe that, moments before, he had been the magical, acrobatic clown, the focus of the room. Now, no one would glance at him twice. Sally felt an unreasonable, complicated pang of loss. She was almost angry, as if she'd been fooled and led astray.

She fumbled her own mask off and surveyed the room. Francine was across the way, blinking dazedly. Her companion, the Amazon, had pouches under her eyes and looked older and less formidable than before. The faces of the others, faces that had been so mysterious and intriguing, so much like characters in a dream, were naked and reduced.

Michele stood beside her. She was almost embarrassed to look at him, afraid she would betray her disappointment. "So the scoundrels go home to bed," he said.

"You give a party like this every year?"

"Since Carnival was revived. Many Venetians say they hate Carnival, with its crowds, noise, and confusion. They close their houses and leave until it's over. But I love crowds, noise, and confusion, and I give the Scoundrels' Ball in celebration of them."

He moved away to say good-bye to his guests, and Sally sat on the sofa in front of the dying fire. She ran her fingers through the fringe of her shawl.

People called "Ciao!" The room smelled of smoke. Boats were starting up outside. She felt let down, exhausted, full of apprehension. As long as the masks were on, nothing was real. Now she was no longer a corpse or a señorita, but a girl from Tallahassee who was in trouble a long way from home.

She heard the door close. Michele came and sat on the arm of the sofa. "Now we can talk," he said briskly. "First, I want you to know that I will do my best to protect you."

Sally frowned. "Protect me?"

"The law recognizes only its own definition of justice.

But we know, don't we, that there is also a fundamental justice of the heart?"

Sally stared at Michele. His unremarkable face was almost radiant with sincerity. "The what?"

Michele leaned toward her. "I am saying I will help you," he said. "But we must agree on what to tell the police."

Sally guessed she had lost the thread of the conversation. Michele went on, "Nobody could blame you. No thinking, feeling person could blame you at all."

Blame her? Sally thought she understood. He must be talking about how she had dressed up and gone to a party right after Brian had been killed. "It wasn't the right thing to do. I wish I hadn't," she said.

Michele's eyes were very bright. "No one but the two of us need ever know."

Sally was glad he wouldn't tell the police. What she had done *did* look heartless, and she was still bewildered by it. Then something occurred to her. "Francine saw me. She didn't recognize me, but she might realize if she thinks about it later."

"Francine saw you?" Sally noticed he didn't say, "Who's Francine?"

"Yeah. We talked a little."

Michele appeared nonplussed. "That makes it more difficult. If Francine was at the Rio della Madonna also, and she saw you and talked with you, how do we know what she will tell the police?"

"The Rio della Madonna?" Sally said slowly.

"The canal where I found you. Where Brian—"

Sally shook her head vehemently. "No! I meant she was here. Francine was here at your party."

"Was she really?" Michele fell silent for a short while. Then he said, "So there wasn't another witness. Good. Nobody to refute your story—or, rather, our story."

Sally felt extremely tired. She was too tired to want to recognize what Michele was talking about, but she knew she had to. "What do you mean?" she asked.

Michele got up and stood with his back to the fireplace. Behind him, embers pulsed and died. "You had ample reason for what you did," he said smoothly. "Brian treated you abominably. He himself admitted as much. It must have been intolerable for you."

Tears sprang in to Sally's eyes. "Oh, it was!" she cried out. "It was terrible! It really was!" To her horror, she began to sob, her body heaving, tears pouring down her face in warm, mortifying streams.

Michele was at her side instantly, kneeling, dabbing at her face with a white linen napkin. Sally saw gray smudges from her eye makeup on the cloth. "And finally you couldn't bear it," he murmured. "You couldn't bear it, so you took the opportunity to free yourself."

Sally's sobs ceased abruptly. "I what?" she gasped.

"You took the opportunity—"

Her head was shaking vehemently, as if of its own accord. "No. No. I didn't."

Michele, sitting back on his heels, looked perplexed. "Why do you deny it, Sally? I have said I understand and will help you."

Sally couldn't speak. She swallowed, and the swallow made a squeaking sound. After a while, she said, "Oh."

Michele stood. He handed her the napkin. "You feel better now?"

"Listen. I told you about the mirror-man." Sally's voice was jerky, as if she'd forgotten how to talk. "Brian was in the water when I got there, and the mirror-man was leaning over him."

"If only I had seen him, too," said Michele regretfully. "As it is, I saw only you bending over Brian. And of course, when you say what you did wasn't the right thing to do, and you cry and tell me your situation was unbearable, why"—he spread his hands wide—"what am I to think?"

This must be what drowning is like, Sally thought. She

said, "The mirror. The broken mirror on the staff. It was there. You saw it."

Michele shrugged. "I saw it. But can you prove you didn't bring the staff there yourself?"

He seemed gigantic, looming above her. She gazed up at him. Her lips moved wordlessly.

The next moment, he bent and put his arms around her. "My poor, darling Sally," he said. "Forgive me for showing you how careful, how extremely, absurdly, careful you must be."

Sally was numb, almost unaware of his encircling arms. "I didn't kill Brian," she said.

"No, no, no." His tone was one he might have used with a fretful but beloved child. He pulled her shawl tighter around her shoulders. "The boat is ready," he said. "Come along. Come along."

FRANCINE
AND URSULA

SLOUCHED IN THE open back of the boat, her head ringing with the damnable buzzing of the motor, Francine looked at Ursula, the Amazon, with a feeling approaching dislike. Ursula had on sunglasses, and a fur coat over her breast-plate. Her hair was whipping in the wind, and she was smiling dotingly at Francine.

Admittedly, it was thanks to Ursula that Francine had been able to disappear when she needed to, but now Francine was less desperate. Her next moves were going to be delicate, and she didn't want them hampered by Ursula.

Francine had discovered early in her acquaintance with Ursula that Ursula cared nothing for ideas. The kind of ideas Ursula got were ideas about having Francine dress in a white, high-necked nightgown, brush her hair so it floated around her head, and lie in a narrow bed with a crucifix on the wall over it and pretend not to know what Ursula wanted when she crept into the room.

With Francine's help, Ursula had enjoyed herself immensely, and when she was enjoying herself most, she referred to Francine as Silvia, with gasps and even a few quickly dashed away tears. All this had been fine with Francine. Her sexual experience was wide and fairly indiscriminate, but her true passion was for the intellect. Ultimately, the physical bored her, so she had been happy when Ursula announced that it was time to go to Count Zanon's masked ball.

Ursula wanted Francine to change disguises so the two of them could go to the party dressed as nuns, but Francine insisted on wearing her Sartre costume. She allowed Ursula to give her a mask, but that was all.

As they got ready, Francine smoked a cigarette while Ursula, sitting in front of a light-encircled mirror, patted her face with lotion.

"Jean-Paul Sartre contended that when another person looks at us we become objects," Francine said.

"Mmf." Ursula was massaging lotion into her neck.

There was a short silence. Finally, Ursula said, "Interesting."

"Yes, it is. And what classical myth does that remind you of?" Francine demanded.

Ursula took Francine's cigarette and sucked in a long drag. She expelled the smoke toward her reflection, and the smoke curled back at her. "Classical myth? My God, *cara,* do you know how many years it has been since I was at school?"

Francine had expected nothing better. "This idea—the idea of becoming a fixed object when another looks—doesn't it suggest the myth of the Medusa, whose glance turned others to stone?"

"Certainly. Of course it does." Ursula's eagerness to please was obvious.

"Yes, certainly." Francine leaned forward. "So couldn't we say—"

Ursula had been staring into the mirror, flicking with a painted fingernail at a patch of peeling sunburn on the side of her nose. She turned to Francine. *"Cara mia,* why do you worry about unpleasant things like Medusa? What counts isn't the head, but the heart." She put her hand on her bosom. "The heart, my darling."

Ursula was hopeless. During the entire night at the party, she had watched Francine closely. When Francine refused to dance, Ursula pouted and danced by herself, but she kept her eye on Francine even then. The result was that, after all, Francine hadn't had a very good time.

Now, Ursula was leaning over to bawl something in Francine's ear over the noise of the motor. "The woman in the Spanish costume! The señorita! Who was she?"

Francine shrieked back, "I don't know!"

"No? The way the two of you were talking I thought you knew her!"

Francine shook her head, and Ursula sat back, but the question made Francine think. The señorita *had* looked familiar. She had also, it seemed to Francine, been rather forward and prying in her questions—wanting to know what had happened to Francine's friends, how they had been separated. It was so typically American to ask personal questions as if one had a right to know everything. Francine had noticed it many times with Brian and Sally—

She sat up straighter, squinting into the brisk wind. The señorita had reminded her of Sally, which was utterly ridiculous. Francine hadn't seen the señorita's face close up, just glimpsed it from across the room after the unmasking, but the señorita had been much more beautiful than Sally. The voice—she had no particular recollection of Sally's voice. Besides, Sally would never have the nerve to put on such a costume, to carry it off with any sort of aplomb. What had the señorita said, so casually? "Are you a friend of Michele's?" Unsophisticated Sally could never have spoken of a Venetian count in such familiar terms. Being completely awed by a title was even more typically American than asking rude questions. The señorita, even though American, was obviously much more a woman of the world.

The boat had reached Venice, and they were moving

slowly past the stone lions that guarded the Arsenale. The morning was lighter now, though still muffled in gray chill. A few people were about, walking briskly along, their breath condensing in white puffs.

Normal conversation was now possible. "Where will the boat stop? San Marco?" Francine asked Ursula.

"Not at all. I will have him take us directly to my door."

Francine shook her head. "I'm not coming back with you now."

Ursula's lower lip sagged. "But of course you are! You're terribly tired. You must have a good sleep."

"Yes, that's right. I have to go to my *pensione*."

Ursula gripped Francine's arm. "You'll come later today? For lunch? For tea?"

"Yes. Later."

Ursula let go of Francine's arm but continued to regard her dolefully. *"Cara,"* she whimpered.

"Later."

"What's the name of your *pensione?* You never told me."

Francine hesitated. She remembered a sign she had passed, she couldn't remember where. "Albergo Lorenzo."

"Lorenzo." Ursula lingered wistfully on each syllable. "I will be waiting impatiently for you."

After leaving the boat and Ursula, Francine walked through the nearly deserted Piazza. Sweepers were cleaning up the cans, bottles, paper, confetti, broken glass, and other trash that littered the pavement. Two people in costume drifted by—a tousle-haired witch and a balding clown holding hands, their heads leaning close to one another.

She walked through the cold, quiet streets, the squares with their empty bandstands, past masks staring blankly from closed shop windows, until she reached a *campo* near the Rialto Bridge. Among the buildings sagging against one another on the little square was her *pensione*, the Al Ponte. As she crossed toward it, a man sitting at the base of a stone wellhead in the center of the *campo* got up. He took a few steps toward her and said, "Francine?"

She stopped and peered at him. She knew him, yet she couldn't think who he was. Suddenly she realized it was Tom. He had shaved off his beard. The plumpish contours of his cheeks, the fleshy chin, were completely unfamiliar.

"I've been waiting for you," he said, and came closer.

Involuntarily, she took a step back.

"I want to talk with you," he said, and when she still didn't reply, he added, "Please."

She nodded. "All right. But we must be very quiet."

"Yes," he said, and followed her into the sleeping *pensione* and up the stairs to her room.

IN THE *PENSIONE*

Tom RUBBED his chin where his beard used to be. He couldn't get used to the cold air on his naked face. A draft was coming from somewhere. He peered around Francine's little room, with its faded wallpaper and its sagging but neatly made bed. A window might be open. "Isn't there any heat in here?" he asked.

Francine didn't answer. As if to belie his feelings of chill, she loosened her tie, took off her suit jacket and dropped it on the bed, then rolled up the sleeves of her rumpled white shirt. She sat on a wooden chair next to the window and crossed her arms. "What do you want?" she said.

Tom wished he had a tape recorder. He wanted to get everything. "I've got bad news," he said.

He hadn't realized he was still caressing his chin until he felt goose bumps rise under his fingers at his words. He took a breath.

Francine said, "Brian is dead."

Tom felt the goose bumps subside. "How did you know?" he demanded.

She shook her head. "How did *you* know?"

Bitter disappointment invaded him. "I know, that's all," he said belligerently.

"*Please* be quiet!"

Infuriated, Tom turned his back on her. He caught a glimpse of his reflection in a little Venetian-style mirror, festooned with blue glass flowers, hanging on the opposite wall. God. There he was without his beard. His hand rose inexorably to his face.

Behind him, Francine said, "I suppose you've been talking to the police."

He continued to watch his reflection as he said, "You know better than that. Did I talk to the police in '68? I don't talk to those assassins." Tom was pleased with his speech, but not with the way his jowls shivered as he gave it. He looked toward Francine. "Why? Have you?"

"Don't be absurd."

This encounter wasn't progressing as Tom had hoped. It would hardly contribute to a study of the group in crisis in the face of violent death. He tried another tack. "Brian dressed as Medusa," he said.

Francine shifted her body impatiently. "Yes. Even his final gesture was a mockery."

"A mockery?"

"Of me. Of Sartre."

Tom wished he could take notes. "Dressing as Medusa was a mockery of Sartre? How?"

Francine tightened her crossed arms. "You wouldn't understand."

Tom could tell she wasn't about to explain voluntarily. He'd have to trick her. "I don't think it had anything to do with Sartre," he said. "I think the Medusa was a symbol of Brian's sexual ambiguity. I mean, Freud said the Medusa represents the female genitals."

"Freud is the only person in the world who was stupider than Brian."

"No, really. See, the snakes are pubic hair, and—"

"And presto! We have the woman whose visage turns others to stone." Francine's tone was scathing.

Tom stared. "So it was you," he said.

"Me?"

"That poem. *The woman whose visage turns others to stone*. What a monstrous act of hostility."

"You're mad," said Francine promptly.

Tom took a step toward her. "Who do you think you are? Sending me poems, jerking me around?"

"Stop shouting!" said Francine in a furious whisper. "I didn't write the poem. I didn't know Brian would dress as Medusa, did I? I received a copy, too."

Tom thought about it. "Yeah, but if you had done it that's exactly what you'd say."

Francine shrugged. She got up, went into the bathroom and closed the door. Tom heard the toilet flush, and water running. He could still feel a draft on his face. He checked the window, but it seemed to be tightly closed.

Francine emerged from the bathroom, rubbing her face with a towel. "I wonder where Brian and Sally were staying," she said meditatively.

"Albergo Rondini." Distracted by the mysterious draft, Tom had spoken without thinking. He stood very still, hoping Francine hadn't caught what he'd said.

She stiffened. *"I see."* She crossed to face him. "Albergo Rondini. And how would you know that? You haven't been spying, have you?"

"Wait a minute," Tom said.

"Yes. Yes you were," she said slowly. "You had on a silver robe with symbols on it, didn't you, and a silver mask with a white beard. I saw you in the Piazza, and now I remember that I saw you here, too. Right outside, hanging about in the *campo*, spying on me. You're a cheat and a spy."

"Now look, Francine—"

"A pathetic, filthy spy."

"Shut up!" Tom bellowed, and Francine hissed, "Keep your voice down!"

Breathing heavily, they regarded each other. Then Francine said, "I saw you somewhere else, too. At the Rio della Madonna."

Tom saw the scene again. Brian's streaming body, his ruined face. The murmurs of the crowd, a woman whimpering, a man saying in a British accent, "Killed him, by God." Tom looked at Francine's trousers, her loosened tie. She'd been padded. That had fooled him.

"I was there, and so were you," he said. "I recognize you now." The frustration of the past hours, days, years boiled up. "What were you dressed as? A troll? A troglodyte?"

Francine's eyes were wide. "Get out," she said.

"A troll! A spiritually deformed freak—"

"Get out of here!" Francine screamed. "You're a fool! You understand nothing! Nothing! Nothing! Nothing!" She stamped her foot, hard, with each repetition of the word.

He heard voices in the next room, and a door opening and closing somewhere in the house. He crossed to the door. "Don't call me a fool. I'm warning you," he said.

They exchanged a last, furious look before he left, giving the door a shivering slam behind him.

ANOTHER SLAMMED DOOR

Tom stormed down the stairs, brushing past a beefy, sleepy-looking—and possibly also angry-looking—man in a red terrycloth bathrobe who was on his way up. Outside, he didn't allow himself to run, but walked briskly away at a pace calculated to put him out of the immediate neighborhood before the beefy man had a chance to get dressed and come after him, if that's what the beefy man decided to do.

Tom was trembling. At this rate, Brian's death would be a complete waste, and Tom's efforts and humiliations would count for nothing. Why had Tom said those two words, "Albergo Rondini"? It was as if he were trying to sabotage himself. He'd heard of criminals doing that, out of guilt and a subconscious desire to be caught.

Tom didn't want to be caught. He wanted to do everything right—starting now—and pull this off.

Albergo Rondini. Like a jackass, he'd said it. As much as he'd tried to forget the damn place, forget the snotty concierge saying, "Can I help you, sir?" and "I'm afraid you'll have to leave now. Perhaps you can locate your friends tomorrow." Tom flushed. What was the two-bit Albergo Rondini doing with a concierge who acted as if he worked for the Gritti Palace Hotel?

At least Francine hadn't gone to the police. That much was very fortunate.

Tom stopped abruptly halfway up the steps of a bridge. A man wrestling a dolly loaded with empty soft drink bottles up the steps behind Tom looked at him inquiringly and laboriously pulled the dolly around Tom's motionless body.

Sally. Shit, yes, Sally would talk to the police. And not only that. When the police started asking questions at the Albergo Rondini, and the concierge started telling his story, and Sally said, "Oh, that description sounds like Tom—"

God damn Sally. She was as much of a troublemaker as Brian.

Tom entered a brightly lit cafe, where a few men who looked like workers were clustered at the bar drinking espresso. He sat at a Formica table next to a jukebox and ordered cappuccino and rolls. His hand kept straying to his face, his fingertips moving over the flesh and incipient stubble. He didn't like the cold air, the rough feeling where the hairs that protected him so long had been rudely and precipitously chopped off. He looked at his distorted reflection in the polished chrome of the juke box. With his beard, he had looked wise. Without it he was afraid he looked like what Francine had said he was—a fool.

He finished his cappuccino and wiped the foam from his naked upper lip. He wasn't far from the Accademia Bridge. If he crossed there, it would be only a short walk to the neighborhood of the Salute church, where Jean-Pierre's hotel was located. He would start again.

A watery sun was breaking through the mist as he climbed the wooden steps of the bridge. He stopped in the middle, leaned on the railing, and gazed toward the point where the Canal opened into the Basin of San Marco, at the gleaming golden globe on top of the Customs House. A barge piled high with refuse churned along beneath him. Then a gondola slid by, and Tom caught a few bars of the tune the gondolier was whistling. The passengers were a man and woman muffled in hats, coats, and scarves. They were holding hands. Two suitcases sat in front of them in the gondola.

Taking a romantic gondola ride to the train station, Tom thought. The idea made his chest ache. He crossed to the other side of the bridge to watch them a little longer. Tom had an instant of knowing that he would give anything— anything—to change places with the man in the gondola holding the woman's hand.

He wondered what he was hanging around here for instead of going on to see Jean-Pierre. Tom's face was chilly again. He'd have to buy a wool scarf to wind around his neck and chin. Or a mask. A mask would keep the air off.

When he got to Jean-Pierre's hotel, he checked the breakfast room first, but Jean-Pierre was not among the people drinking *caffelatte* and eating rolls and jam at the crumb-littered tables. Tom trudged upstairs. He had gotten everybody's room number when he called around. He found Jean-Pierre's room and knocked on the door.

There was no answer. He knocked again, more forcefully, and said, "Jean-Pierre?"

Tom heard footsteps, and then the door opened and Jean-Pierre looked out. His face was bloated, his eyes swollen nearly shut. Tom knew he looked shocked at Jean-Pierre's appearance, and he could see his own surprised expression mirrored in Jean-Pierre's puffy eyes. Then he remembered. "It's Tom," he said. "I shaved off my beard."

Jean-Pierre was dressed in slacks and a pullover. He stood back to let Tom in. His room was in complete disarray—the bed not just rumpled, but sheets and blankets wadded, pummeled-looking pillows flung on the floor. On the floor, also, crumpled under a chair, was a black-and-white Pierrot costume. A mask with a tear embedded in the cheek lay in a corner. Tom had, he remembered abruptly, predicted to himself that Jean-Pierre would dress as Pierrot. He had been right. Yet now he realized that his own reasons for thinking of Jean-Pierre as Pierrot and Jean-Pierre's reasons were probably completely different, and that he couldn't imagine what Jean-Pierre's reasons might be.

He looked again at Jean-Pierre's face. "What happened to you?"

Jean-Pierre didn't answer. He leaned against the dresser.

It was time to begin. Tom cleared his throat. "About Brian," he said.

Jean-Pierre held up his hand palm out, like a policeman stopping traffic. "I will not speak about Brian," he said. His voice was barely louder than a whisper.

"I came to ask you—"

Jean-Pierre shook his head. "I have told you I will not speak about it."

"Look, Jean-Pierre—"

"You look." Jean-Pierre's voice cracked. "I will not say anything, I will not listen to anything. You came here, yes. but I do not have to talk with you or hear you or see you."

Tom's anger flooded in again. "Right. You don't have to talk with me or hear me or see me," he said. "I don't even have to talk with you or hear you or see you." He turned on his heel and left the room, slamming the door behind him.

His fury was molten. He flung himself downstairs and out into the pale sunshine. The bells of the Salute began to peal.

A NEW MASK

THE SOUND of the slamming door reverberated through the room as Jean-Pierre collapsed on the bed. He had been sure it was the police. How had Tom found him? Breathing through his mouth, he blotted perspiration from his forehead with the palm of his hand.

In a little while he felt calmer, if a state of dull agony could be called calm. Thank God Tom was gone. His face had looked naked without his beard—unprotected, like a newborn animal. Jean-Pierre sat up and looked in the mirror. Horrible.

Gazing at his swollen face, Jean-Pierre wondered why he didn't take the next obvious step and kill himself. Why continue to breathe the grief-laden air in this hotel room, to look at his wretched reflection, to feel this torture that would never abate? That he could descend the stairs like any other human being and eat breakfast, that he could walk in the winter sunshine on the streets of Venice, was unthinkable. Yet he knew that was exactly what he was going to do.

Exactly, yet not exactly. He would eat and walk like any

other human being, but he himself would know that he had been transformed, as if the composition of every chemical in his body had been altered.

He couldn't forget the poem. The hateful, taunting Medusa poem that had poisoned and changed him. One person, and one person only, had reason to taunt Jean-Pierre, and that person was Sally. Sally had been so quiet, so sly, waiting in the background. She had brought on the destruction of what had been so beautiful, and it was that knowledge, the knowledge of who was to blame, that was keeping Jean-Pierre alive.

It was time to go to breakfast now, but he didn't want to be seen with his face like this. It was less a matter of vanity than an unwillingness to call attention to himself. He could have breakfast sent up, but that would mean waiting, and all at once he was claustrophobically anxious to get out of the room.

He could wear a mask. Carnival revelers often wore masks and costumes at breakfast. To put on his Pierrot mask was unthinkable, though.

He remembered that a French champagne company was giving away thousands of yellow cardboard eye masks imprinted with the company's name. They were passed out in the streets and left in cafés and hotels, and there was a bowl of them on a table at the end of the hall.

Jean-Pierre slipped out and took a mask from the bowl. Back in his room, he tried it on. It was flimsy, the elastic wouldn't last long, but it would do until he could get a better one. When he wore it, his face didn't look quite so awful.

He took one of the hotel's plastic laundry bags from the closet. In it he crammed his Pierrot costume and mask. He wadded the bag up and wrapped it in his jacket. Then he went downstairs to breakfast.

ON THE GIUDECCA

ROLF WAS ASLEEP, or almost, but a bar of sunlight was teasing his eyes. He tossed, trying to escape it, and raised a cloud of dust from the couch on which he lay in his sleeping bag. As the dust invaded his nostrils, he sneezed, and his eyes flew open.

Shit. He sneezed again. Downstairs the kids were screaming at each other, and then Rosa joined in with *"Basta! Basta!"* What was it about Italians, that they had to conduct their business at the top of their lungs? If they weren't yelling, they were singing.

As if to prove his point, the sound of a man's voice warbling a song drifted from outside. Sleep? Forget it.

Rolf fumbled in his backpack for his cigarettes, found them, and lit one. He propped his head on the arm of the couch and expelled smoke into the already stuffy air of the attic storeroom that was also, at the moment, his bedroom. The place was piled with old trunks, battered suitcases with peeling stickers from Naples and Sorrento, colored Sunday supplement magazines from years past, a broken lamp whose shade hung at an angle. Still, it wasn't a bad place to be, which is what Rolf had realized when he rushed in late yesterday afternoon all hot to get out of town.

Where would he go? He wasn't going back to Paris, but he couldn't think of any obvious alternatives. Money was a consideration. He had told Gianni and Rosa he'd be here till Carnival was over, and that wasn't until tomorrow. He could stay here for free and think about the next move.

Nobody could connect him with Sally's death. The weird-looking bride had seen him bending over the body, but what she had seen was a guy with a black hood and a mirror-face. Nobody knew that apparition was Rolf. When he'd dressed in his costume yesterday, Rosa and Gianni were out. Nobody had been around except a cat slinking along the side of the building and some kids kicking a ball to each other down the street. Now the mirror-man was gone—as dead as Sally.

Most important, Rolf needed to do some investigating here in Venice. Someone in the group—at least one of them—had discovered where Rolf was staying. Granted, that wouldn't have been the most difficult thing in the world to do. Anyone could have asked Louis at the bistro, and Louis, being the accommodating, jovial fellow he was, would've given out the address on the Giudecca without a second thought.

What bothered Rolf was, why would anyone ask? It was breaking the rules, which they'd vowed not to do, but Rolf didn't care about the damn rules. He just didn't at all like the idea of someone snooping around, asking about him in order to send him a poem about Sally.

Who can predict what she'll change about you? Rolf couldn't tolerate it. It might be dangerous to stay, but if he left, he'd never know who knew about him, or where that person might turn up again.

So. He was here like a rat in a hole, and he'd better move before whoever it was moved on him. The person had had no trouble at all delivering a poem to him yesterday, in a nice white envelope. Unfortunately, one of the kids had answered the door and taken it. Neither of the boys spoke English very well, and the one who'd accepted the poem seemed especially dumb. Rolf had been over the episode with him several times to no avail, the kid with his closed, sullen face, sitting half off his chair, glancing longingly toward the living room where the TV was playing full blast:

"Who brought the envelope?"

"A boy."

"Do you know him?"

"No."

"You never saw him before?"

"No."

"What did he look like?"

Long hesitation. "A boy."

"Was he older or younger than you?"

"What?"

"Was he *older* than you?"

"Yes." Throat clearing. "I think so." And on and on. In all probability, the boy who looked like a boy was some urchin hired for the job and wouldn't know much, although Rolf would give a great deal to lay hands on him, even so.

Rolf put out his cigarette in the butt-filled ashtray on the floor by his backpack. His hand strayed to the backpack's webbing strap. Maybe he *should* get out. He hefted the backpack slightly, then put it down again and lay with his hands clasped behind his head.

No. He wasn't going to run. Somebody knew too much, and Rolf couldn't have it. He would stay and find out what was going on. The decision made, he felt better.

Some time later he dressed and went downstairs. The kids had gone out—to school, he guessed—and Rosa was in the kitchen rolling out pasta. She was friendly, dark-eyed, sallow-skinned, putting on weight around the hips. She wore a green wool sweater fraying at one elbow and a heavy gold cross around her neck. She spoke a few words of English and French, and Rolf spoke a little Italian, so they got along fine.

Rolf's decision to stay in Venice and fight had made him feel exceptionally good, he realized as Rosa poured him a cup of coffee. When she put the cup in front of him, he said, with effusive mock gallantry, *"Tante grazie, Signora,"* and kissed the chapped back of her hand.

"Prego, Signor." She giggled, pulling her hand away. He noted with satisfaction the flush rising on her plump cheeks.

He drank his coffee and ate bread and butter, watching as, her back turned toward him, she continued with her work. She seemed to shift her weight rather often from one hip to the other. Watching the outline of the movement against the back of her skirt, Rolf started to smile to himself.

When he'd finished eating, he made a great show of taking his dishes to the sink and starting to wash them. Noticing what he was doing, she protested, "No, no! I do!"

"Sì, sì! I do!" he mocked, grinning, running hot water in the dishpan to make a soapy froth.

"No!" Laughing, she grabbed at his cup and saucer as he slid them in the dishpan.

"Sì." He caught her wrist and, with his other hand, picked up a pile of soapsuds and blew them at her. A few bubbles landed on the front of her sweater.

She gave a cry of delighted outrage, picked up her own handful of bubbles, but was laughing too hard to blow them at him. Rolf took that wrist too, and blew them back at her. Bubbles flew around them, clinging to her dark, curly hair.

"Terrible! Very naughty!" she gasped, her face glowing.

"Very naughty," Rolf agreed as he slid his arms around her extremely warm body.

Yet even as he tasted Rosa, held her, pushed himself

against her, murmuring what he hoped was the Italian word for "upstairs," Rolf found himself thinking of Sally. The image of her skinny, cold, dead body only increased his need and desire.

THE PIERROT
COSTUME

THE SUN SPARKLED on the green expanse of the Giudecca Canal and reflected brilliantly off the white bulk of an arriving cruise ship. Rolf, walking along the Fondamenta Santa Eufemia to get the vaporetto across to the Zattere, thought it was a nice enough day to have a coffee outside. Maybe he'd do that at one of the cafés near the Accademia Gallery.

Rosa had been disappointed at his leaving her so soon, but Rolf had never understood what was so appealing about the cuddling, the tracing the outline of nose, lips, chin, with a forefinger, the sticky, worn-out kisses and soft murmurs afterward. A cigarette, or even two, was fine. After that, he started to feel moody just lying around, and somebody's eyes brimming and a few hurt looks weren't going to make him stay.

Besides which, Rosa might be a little pissed at him now, but he knew she was going to be at him every minute Gianni was out of the house, because she had been so ready. When they were ready like that and you got them going, they couldn't stop even if they wanted to.

A boat was approaching, and he ran for it. Even this early, a clown with a painted face, wearing a red fright wig, was among the passengers. The clown wore an overcoat on top of his costume and carried a trombone case. Looking at the clown's exaggerated mouth, bright red against white greasepaint, and his heavily outlined eyes, Rolf felt that his own face was naked. If he was going to stick around Venice, maybe he should get another mask.

The clown had dark brown circular freckles drawn across his nose and cheekbones. The freckles reminded Rolf of Sally. He shifted his eyes from the clown to the churning water beside the boat, watching it until they reached the Zattere.

He got off and looked around. A couple of places were serving coffee at outside tables, but he didn't want to sit looking back across at the Giudecca. He'd rather put a little more distance between himself and Rosa. He wandered along the Rio di San Trovaso across from the gondola works, cut behind a palazzo, and emerged into the *campo* in front of the Accademia Gallery, with its newsstand near the foot of the Accademia Bridge and a couple of cafés overlooking the Grand Canal.

He wondered if there would be anything in the local papers about Sally's death. He couldn't really read Italian, but he could pick out enough to make it worthwhile to buy a paper. He wandered toward the newsstand and had almost reached it when he saw Jean-Pierre entering the *campo* from the opposite direction. Rolf was sure it was Jean-Pierre, even though Jean-Pierre was wearing one of those yellow cardboard masks that were given away everywhere.

Rolf shrank behind the wire rack of postcards, next to the banks of magazines in four languages, and peered out at Jean-Pierre. Jean-Pierre gave no sign of having seen him. He was carrying a white plastic bag under one arm.

The bag was stuffed full. As Rolf watched, Jean-Pierre turned and began to climb the steps of the Accademia Bridge.

Lingering by the postcards, Rolf debated what to do. He hadn't hailed Jean-Pierre because it was possible that Jean-Pierre was his enemy, the author of the poem. Rolf couldn't trust any member of the group, and he would stay away from them until he was sure of his next move.

Jean-Pierre's appearance, though, might be an opportunity to find out what was going on. Maybe Jean-Pierre was on his way to see Brian. Rolf was surprised, in fact, that Jean-Pierre wasn't with Brian now, but maybe Brian had had a bad reaction to Sally's death.

Jean-Pierre had reached the top of the bridge. Seconds from now, he would be out of sight. Rolf left his hiding place and started for the bridge, following Jean-Pierre.

Luckily, quite a few people were out by this time, enough so Rolf could lose himself among them. Still, he would have given a great deal to have a mask, as extra protection against discovery. He would get one the first chance he had.

So where are we going, sweetie pie? Rolf sneered at Jean-Pierre. Rolf had had no respect for him since he'd gone gaga over Brian. That slavish, sickening devotion was imbecility. Rolf might have his problems, he'd be the first to admit it, but slavish devotion had never been one of them. It was, in a way, the opposite in his case. He didn't want to be anybody's slave. He wanted to be in control. And if the woman—an innocent type like Sally—was scared, terrified—

Rolf switched his mind off that subject and concentrated on Jean-Pierre. They had crossed the bridge and were passing a flower stand where bunches of yellow mimosa, iris, and salmon-colored roses sat in tubs on the pavement. Jean-Pierre plodded on, clutching his bundle, head bent and shoulders rounded. He was the very picture of a defeated jerk, although he should've been riding high with his competition out of the way.

They moved into the large, airy Campo Francesco Morosini. Costumed children chased each other while their mothers, wearing dark winter coats and carrying shopping bags, stood talking. A couple of cafés here were serving outside, but for the moment Rolf had given up on coffee alfresco. He followed Jean-Pierre into the passage in front of the Santo Stefano Church, then down a little shop-lined street.

And then, God damn it to hell, right to a dead end at a canal.

Seeing Jean-Pierre stop abruptly, Rolf skidded to a halt as well. When Jean-Pierre turned around, which he was sure as hell going to have to, he'd be staring Rolf in the face if Rolf didn't do something right now. Of course, this being the most inconvenient city in the world, there were no handy side streets or alleys. Rolf ducked into a little shop with sausages hanging in the window and waited for Jean-Pierre to pass on his way back.

Rolf waited. A man wearing a white apron asked him something in Italian and Rolf gestured to him to shut up. He craned his neck past the sausages, watching for Jean-Pierre, but Jean-Pierre didn't return.

Jean-Pierre could've sat down on the stones to enjoy the sun. He could've jumped into the canal. Those were the only two alternatives Rolf could think of, because Jean-Pierre couldn't possibly have come back without Rolf seeing, although Rolf began to feel that Jean-Pierre had managed it somehow.

The man in the apron was right behind Rolf, talking in Italian again. His hand was on Rolf's arm, giving Rolf a little shove. Rolf shook him off and went to the door. He'd take a short look to make sure Jean-Pierre was still there.

As the man, still close behind him, began to yell, Rolf stuck his head out the door. He stuck it practically in the face of Jean-Pierre, who was returning from the canal. Jean-Pierre's eyes were on the ground and he no longer held his plastic bag.

Rolf jumped backward. He bumped into the man's soft stomach, and stepped on the man's foot. The man's voice was raised even higher in what was clearly pain and outrage. Rolf turned to him and said, "Can't you shut up for a second?" He checked that Jean-Pierre wasn't looking back, had apparently not noticed him at all, but was proceeding down the street at a steady pace. Then he slipped through the door, followed by the man's cries, which were muffled as the door closed.

Rolf was in a quandary. He could either follow Jean-Pierre, who would be out of sight very soon, or search for the plastic bag. Whatever was in the bag, Jean-Pierre had wanted to get rid of it someplace where it wouldn't be connected with him. If it was garbage or something equally boring, why carry it all this way? Maybe he had given it to somebody. If he had, Rolf had better hurry if he wanted to see who it was. Rolf opted for the bag and rushed to the place where the street ended.

There was the canal, glinting in the sun. Steps led down to water level. And on those steps were piled quite a few well-filled white plastic garbage bags.

Rolf wished he could get his hands on Jean-Pierre. He would shake Jean-Pierre until his teeth rattled. How was Rolf going to find Jean-Pierre's plastic bag among all these plastic bags? A Coca-Cola can that had escaped the cleanup lay at Rolf's feet. He picked it up and hurled it into the canal, taking some satisfaction at how ugly it looked floating there.

Then he got an idea. Jean-Pierre's bag had looked much like these bags, yes, but it hadn't been nearly as large. These bags were neatly closed at the top, so Jean-Pierre probably hadn't shoved his bundle inside. Perhaps he had simply pushed it in among the others. Rolf approached the pile and began tossing bags aside. In barely a minute he had uncovered the bag that Jean-Pierre had been carrying.

Here was a bonus: Printed in small black letters on the white plastic was the name of a hotel, Hotel Romanelli, and an address. More than likely that's where Jean-Pierre was staying. Rolf opened the bag. Inside was a mass of white satin and black net that turned out to be a Pierrot costume. Along with the pajama-style trousers and billowing top with its black net ruff were a black satin skullcap and a Pierrot mask with a fake-diamond tear.

Jean-Pierre had dressed as Pierrot? On the face of it, that didn't make sense. And why had he walked across town to get rid of his costume—or gotten rid of his costume at all?

Thoughtfully, Rolf stuffed the costume back in the bag. He put the bag under his arm and strolled toward the Campo Francesco Morosini. He was ready for his coffee.

SALLY PACKS UP

SALLY SAT on the bed where Brian had made love to her the night before he died and stared at the two open, empty suitcases. She was wearing jeans, running shoes, and her sweater with the geese flying in front of the moon. Her hair, no longer piled in the señorita's topknot, hung past her shoulders, and there was no trace of makeup on her face. Her clammy hands, palms together, were pressed between her knees.

Brian had been murdered. The policeman with luminous, chocolate-colored eyes had explained how it happened, with a lot of translating help from Michele. The policeman had acted very grateful to Michele, very deferential.

Brian had been hit in the face, a blow hard enough to break his nose despite his mask

"He is hit—so," said the policeman, making a chopping motion across the bridge of his own nose. "He is stunned, you know, he stumbles forward—"

Michele, soberly dressed in a dark gray suit, a yellow rosebud in his buttonhole, interrupted with a flood of Italian.

The policeman answered in an apologetic tone, still looking at Sally.

"I have asked if you can be spared the pain of this recital of details," Michele said.

"No. He can go on," said Sally.

At a nod from Michele the policeman proceeded. "He stumbles forward, falls into the canal. His mask is cracked, but it does not come off. He is wearing on his head this— these snakes, which are heavy. His face, you see, is in the water."

Sally stared at a blue crockery mug on the policeman's desk. She was studying the mug so carefully that she didn't hear what the policeman said next, but she knew without hearing him. Brian fell into the canal. Dazed, his nose broken, wearing a heavy headdress, he couldn't lift his head. His mask filled with water and blood, and he drowned.

Michele spoke sharply, in a tone of command, and someone brought her water in a paper cup. After she had taken a swallow she said, "What was he hit with?"

The policeman shrugged slightly. "Very possibly the staff that was lying there, although we have no conclusive proof that was the weapon."

So it could just as easily have been the bat a Harlequin wears tucked in his belt, Sally thought. She didn't look at Michele, but she could feel his presence, not two feet away.

Sally didn't know if Michele really believed she might have killed Brian, or if he'd wanted her to think he did. In any case, she had insisted on telling the policeman the truth—about the game, and Brian's saying he was afraid, and the message in his glove, and finding the body, and seeing the mirror-man. Her words seemed to disappear into the policeman's eyes as if they were sliding into two vats of chocolate, leaving no disturbance on the surface. When she finished, he asked her not to leave Venice.

Michele broke in with more Italian conversation, at the

end of which he turned to her and said, "I have told him you'll be staying with me."

"With you? But why can't I stay at the hotel?" The words escaped before Sally knew she was going to say them. She looked from the policeman to Michele.

Michele shook his head. "You must not be alone, Sally. It will be no inconvenience for me to have you." The policeman was nodding, his demeanor indicating that Sally was fortunate to have Michele being so kind to her. Michele was rich, and a count. Sally knew the policeman was impressed.

Sally had called her parents. Maybe it was chickenshit of her, but she'd asked them to call Brian's mother and father. Her parents were coming over here as soon as they could get flights, which might not be immediately, because getting into Venice at the height of Carnival wouldn't be easy. Sally didn't think they had passports, either. She didn't remember much about the conversation, but she knew her father had said, "You'll come back here with us, sweetheart."

Now, Sally sat on the bed in the Albergo Rondini. The police had been through the room. Whatever was left belonged to Sally.

She stood up. This was going to be pretty bad. Trying not to think about it, she opened the drawer where Brian had put his things and looked at the jumble of underwear, socks, the white cable-stitch pullover his mother had knitted. She couldn't do it. She closed the drawer and looked in the big, musty-smelling armoire that served as a closet. His jeans and jacket were on hangers, his running shoes on the floor below. Breathing shallowly, she took the jeans, jacket, and shoes and put them in Brian's suitcase. Then she sat on the bed and put her head on her knees to wait until the roaring in her ears went away.

As it abated, the telephone rang. When she answered, Michele's voice said, "Are you packed?"

"Not yet."

"Are you sure you wouldn't like me to come up and help?"

"No. I'll be ready in a minute."

"I'll be here."

She put the phone down and went to the drawer again. She took handfuls of Brian's things and put them in the suitcase, not folding or straightening, trying not to look at them. When she went into the bathroom and picked up his razor, shaving cream, and deodorant, she started to cry. Her knees gave way and she sat on the side of the tub, shaking. Tears fell on the bathmat. When she tried to blot her eyes, the can of shaving cream was cold against her face.

The eruption subsided, and she was left with the idea that she didn't want to stay with Michele.

She got up and finished packing Brian's things. She closed his suitcase and rested her hand on it, thinking.

Michele was too smooth, he changed too fast—a crazy Harlequin one minute, a proper, upstanding citizen helping the police the next. Sally felt she'd been railroaded. She wouldn't stay with Michele. She'd find another place. She began flinging clothes into her suitcase, including Antonia's señorita dress, which Sally had hung neatly in the closet when she came here to change before going to the police.

She put her toothbrush in its plastic travel case, tossed it in her suitcase and closed it. She'd find another place. She wouldn't argue about it with Michele, either. She'd go down the back stairs, or something, leave him waiting in the lobby. She pulled on her coat, jamming her hands through the sleeves. Then she picked up both cases and opened the door.

Michele was leaning against the wall opposite her doorway. He smiled slightly when he saw her and said, "You're ready, I see. Shall we go?" The next moment he had the suitcases, and they were walking down the hall together.

THE LETTERS

SALLY SAT cross-legged in her sock feet on the green brocade coverlet of Antonia's bed. She was disgusted with herself for coming back here, and the disgust took the form of leaden weariness. Her thwarted determination to escape had been the dying flare of her energy. Too keyed up to rest, she stared at the shifting patterns the sunlight, reflected off the Grand Canal, made on the walls.

She contemplated Brian dead, his beautiful face ruined. She had looked only a second, half a second, when she identified him for the police, but the terrible image hung inside her eyelids. His face an unnameable color, his features seeming slightly off center, he had looked worse than any Medusa.

The dancing light played over a painting of fruit, making a lemon shine out. Sally watched to see if the light would jump to the apple next.

She hadn't loved Brian, she saw that now, and he hadn't loved her. She had married him because—well, because he was handsome, and he'd asked her, and it seemed to be time. She could guess at why he had married her. He must have been trying to escape from what he was, and Sally was the closest thing to an escape route he could find.

The light danced on the apple, then back to the lemon.

Sally wondered who had killed Brian and why. She herself, she realized uneasily, had the best motive as the humiliated wife. Did one of his friends in the group hate him enough to want him dead? Or had it been a chance meeting, a quarrel with a stranger? Or, since Brian had been disguised, was his murder a grotesque case of mistaken identity, his killer after someone else, not Brian at all? Sally thought of the black figure with the flashing mirror-face. She drew her knees up and hugged them to her chest.

She hadn't loved Brian, and he had treated her badly, but he hadn't deserved to die like that, to suffer obscenely and leave behind only a jumble of clothes in a suitcase.

The jumble began to prey on Sally's mind. She had wadded his clothes, shoved them into the suitcase every which way. His mother might open it and see them in a mess. Out of respect for Brian, and his mother, too, Sally would straighten and fold them nicely.

Relieved to have something to do, Sally took Brian's suitcase out of the closet and put it on the bed. She braced herself against the sight of his things, but having a purpose, a goal, steadied her. She emptied the suitcase and began to repack it—shaking out, smoothing, folding, stacking. The simple rhythm of the task was calming.

She did feel a pang, and the sting of tears when she picked up his running shoes. He'd had them since long before she'd known him. Once brilliant blue, they were faded and grimy now, nearly worn out. She straightened the dingy laces.

Nobody would want them, not even Goodwill. On one of the shoes, she noticed, the innersole was coming loose. Sally pulled at it, to see if it were still connected at all, and it came out in her hand. Left in the shoe, pressed down to conform to its shape, was an envelope.

Sally wished violently that she could replace the innersole and forget about the envelope. She hadn't seen it. She didn't want it. She had had enough, and more than enough.

She pulled the envelope out of the shoe and found another beneath it. There were four in all—small, flimsy ones. She recognized them as the letters that had disturbed Brian when he received them in Paris. They were addressed in a hand she didn't recognize, and were postmarked Paris, four or five days apart.

Each envelope contained a sheet of thin paper, folded once. In the middle of each sheet, in the same handwriting as the address, a short sentence was written. There was no salutation, no signature. In date order, the messages read:

Desire is defined as trouble.

Fear is a flight; it is a fainting.

Slime is the agony of water.

To be dead is to be a prey for the living.

Chills prickled at Sally's body despite her sweater, despite the fact that the room had seemed plenty warm a few minutes ago. She replaced the letters in their envelopes. She stuffed them into the bottom of her tapestry drawstring handbag, and pulled the drawstrings tight.

As she finished packing Brian's suitcase, she began to shiver. The shivering got bad, so she turned back the brocade bedspread, crawled in under the blankets and lay there, smelling the scent of magnolia, watching the play of the light on the ceiling of the room.

BRIAN

IF THE DEAD could see and hear, Brian would see colors shifting, bodies moving. He would hear the comically off-key music played by an oompah band of clowns on the Calle Larga 22 Marzo. The clowns danced as they played, the trombonist kicking his feet, the clarinetist shuffling heel-and-toe. The bass drummer's drumsticks swirled with multicolored ribbons as he flourished them between beats.

Because Brian was dead, he saw past those clowns to the clowns within them, and past the inner, private clowns to cold nothingness. He heard past the music to profound, insupportable silence. He saw ribbons of air around the colored ribbons. If dead people could dance, he might have danced with the clowns, but rage never stops to dance.

In the Campo San Maurizio the mask makers had spread their wares on canopied tables. Chaste skulls represented death, but Brian could have told them death was nowhere near as clean as that. What could a skull, severely beautiful, express about vile, sliding fluids and matter that was spongy with putrefaction?

Masks lay on the tables, noses pointing upward, like

141

half-submerged heads. Others hung from the canopy supports and gazed down with immobile, hollow-eyed disdain. Among the golden lions with swirling manes, the sharp-beaked birds, the expressionless doll-faces painted with flames or flowers, would be a mask for a dead person to wear. He only had to find it.

Brian drifted through the world of masks. He had no need of horror. Once he was past the chilly barriers, horror became the element he moved in. Pain was irrelevant. All that remained was the idea that he shouldn't be dead.

The mask nodded at him from the nail where it hung by one eye. Brian and the mask recognized one another.

Brian was washed away from the mask market. He flowed out of the Campo San Maurizio. The mask would hold up this putrid, slippery collapse, support the repugnant jelly he was becoming. It would take him where he had to go.

CONFRONTATION

SALLY THOUGHT she had slept a little. She had, in any case, closed her eyes and later opened them with the conviction that she must go, now, and take the letters she had found to the police. The letters weren't exactly threats, but they were creepy, and obviously they had worried Brian. He had hidden them in his shoe, Sally guessed, because he'd wanted to have them handy but didn't want anyone else to see them.

It occurred to her that somebody might try to get them back.

Sally brushed her hair, splashed water on her face, and put on her jacket. When she opened the door, she half expected to see Michele watching, but the hall was empty, the house quiet. Her handbag slung over her shoulder and anchored firmly with her elbow, she tiptoed down the hall and descended the staircase.

The long ground-floor room seemed deserted. A door in the opposite wall stood ajar, but she heard no sound. She was halfway down the room when a man wearing a light blue smock pushed the opposite door open wider and said, *"Signorina?"*

Sally should have known. She'd even seen the man before, she remembered, when Michele had first brought her here. He was one of Michele's servants.

She pointed to the door that led to the garden. "I'm going out." The man gazed at her benignly. She raised her voice. *"Out."* She took a step.

"Momento, Signorina," he said. He reentered the room he had come from, leaving the door open. Sally could see, now, that it was a sort of lounge, with a couch and a television set on a table. The man must be some kind of doorkeeper.

His eyes on her, the man spoke into a telephone mounted on the wall. After he hung up, he shrugged apologetically. *"Momento,"* he said.

Sally looked out the window at the bleak little garden with its wellhead, gravel paths, and tile-roofed shed, while she waited for Michele's steps on the staircase. She heard them almost at once—light and very fast. He burst into the room and said, *"Grazie, Sandro,"* to the man in the smock. He had a newspaper in his hand and wore Ben Franklin glasses on the end of his nose. "What is this, Sally? Where on earth are you going?" he asked.

"Back to the police."

Michele removed his glasses and put them in his breast pocket. "May I know why?"

Sally's elbow pushed her handbag closer to her side. "I forgot to tell them something."

Michele's eyes flickered to her bag as he said, "Did you? Then of course you must go back. Can you wait a moment, while I get my overcoat?"

She shook her head. "I want to go by myself."

She almost thought she saw a flash of approval, or even amusement, in his eyes before his face took on a worried look. "Sally, you know that is not wise." He took her by the shoulders. "You don't trust me—no, of course you don't. But I wish you would listen to my advice."

Maybe he was right, Sally thought. Maybe she shouldn't be walking around Venice alone, with her husband murdered and weird letters in her purse. On the other hand, maybe she'd be better off doing that than staying here and letting Michele make her decisions for her. "Just tell me the quickest way to get there," she said, braced for his protests.

He held her eyes for a long moment, then said resignedly, "I can see I needn't argue. Most probably you are right, and I'm acting like a foolish old woman."

Sally was amazed by his sudden about-face. As he ushered her to the door, giving directions that she barely heard, she started to feel distinctly apprehensive. If he renewed his offer to go with her, she thought she might take him up on it.

He didn't. In the next minute, she was walking out into the chilly garden. Michele clapped her on the back. "Don't be long. Maria will have coffee and pastries for you when you return." The door closed behind her.

Now there was nothing to do except carry out her plan and take the letters to the police. Sally took a shaky step. She wished she were back in Antonia's bed, or having some of Maria's coffee. She pushed herself forward, through the garden, past the wrought-iron gate, and out into the street.

She felt stronger as she walked. The sun was still bright, although a few clouds scudded overhead. She was doing the right thing, at least she knew that. The messages in the letters drummed in her head, making a rhythm to accompany her steps: *Desire is defined as trouble. Fear is a flight; it is a fainting. Slime is the agony of water. To be dead is to be a prey for the living.*

She had moved from the dead-end lane that led to Michele's palazzo into a more populated street. A small crowd had gathered to watch a young man with a painted face playing a trumpet, using a foot pedal to pound a drum,

145

and manipulating a marionette all at once. Seeing the happy, marveling faces of his audience, Sally felt cut off. Those people didn't have to think about murder and going to the police. They weren't worried about desire and fear and slime and death. She trudged on.

The next corner, she thought, was where Michele had said to turn, but she wasn't sure. She looked around for a street marker, or something to jog her memory about the route.

Her eyes slid over, then returned to, a figure standing in an arched doorway a few yards away. It wore a white robe, a blank, expressionless white mask, a headdress of bobbing appendages.

Sally stared. It was a Medusa.

The costume wasn't the same as Brian's, not even close. The snakes were lengths of springy white electrical cord that swung and dipped crazily, but the effect, for Sally, was horrible rather than funny. The Medusa was looking at Sally. Its gaze felt like an assault.

Even as Sally's mind told her Medusa was a legitimate costume, that there could be many Medusas at Carnival, that this ghost-Medusa had nothing to do with Brian, she was backing away. The Medusa took a step toward her.

Sally panicked, fleeing blindly, pushing her way past people with no idea where she was going. She wouldn't look back. She couldn't bear to see the crazily waving headdress behind her.

PURSUIT

PEOPLE LAUGHED and pointed as Sally ran past. She realized, with deepening terror, that she and the Medusa had been taken for participants in some sort of antic street theater. The Medusa, for them, was a comic monster, and Sally's flight was part of the comedy. She wanted to scream the truth, beg for help, but she knew, with nightmare certainty, that they'd believe her fear was part of the act.

She might have gotten away had it not been for a group of laughing dogs, one of whom jumped into her path and caught her neatly, his brown plush paws closing on her upper arms.

"No!" Sally screamed. The eyes looking at her from over the protruding muzzle were mirthful. His companion dogs cheered.

The dog turned her around and presented her ceremoniously to the waiting Medusa. Sally saw hate in the Medusa's eyes. She pulled back, prompting guffaws from the dogs. "No," she said again as the Medusa gave a slight bow of thanks and led her, accompanied by scattered applause, into a side passage.

The passage was empty except for a crumpled sheet of newspaper blowing toward them. Sally took a breath to scream but the Medusa's hand fastened over her mouth, pulling her head back so far she nearly gagged. Trying to free herself, she thrashed her arms and felt her purse slip, heard it fall with a soft plop to the pavement despite her belated effort to arrest its slide.

The Medusa marched her forward. She knew the eyes, she thought, even though she'd seen them so briefly. She wrenched away, contorting her body, stumbling forward. She reached the end of the passage and dodged around the corner, but she was off balance and hadn't regained full speed and the Medusa caught her again.

This time she did scream, her "Help!" squeaky and quickly cut off when the Medusa's hands closed around her throat. As she struggled, her head snapped back and hit the stone wall behind her. Jarred to the teeth, she scrabbled at the Medusa's hands, feeling saliva flood her mouth.

Intent on the struggle, her strength ebbing, Sally was unaware of Michele until he was upon them, tearing at the Medusa's robe, pulling the Medusa away.

The Medusa didn't struggle with Michele, but seemed to hesitate, swaying. Then it turned and ran back the way they had come, disappearing around the corner.

Sally's knees gave way. She slid down the wall and sat heavily on the pavement. Her head hurt. Her throat hurt.

Michele knelt beside her, saying breathlessly, "Sally, are you all right? I followed because I was worried. Then you began to run and I nearly lost you."

Sally didn't think she was all right. She whispered, "Go after it."

"But are you sure—"

"Go on."

As soon as Michele darted away, Sally was overtaken by abject fear. She shrank against the wall, terrified of seeing again the macabre head with its dancing snakes, the expressionless white mask, the poisonous eyes of the ghost-Medusa. It could circle around and approach her, emerge from a doorway, elude Michele and appear, like her worst fears realized in a bad dream.

She longed for Michele to come back. Michele had saved her. The paving stones were cold under her palms.

Finally, Michele returned. He was carrying her handbag. "I couldn't see even a trace," he said. "Once the headdress was taken off, it would be very hard to find in a crowd. I'm sorry." He handed her the bag. "This is yours, isn't it?"

She almost didn't have the strength to pull it open and look inside. The letters were gone.

Michele was watching her. "Something is missing?"

Sally was too exhausted and demoralized to talk about it. She shook her head. It hurt to shake her head. She leaned back against the wall and closed her eyes. "Nothing special," she said.

Neither of them spoke. Then Sally said, "You saw it. A Medusa."

"Yes, I saw."

They waited until Sally felt able to walk. Then they started back to the palazzo.

A VISIT FROM
MICHELE

FRANCINE HAD just gotten out of the shower when she heard a light tapping on the door of her room. She pulled on her bathrobe, black satin printed with scarlet poppies. To her curt demand, in English, to know who was there, the response came, "Please open the door. I'd like to talk with you."

"Who are you?"

"A friend of friends of yours."

Francine opened the door a crack and peered out. Standing in the hall was a slim man with neatly barbered brown hair. He wore a gray suit with a yellow rosebud in the buttonhole and carried an overcoat on his arm. His face, with its light brown eyes and straight nose, was conventional, safe-looking, not very interesting. There was something extremely familiar about him.

"Who are you?" she said again.

"A friend of Brian's," the man said.

Francine stood completely still. The man put out a hand and pushed gently on the door. "May I come in?"

Francine stepped back, and he entered the room, closing

the door behind him. She pulled her robe closer around her. The man stood looking at her, a pleasant expression on his unremarkable face.

Francine sat down on the bed. "Are you from the police?"

He hesitated before answering, "No, I'm not. Although I expect they will be here shortly."

"Perhaps." She took a cigarette from a pack on the bedside table and lit it.

The man put his overcoat on a chair. "You know, then, that Brian has been murdered."

"Yes."

There was a challenge in the monosyllable, and the man took it up. "You don't seem sad."

She lifted one shoulder. "Brian was an ignoramus and a troublemaker. I don't pretend to feel what I don't feel."

"You are brave. If you speak that way to the police, they may believe you killed him yourself."

She said nothing. He leaned closer. "Did you?"

She laughed harshly. "Do you expect me to say yes?"

"Only if it's the truth. I see you are a woman committed to the truth."

"Yes, I am. And you?"

"I am committed to the false. It's a Venetian characteristic. We paint wood to look like gold, and paper to look like marble. And the wellheads you see in the *campos?* You thought, I suppose, there were wells beneath them. Not at all. They are simply the tops of columns stolen from elsewhere by marauding Venetians, brought back and set up to *look* like wells."

The man had a triumphant air, as if he had proved an important point.

Francine said, "That's disgusting."

"Not at all," said the man earnestly. "If Brian's killer had tried to knock him down a well, instead of into a canal, Brian would still be alive."

Francine studied this familiar, ordinary-looking man.

She wanted to dismiss him as an idiot, but in fact she was intrigued. "Who are you? Were you really Brian's friend, or did you say that as part of your commitment to the false?"

He smiled. "You are clever. No, I was not Brian's friend, any more than you were yourself."

Francine said, "I hate to be mocked."

He pulled an exaggerated long face. "Then we won't get along very well together."

"Brian mocked me. He dressed as Medusa. It was intended as a mockery."

"A mockery of—"

"A mockery of Jean-Paul Sartre and of those who admire his ideas." Francine took a furious drag on her cigarette and expelled the smoke sharply toward the buttons on the man's jacket.

The man seemed to be thinking. At last he said, "I saw you in the Piazza yesterday. Sartre."

Francine didn't answer.

"That's who you were. Sartre," he said. He sounded very pleased with himself. "You weren't a troll at all."

Francine winced. "I certainly was not a troll. I was Jean-Paul Sartre," she said.

He crossed to the bed and sat next to Francine. He took her hand. "How interesting it must be to talk with you!" he said excitedly.

Francine burst into loud sobs. She burrowed her head against the man's neck. He removed the cigarette from her clutching fingers and put it out in the ash tray. Then he smoothed and patted Francine's back murmuring, "My poor girl."

"You don't know what it's like," cried Francine. She grasped his lapels, dislodging his rosebud. "To be possessed, completely *possessed* by his ideas, and nobody—"

"Poor thing," he said. He brushed some of Francine's hair out of her eyes and kissed her forehead. "I kiss all those ideas," he said.

Francine held on to him, her body heaving. At last the tears subsided and she rested, sniffling, with her head on his chest. "It *is* interesting to talk with me," she said.

"I'm looking forward to a long conversation," said the man. He continued patting her back gently and said, "Will you tell me about Brian's death?"

Francine recoiled. "I don't know anything."

The hypnotic patting on her back didn't stop. "What did you see?" he asked.

"Just Brian. Dead. When they pulled him out."

"Ah." He continued to pat her back, in an absentminded way.

She looked up at him. "Were you Brian's lover?"

"Lover." He chuckled softly. "Desire is defined as trouble."

For a few moments, Francine didn't move or speak. Then she said, "Tell me who you are."

"My name is Michele."

Michele. Francine had heard the name recently. She had heard it—

He released her and stood up, straightening his jacket. "I must go."

Fear crawled along her spine, but she could feel, bound up in it, the sensation his hand had created when he touched her. "Please don't."

He inclined his head. "I must. But our visit has been very interesting." He took her hand and kissed her knuckles. "I want to talk with you soon about Sartre."

After the door shut behind him, Francine found his yellow rosebud where it had fallen on the bed. As she smelled it, the petals cool and smooth under her nose, she remembered where she had heard the name Michele.

RETURN TO URSULA

THE MAP OF Venice rattled in Francine's hand, and she cursed the wind, the map, and her own nerves. She must be steady. Steady, calm, and as wise as Sartre. The map didn't stop shaking altogether, but at least she could read it now.

Francine knew she was moving in the right direction but wasn't sure of the exact address. She had hardly bothered to notice landmarks before, although she did remember a gondola stand in a side canal and a ridiculously ornate church near the palazzo where Ursula had the top floor. She folded the map and picked up her suitcase.

Leaving the *pensione* had been natural, after the scene Tom had made early this morning and the insults she had taken from the landlord afterward. Leaving was a good idea for other reasons as well, and she'd done it just in time. As she was coming down with her suitcase, she had heard her name mentioned in the midst of a low-voiced Italian conversation being carried on at the desk. Looking down through the banisters on the first landing, she had seen a man in an unfashionable brown overcoat leaning over the registration book. Michele hadn't been a police-man, but the man in the brown overcoat undoubtedly was. The landlord continued talking, gesturing toward the stairs, and Francine hastily and very quietly retraced her steps and hurried down the back way.

The streets were already filled with people in costume. The good weather had drawn a big crowd. In a *campo* two young men were setting up a puppet theater, and the sound of a violin floated through the air. Francine, with more serious matters on her mind, was in no mood for this cheerful, colorful scene, so much like a cheap operetta.

At last she caught sight of the church with its facade of hideous statuary. Yes, and there was the gondola stand. Now she knew exactly how to find the place.

The maid who answered Ursula's door spoke only Ital-ian, but she managed to convey that Ursula was out. A small, mousy woman, she eyed Francine's suitcase du-biously, but eventually consented, through shrugs and sign language, to let Francine wait.

Smoking a cigarette, sitting on a slippery blue silk chair in an anteroom, Francine tried to make sense of what was going on. Her mind went back to breakfast on Torcello. "Are you a friend of Michele's?" the señorita had asked. Of course, now that Francine had made the connection, there was no doubt that Michele was Count Zanon, whose party she'd attended. She had even seen him, from a dis-tance, without his mask, but the crowd, her lack of sleep, and the Harlequin costume he'd been wearing had con-fused her, and she hadn't recognized him when he'd come to the *pensione*. His face, anyway, was unremarkable, or so she had thought at first.

Michele had said he was a friend of friends of Francine. The señorita, Francine now remembered vividly, had re-minded her very much of Sally—except the señorita had been more beautiful and sophisticated. Watching cigarette smoke drift around the multi-colored glass garlands of Ur-sula's chandelier, Francine wondered if the señorita could possibly have been Sally. She decided that, unbelievable as it seemed, she could. The more Francine thought about it, the more certain she became.

But how had Sally gotten on such familiar terms with Count Michele Zanon? And the señorita costume—was that the disguise Sally had picked to express her true self? Francine began to toy with the absurd idea that Sally's plain, pale, withdrawn aspect in Paris was the disguise, and that all along Sally had lived a double life in Venice as the—what?—say, the friend of Michele Zanon. "Are you a friend of Michele's?" Sally had said that to Francine. Furthermore, Sally must have known exactly who Francine was, since the tiny black mask Francine had been wearing was no disguise at all.

Francine put out her cigarette in a crystal ashtray. She felt badly used, tricked by Sally. As for Michele—Francine must find out a great deal more about Michele Zanon.

She heard a key turning. The front door opened and a greyhound bounded into the room, his nose and mouth covered by one of the straw muzzles Venetian dogs wore. He skidded to a stop when he saw Francine and stood, flanks quivering, as Ursula came in. Ursula had on her fur coat. A red leather leash trailed from her hand. When she saw Francine she dropped the leash and cried, *"Cara!"* She threw herself at Francine, and Francine was smothered by fur and a sweet, heavy scent. Then Ursula took Francine's face between her hands and said, "I've been searching desperately for you. I couldn't wait, I couldn't bear it. *Cara,* at Albergo Lorenzo they never heard of you! I was wild with despair!"

"A misunderstanding," said Francine. "I'm here now, in any case. I've brought my things, hoping you'll let me stay."

"My darling—" Ursula's voice broke and she clasped Francine again. Then she was calling the maid, unmuzzling the dog, leading Francine out to a tiny roof garden with leafless trees in tubs, an ornate white cast-iron table, a statue of a naked boy holding a seashell. Soon, Francine and Ursula were sitting at the table sipping Cinzano.

After further expressions of Ursula's joy and descriptions of the suffering she had gone through, Francine said, "Tell me about Count Zanon."

"Michele? Why?"

"I'm curious, having gone to his party."

Ursula arranged her coat around her shoulders and tapped her front teeth with her fingernail. "Michele," she said meditatively. "He's Michele, that's all. Everybody knows him. We call him Michelazzo, which means he is a bit naughty. The Venetians have a saying that the good life is *La Vita de Michelazzo—magnar, bever, e andar a spasso*. The life of Michelazzo is to eat, drink and walk around. That's Michele. That's all there is to say about him."

"Is he married?"

Ursula shot Francine a sharp look, then laughed shrilly. "Are you looking for a rich husband? Well, I'm sorry to tell you he *is* married—in a manner of speaking."

Francine raised her eyebrows. "Oh?"

"His wife lives in Milan. She comes back from time to time, and when she does they go everywhere together, but —you know. It's a boring story."

"What's she like?"

"Antonia is exquisite. Also very rich. Most of the money is hers. I'm sure she has many, many lovers in Milan. She deserves them, the poor darling."

"Why do you say that?"

"It's idle gossip, really." Ursula smirked. "When she first went to Milan, people said it was because Michele had lost—certain abilities, certain capacities. In the physical line. You do understand?"

Francine felt her face flushing under Ursula's close inspection. "Of course I understand."

"I think Antonia got rather desperate about it and told a close friend, and the friend was indiscreet. It's difficult to know who's trustworthy, isn't it?"

"Since then, since she left, he's had no—"

"I couldn't say," said Ursula brusquely. "I haven't wasted my time worrying about something as dull as the life of Michele Zanon. But do you know, *cara,* what I *was* thinking—"

Ursula leaned forward, her head close to Francine's. Francine sighed inwardly and tried to prepare herself.

IN THE SCUOLA DI
SAN GIORGIO

TOM SAT on a bench in the small, shadowy Scuola di San Giorgio degli Schiavoni. He was aware of the low drone of conversation as the caretaker sold postcards and guidebooks, and of the masterpieces by Carpaccio that lined the walls. He was only slightly bothered by the air on his naked face.

Tom was completely absorbed in planning his book, the companion volume of *From the Barricades*. The connections were coming together. Both books were portraits of people caught up in crucial events. In '68 it had been political upheaval; now, it was murder. Clearly, crisis was needed to unleash Tom's creativity. No wonder he had had trouble working all these years. He had missed the jolt of adrenaline that danger gave.

He couldn't deny that the project had gotten off to a rocky start, and he hadn't written anything yet, although he was going to get down to it soon. Actually, since he'd quarreled with Francine and Jean-Pierre, he had little to write so far. He had imagined they would cling to him for support, tell him all their thoughts. It hadn't started that

159

way, but Tom would make it work out. He had to.

"Pardon, monsieur." A Frenchman in an oversize baby bonnet, carrying a bottle with a huge rubber nipple, pushed past Tom to get to the paintings on the other side of the room.

Another factor hampering Tom's work was his determination to stay away from his hotel in order to avoid the police. His feverish wanderings had brought him to the Scuola di San Giorgio. He had entered this unprepossessing building next to an out-of-the-way canal because he saw other people going in and he needed to get the cold off his face. He had even bought a guidebook.

He got up and wandered around, glancing at the pictures. He should go now. He had to return to the hotel sometime. He reached the door and looked at the last painting.

The guidebook said it was called *The Vision of St. Augustine*. The saint was in his study, a pen in his hand, gazing at a bright light at the window. The study was sumptuous, spacious. Open books lay on the floor. There was a reading lectern, shelves. A fluffy white dog with bright black eyes sat to one side.

Tom was irritated. Who couldn't be a saint in a place like that? Naturally, Saint Augustine could work, at that fancy table covered with green leather! Saint Augustine didn't have a wife and a kid and a tiny apartment near the Tour Montparnasse.

Also, and this was the worst part, Saint Augustine *did* have a thick brown beard.

Tom shoved his hands into his pockets and left the Scuola di San Giorgio.

When he got back to the hotel, the desk clerk said, "This is for you, *Signor,*" and handed Tom a card along with his key. The card was a calling card, large and square in the European style. On it, in curving black letters, was printed, "Michele Zanon," and an address.

Tom looked at the card. He turned it over. On the back

was scribbled, "Please meet me Florian's. Until noon." Was Michele Zanon a policeman? He said to the clerk, "You must've put this in the wrong box. I don't think it's for me."

The clerk nodded a vigorous affirmative. "It's for you. Count Zanon asked for you by name."

Tom studied the card again. "Count Zanon?"

"Yes, *Signor.*"

Tom wondered if this card were a trick. He turned to the clerk, who was still nodding, his manner considerably more unctuous now than it ever had been before. "You know this Count Zanon?"

The nodding picked up speed. "Certainly. I have seen him often. He is well known in Venice."

Tom tapped the edge of the card on the counter. It could be an elaborate trick. But if the clerk wasn't lying, Tom guessed that this Count Zanon had indeed been here asking for him and would wait at Florian's until noon for him to show up.

Tom reached the Piazza San Marco in plenty of time. Florian's was suffused with mellow golden light and the warm smells of coffee and chocolate. Although it was filled with chattering patrons, many in costume, the waiter reacted instantly to Count Zanon's name and led Tom to a table where a slight, well-dressed man was finishing an espresso.

When greetings had been exchanged and more coffee ordered, the count said, "You are kind to have come. Thank you."

"Sure. What's it about?" Tom said warily.

"First, I must offer my condolences on the death of your friend, Brian."

Tom felt uncomfortable. He wondered if a Venetian count could be an undercover policeman. "Are you a cop, or what?"

The count shook his head. "A bystander. But I had another motive for wanting to meet you, too."

Tom waited.

The count leaned forward. "I am a great admirer of your book, *From the Barricades.*"

This was more like it. Tom settled down, the way he always did on the occasions, rarer and rarer now, when people made such remarks. The count, who had looked like a wimp, seemed to become more substantial. "You are?"

"Yes, indeed. I was fascinated. What a time that must have been!" The count's face was flushed, his eyes shone with candor.

Tom could see that this man understood May of '68 and its importance. "Well, Mr.—Count Zanon—"

"Michele."

"Well, Michele—"

Tom continued for some time. Another round of espresso was bought and drunk. Tom enjoyed himself. He noticed he was rubbing his cheeks less.

When Tom eventually ran down, Michele let some moments pass before he said, "And Brian was one of your disciples? Surely it was a terrible blow to lose him."

Tom shook his head. "That kid. May of '68 meant nothing to him." Seeing Michele's look of surprise, he added hastily, "Of course I'm sorry he's dead."

"Of course."

A breath of irony in Michele's tone made Tom say, "What is your interest in all this? Did you know Brian?"

"Slightly. His murder was bizarre, don't you think?"

"Yeah. It really was."

"Although, you know"—Michele sounded meditative—"apparently there had been incidents before."

Tom wished Michele would get off the subject. He waited a long time before saying, "There had?"

"Yes. This morning I was at the Albergo Rondini, where Brian stayed. The hotel staff was distraught about the murder, as you can imagine. One of them told me that a bearded man had been ejected from the hotel the night before last because he was lurking around suspiciously."

Tom wished he could move from Michele's line of sight. He became aware that he was rubbing his face. He took his hand away. "No kidding."

"Yes. No one knows who the bearded man was, but now they're all sure there was a connection with the murder."

The air in Florian's was stuffy. "I've got to go," Tom said.

Michele said, "Fear is a flight; it is a fainting."

Tom stared at Michele. Then he said, "I guess so." He got up, and started for the door.

JEAN-PIERRE
AND THE JESTER

A YOUNG ACROBAT in a jester's costume had drawn a crowd in front of the San Moisè Church. His face was painted white, his lips an exaggerated red Cupid's bow. With every movement of his long arms and his graceful body, tiny gold bells attached to his cap and his red-and-green motley jingled. Their sound blended with his musical accompaniment, recorders played by two young men in velvet berets decorated with plumes.

The Jester balanced on his hands, let his legs descend into a beautifully arched backbend, came upright, then slid into a split. Cameras clicked. He rose to his feet, pirouetted, then climbed to the shoulders of one of the recorder players. He stood upright, a figure of unbelievable brightness against the gray facade of the San Moisè. The next moment he was a blur of red and green as he flipped to the ground, somersaulting in midair, his red-slippered feet landing lightly on the paving stones.

Jean-Pierre, at the edge of the crowd, joined in the applause. He couldn't take his eyes off the Jester. The Jester was everything Jean-Pierre was not. Jean-Pierre was leaden, swollen with grief and anger, clumsy. With every movement the Jester radiated lightness, agility, joy. As the Jester cartwheeled, contorted, spun with increasing abandon and defiance of gravity, something in his performance reminded Jean-Pierre of his early days with Brian.

In a moment this will pain me, Jean-Pierre thought, but the pain was miraculously suspended. Jean-Pierre remembered Brian's body quickening under his mouth, remembered Brian's strong, straight legs, the way the sweat-soaked curls clung to his forehead. In that moment of suspension Jean-Pierre was flooded with a driving excitement that was almost like ecstasy.

When the pain did come, it was gentler than before. Through the eyes of his mask, Jean-Pierre gazed at the Jester with gratitude for the relief he had thought he could never, even for an instant, feel. When the Jester bowed low to enthusiastic applause and passed through the crowd carrying the velvet cap of one of the recorder players, Jean-Pierre put a twenty-thousand-lire note on top of the other, much smaller, offerings.

The Jester looked keenly at Jean-Pierre. He said, *"Molto, molto grazie"* in an accent Jean-Pierre recognized as French.

Jean-Pierre replied in French, "I enjoyed watching you. You were marvelous."

The Jester shrugged deprecatingly. "You're very kind." He moved away to offer the cap to others.

The crowd was breaking up. Jean-Pierre stood for a while longer, watching the Jester collect money and the recorder players put their instruments in cases. At last he wandered away, looking idly in nearby shop windows. In a few minutes he heard bells beside him and turned to see the Jester.

The Jester smiled and said, "You're from Paris?"

"Yes."

"Me, too. Sometimes I perform in the plaza in front of Beaubourg."

"I'll look for you there."

They walked along together. The Jester said, "There are many generous people at Carnival, but few are as generous as you."

"Not many performers are as excellent as you."

Wandering, they talked about inconsequential things. The Jester's bell tinkled as they walked, surrounding the two of them with a web of sound. At last the Jester said, "Do you know what I would like?"

"What?"

"I would like to see your face without the mask."

Jean-Pierre shook his head. "I look awful today. I'm wearing the mask because I don't want to show my face to anyone."

"I'm sure it isn't awful at all. Please?"

"I can't."

The Jester smiled in a wheedling way. "Even if we went somewhere private? So no one but me could see you?"

Jean-Pierre looked at the Jester. The Jester touched Jean-Pierre's shoulder. "Please?"

After a moment Jean-Pierre said, "All right. We can go to my hotel."

When they reached the hotel, Jean-Pierre took no notice of the conventional-looking brown-haired man in a gray suit who was leaving as they entered. Jean-Pierre had taken his key with him, and he did not check for messages.

When he and the Jester were in his room, the Jester said, "Now."

Jean-Pierre took off his mask and put it on the dresser. The Jester moved toward him. He stood in front of Jean-Pierre. He put cool fingertips on Jean-Pierre's swollen eyes. Jean-Pierre breathed deeply at his touch.

"Someone hurt you," the Jester said. He pressed the tender skin of Jean-Pierre's cheeks.

"Yes."

"Your lover?"

"Yes."

"Love can be brutal, they say."

"It can."

The Jester said, "I'll show you my face, if you like. Would you like that?"

"Yes."

The Jester went into the bathroom and closed the door. Jean-Pierre heard bells jingling, water running. He undressed and turned down the freshly made bed. The sheets were cool and smooth beneath his body.

When the Jester came out, he had taken off his cap, and his face was clean. His brown hair was tousled. He had a small, dark birthmark high on one tanned cheek. He looked very young.

The Jester saw Jean-Pierre and said, "Good." He came to the bed, bent and kissed Jean-Pierre. His mouth tasted sweet to Jean-Pierre, as if the Jester had been eating candy.

Jean-Pierre's crazy ecstasy returned. It knifed through him, accompanied by the sound of bells as he clasped the Jester. Then the bells fell away.

When Jean-Pierre was about to be overwhelmed, he said, "My lover is dead."

Dozing, Jean-Pierre felt the Jester slide out of bed, heard him slip into his tinkling costume. He opened an eye and saw the Jester find Jean-Pierre's wallet and remove the rest of his money. Jean-Pierre saw the Jester take his watch from the dresser where it lay beside his mask. Jean-Pierre closed his eye and listened to the soft opening and closing of the door as the Jester made his exit.

Love can be brutal, but it didn't matter. There was nothing more for Jean-Pierre to care about, or learn. The Jester was welcome to what he could salvage from the wreck of Jean-Pierre, because Jean-Pierre already had all he would need.

ROLF AND MICHELE

As ALWAYS IN Rosa and Gianni's neighborhood, kids were kicking a soccer ball back and forth in the wide, paved area between the cheerless brick apartment houses. The ball sailed Rolf's way, and he grounded it expertly and kicked it back to them. It scudded across the pavement toward a slight man in a gray suit, an overcoat slung around his shoulders, who was leaning in a doorway almost opposite Rosa and Gianni's building. The man straightened and approached Rolf. When he got closer, he said Rolf's name.

Rolf was instantly wary. He studied the man, wondering if they'd ever met before. Possibly, but right now the straight, thin nose, upward-curving mouth and light brown eyes didn't look familiar. It wasn't a face that would stick in your mind. "Yes?" he said, slowing his pace only slightly.

"I wonder if you have time to speak with me? I'm a friend of Brian's."

That stopped Rolf. I should've gotten out. Why didn't I get out? "Yeah? What do you want?"

"I'd like a word with you about yesterday afternoon."

The guy was a policeman, investigating Sally's death. How could he have found Rolf? But wait. A policeman wouldn't say he was a friend of Brian's. And no policeman Rolf had ever seen dressed in thousand-dollar suits. Rolf started walking again. "Fuck off."

Rolf heard footsteps behind him. The man's voice said, "I know you were there."

Rolf halted abruptly and heard the man stop. The drab, ugly neighborhood vanished, became a gray emptiness waiting to swallow Rolf. If Rolf let that cold grayness surround him, he would be lost. He waited, and in a short while he could again see the buildings, the lines of laundry flapping above, could hear the shouts of the children. He turned around. "What are you talking about?"

"You were wearing a black cloak and hood, and you had a mirror over your face."

The grayness was back. Rolf's hands clutched at the white plastic bag containing Jean-Pierre's Pierrot costume. "You're crazy."

The man smiled. "Perhaps I'm crazy, but I'm still correct."

Rolf had to swallow several times. Nobody knew who was behind that mirror, yet this stranger knew. Rolf had been worried about the group, one of them knowing about him and sending a poem, and here came a man Rolf had never seen before who knew Rolf had been behind that mirror. Rolf felt painfully, achingly, exposed, as if he had inadvertently shouted out all his secrets in the Piazza.

"You chose an appropriately Venetian disguise," the man said. "Perhaps you realized that the glass mirror was invented here? The mirror craftsmen were not allowed to leave Venice, for fear they would give away the secret. The secret became known, anyway, as secrets often do."

Rolf scrambled for control. "Talk as much as you like, you lunatic. I have no idea what this is about."

"It takes panache to insist on a claim so easily disproved," the man said. Almost apologetically, he nodded in the direction of the boys kicking the soccer ball. "Before you arrived, I had a conversation with the children over there. One of them told me that you're staying at his home. Yesterday he saw you—or at least, he saw the mirror-man—coming out his front door. I suppose one could claim it isn't absolutely *proof,* but I think—"

Rolf dropped his bag and lunged at the man, but the man stepped easily past his grasping hands. The man's face took on a pink tinge, and he looked as if he were about to laugh.

Rolf stopped. He forced himself to breathe, to clear his head. He picked up the bag. "Maybe I *did* dress that way. That still doesn't mean I was—I was—"

"At the Rio della Madonna? But you were."

The flush on the man's cheeks had deepened. He looked as if he were having a great time. Rolf's chest expanded with fury. "How do you know? You can't prove it."

All at once, Rolf remembered a white figure, a loony-looking bride, with flowers on her head and tattered white material hanging off her. That person had seen him for sure, had stared at him from across the little canal. Rolf said, "Were you the bride?"

The man looked confused. Then realization seemed to dawn. "You mean the *corpse,*" he said. He leaned forward with a confidential air. "To be dead is to be a prey for the living."

The panic and rage Rolf had barely been keeping in check took over. "Get away from me!" he shouted. "I don't care what you saw! I didn't kill Sally!"

The man's brows moved toward one another. "Sally?"

"Leave me alone, you maniac!" If only those goddamn kids weren't around, Rolf would grab this guy and batter him until he was pulp on the pavement, until blood flew everywhere. Rolf would stick his thumbs in the guy's eyes and pop his eyeballs.

The man stared at Rolf in a distracted way. He muttered, "Ciao," turned, and walked briskly away.

Fighting the shakes, Rolf crossed the pavement to the

front door of Rosa and Gianni's house. He saw Rosa framed in a downstairs window, looking out at him.

She opened the door, her eyes wide. She pointed after the man's receding back and said, "I just see. *Il conte Zanon.*"

He stared at her. "You know that man?"

"*Sì, sì.*"

"His name is Count Zanon?"

"*Sì.* Michele Zanon."

"Where does he live? Um—*Dove vive?*"

"Ooh—" Rosa made lavish gestures indicating, Rolf guessed, a mansion. "Beautiful palazzo! So beautiful!"

"*Dove?*"

"*Canal Grande.*" She put a finger on her chin, thinking. "*Imbarcadero San Angelo.*"

All right. Rolf knew who the man was, and he knew where to find him. That's all he needed. He looked at Rosa, who was blushing and nodding. As he'd known it would, her earlier petulance had vanished. Well, she'd done him a hell of a favor. He folded her to him, moving his hands down her back to her round bottom. He kissed her, his tongue deep in her mouth, until she broke away, panting. She pointed outside and said, "Boys. Later."

Good. He wasn't in the mood right now. He climbed the stairs to his room, sat on the couch and lit a cigarette. Staring at the smoke, he thought about Count Michele Zanon.

PART THREE

INTERLUDE

THIS SUNNY DAY is Fat Tuesday, *mardi gras,* the end of Carnival. Tomorrow comes the boredom of Lent. The rains will disintegrate confetti the sweepers have missed, costumes will be aired, folded, and put away, and for the weeks before the summer tourist onslaught it will be possible to get a table at Florian's or Harry's Bar.

For now, Carnival continues. The pace has become feverish, because the cleansing rain and emptiness loom so close. Last chances hover: The last chance to sell a postcard, a ruffled blue net boa, a necklace of glass flowers, a print of old Venice, a striped gondolier's shirt; the last chance to go in costume to a concert, to dance impromptu with a stranger, to walk through the streets behind a bouquet of balloons as tall as the second-floor windows, to stand at midnight in the Bocca di Piazza and listen to twenty angelic-looking teenagers singing motets; the last chance to wear a mask; the last chance to get what you hoped Carnival would give you.

The sun is shining, and the good weather may continue. Perhaps Venice will be so beautiful that it will not matter that very little time remains.

MICHELE RETURNS

SALLY SAT in Michele's salon overlooking the Grand Canal, eating salami, brown bread, and wrinkled black olives and drinking fizzy mineral water. Sun flooded in from the balcony through a wall of leaded bull's-eye glass. It fell on a huge vase of lilies and an Oriental carpet patterned in aqua and gold, and made a path of light over the paintings that were hung one above the other to the ceiling.

She was still achy and jittery after her ordeal with the Medusa, but she had slept—an exhausted, stuporous slumber—and that had helped. When the brown-eyed policeman had left, taking with him her report of the Medusa's attack, Michele had said, "Sally, I must go out for a while. Please rest. Maria is here, and Sandro. You will be quite safe."

Sally had been in no mood or position to argue. She had rested, and she was better for it. When she awoke and wandered out to this room, Maria, the housekeeper whose shoes Sally had worn to Torcello, appeared with the snack, which Sally had been surprised to find herself eager to eat. A few cookies, liberally dusted with confectioners' sugar,

176

remained. Sally didn't want to get sugar and crumbs on the heavy yellow-and-white silk upholstery of the chair she was sitting in, or on the carpet. She wrapped the cookies in her napkin and took them with her out onto the narrow white stone balcony.

The air was fresh and cold, the sky still bright, although occasional rushing shadows showed that clouds were forming. The Canal shone its distinctive blue-green and was alive with activity. Sally leaned on the railing and watched the vaporettos, barges, water taxis, and gondolas below and the wheeling, screaming seagulls overhead. Motors drummed, oars and ropes splashed, people shrieked with laughter or called out to one another. Across the Canal were other palazzos with tall arched or pointed windows, elaborate carved medallions or winged lions for decoration, white balconies like the one on which she stood.

Venice *was* beautiful, if you saw it like this, if you could stand in the sun after a good meal and forget your troubles for a minute or two.

She remembered the words her father had said this morning: *You'll come back here with us, sweetheart.*

She saw the brick house in Tallahassee where her parents lived, where she had grown up. There were pink azaleas in the yard, and trees hung with Spanish moss. In summer in Tallahassee, it rained hard every afternoon and afterward the air was fragrant and soft. In autumn, bushels of pecans dropped off her grandmother's tree.

Sally and her parents would drink iced tea and watch the news on television in the evenings. She'd get a teaching job. Maybe she'd meet some young man just finishing law school, and they'd get married and her life would become what she'd thought it was going to be with Brian.

Except this new young man wouldn't be so handsome. He'd be plain and loyal and good.

Venice was beautiful if you could forget your troubles, but Sally couldn't. Brian had been murdered, and she herself was threatened, and she was alone.

True, Michele had saved her from the Medusa's attack, and her first reaction had been overwhelming relief and gratitude. Now, she'd had time to think.

What had resulted from the episode with the Medusa? Sally lost the letters she had been taking to the police, the threatening letters Brian had received in Paris. Suppose Michele had wanted those letters. Suppose he and the Medusa were in cahoots. Sally didn't know how Michele might have worked it, but she was sure he could have.

On the good side, if the object of the attack had been the letters, there was no reason for Sally to be attacked again. She couldn't take the chance, though. She was trapped.

The sky was becoming more overcast. Sally went back inside.

Suppose Michele and the Medusa were in cahoots, and Michele had ended up with the letters. How could she find out?

She could search around, just see if she found them.

Sally's mother said, *Sally Ann! You will do no such thing.*

Of course not, Mama. I was kidding.

You don't go into people's homes and search their private things!

No, ma'am.

Sally sighed. If she found the letters, it would mean she definitely couldn't trust Michele. At least that would be settled.

She wandered through the dining room, polished and pristine now, a huge bunch of yellow roses on the shining table, and down the hall toward Antonia's bedroom. She tried the doors on the opposite side of the hall. Both were bedrooms with the neat, uninhabited look of guest rooms. With all that extra space, Michele had put Sally in Antonia's room. Sally wondered why.

Off to the left beyond Antonia's bedroom was another hall. She followed it and found a little library. The walls were lined with old-looking books enclosed by tarnished brass mesh. Two cracked leather chairs faced each other in front of a cold fireplace. Beyond tall French windows was a wrought-iron balcony overlooking the garden. A spindly-legged desk held a small portable typewriter and a neat stack of papers under a paperweight of swirling, multi-colored Venetian glass.

Sally walked to the desk and looked down at the stack of papers. The top one was a letter to Michele, written in Italian.

Sally rested her hand on the paperweight.

Sally! Her mother said.

She moved the paperweight to one side.

Sally Ann!

It's okay, Mama. This will just take a minute.

She picked up the papers and riffled through them, looking for the envelopes or the four small sheets with their short, ambiguous sentences. She was searching so intently she almost missed the paper in Brian's handwriting. She leafed past it and had to go back to look again.

The paper had been folded, then straightened out again. Brian's writing was wavery, but it was definitely his writing. A purple stain that looked like wine had discolored one corner of the page.

Brian had written down a poem:

> *The woman whose visage turns others to stone*
> *Changes trusting friends into people alone.*
>
> *The woman who has snakes for hair*
> *Changes faithful lovers to men in despair.*
>
> *There's no way to guess what the woman will do.*
> *Who can predict what she'll change about you?*

Sally read the poem several times. She was still standing there, her search forgotten, when she heard someone coming up the stairs. Quickly she replaced the papers, except for the poem, and put the paperweight on top. She folded the poem and shoved it into the pocket of her jeans, then peered out the door to see Michele just reaching the top of the stairs.

He walked to her swiftly and said, "Sally! Are you all right?"

"Well—my head still hurts a little."

"But you have been quite all right? Nothing further has happened?"

"No. I'm okay."

"Good, good."

Michele, she noticed, seemed highly excited. He took her by the shoulders. "I have something to tell you," he said. "I have found out who murdered Brian."

EXPLANATIONS

ROLF? ARE YOU SURE?" Sally didn't know what she'd expected Michele to say, but it wasn't that.

Michele was pacing up and down the library. Sally sat in one of the chairs in front of the cold fireplace. "He was the mirror-man. He tried to deny it at first. He said"—Michele drew himself up, and a snarl transformed his features—"'Fuck off!'"

In half a second and two words Michele had evoked Rolf so vividly that Sally could see and hear him herself.

Michele's features relaxed. "But of course I had proof. A witness. So he admitted it."

Sally was confused. "Rolf admitted he killed Brian?"

"No, no. He admitted he was the mirror-man. But you yourself saw him leaning over Brian's body. You were telling the truth about that, weren't you?"

Sally saw mockery in the suspicious look Michele gave her. "Yes. But I didn't see him hit Brian or anything."

Michele waved this away. "Perhaps not. But you admit that in all likelihood he is the guilty one? He ran away, after all."

So did I, Sally thought, but Michele continued, "And he didn't go to the police later to tell his story, as you did."

Sally remembered the black-cloaked figure, the mirror-face flashing in the sun. It could've been Rolf. She had no reason to think it wasn't.

"The police were easier to convince than you are," Michele said.

She shook her head. "I guess you're right."

"No. You have doubts. What are they?"

What were they? Sally considered, then said, "I don't know why he would have done it. I don't think Rolf hated Brian. He hardly paid any attention to him."

Rolf didn't pay attention to Brian, Sally thought. Rolf paid attention to me. He had watched her with hooded eyes as they sat in the Café du Coin. Her palms began to perspire now, as she thought about it.

"Ah," said Michele. "That, you see, is the other part of the story."

His excitement seemed to have dissipated. He had stopped pacing and stood next to the desk. "In fact, he doesn't realize it's Brian who has been killed," Michele said. "He thinks it's you."

Sally hated Michele's statement. The hatred lurched through her with frightening savagery. The idea of Rolf's killing Brian hadn't seemed right. The idea of Rolf's killing Brian because he thought Brian was Sally seemed entirely possible. She still couldn't imagine why, but she thought the answer was in the way he had looked at her during those long afternoons at the Café du Coin. The answer had nothing to do with Sally, but with something that was going on inside Rolf's head.

"I shouldn't have told you. I should have waited until they arrested him," Michele said.

"How do you know they'll arrest him? He might get away, since you warned him."

"I had to test him, to be sure. The child who told me he'd seen Rolf in the mirror costume might have been mistaken or lying. I had to see Rolf's reaction."

Sally shook her head. "The police could have done that." Abruptly, she wanted to cry. "Why didn't you leave it to the police?"

Michele frowned uncomprehendingly. "Because it wouldn't have been nearly as interesting."

Sally leaned back in the chair and shoved her fingers into the pockets of her jeans. The poem she had discovered on Michele's desk crackled softly.

Michele resumed pacing. His good spirits seemed to be returning. Sally watched him, trying to think. "How did you know where to find Rolf?" she asked. "I didn't even know myself."

"It was easy." Michele looked pleased. "I called the bistro in Paris where he worked and asked if anyone knew. A very cordial man there seemed happy to give me the address."

"But how did you know about the bistro? I know I didn't—"

"Brian told me."

"Brian?"

"When I talked with him the night before he died."

"When you talked with him?" Sally was stunned. She realized that Michele had told her almost nothing, and she —from confusion? Fear of what she might learn?—had let him get away with it. The spurt of anger she felt was as much at herself as at him. "You didn't tell me you'd talked with Brian."

Michele didn't respond to the accusation in her tone. He sat in the chair opposite hers. He said, "Brian was a terribly unhappy young man."

"Yes."

"He was so stunning, so American, so unhappy. His sadness interested me as much as his beauty."

Michele's face took on a remote look. "We met by chance in a *taverna* near the Fenice. He was alone. We shared a carafe or two of wine, and he told me everything

—about the group, you, Jean-Pierre, the game you were to play. Once he'd started he went on and on. I have never seen a man so obsessed by his own guilt with so relatively little, if I may say so without wounding you, to feel guilty about.

"He felt he had treated you horribly, shamefully. He was also anguished because he couldn't return Jean-Pierre's love with a fervor equal to Jean-Pierre's, and so felt both suffocated and inadequate. Lastly, and very keenly, he felt guilty because he had betrayed the game."

"Betrayed the game? How?"

"At Jean-Pierre's insistence, the two of them told each other what their costumes would be."

"He told Jean-Pierre he was going to dress as Medusa?"

"Yes."

"What was Jean-Pierre going to be?"

"Pierrot."

"Pierrot? But he was supposed to dress as his true self!"

Michele shrugged. "He told Brian he intended to dress as Pierrot."

Sally wondered which of the many Pierrots she'd seen had been Jean-Pierre. One had pushed past her, hadn't he, when she was following Brian after Brian had left the Piazza? A Pierrot with a long, floating ruff of black net?

Michele was looking at Sally. He seemed to be considering something. He got up and went to the desk, saying, "One particular thing was very touching." He moved the paperweight and began to thumb through the stack of papers.

He looked through all the papers, then started over and looked through them again. After he'd finished the second search, he looked at Sally, a smile touching his lips. "I see I'm not the only one who can conduct an investigation," he said. "Sally, what have you done with Brian's poem?"

A VISITOR

SALLY HAD NO idea if Michele believed the stammered impromptu explanation of how she had found the Medusa poem which she offered, sweating, under his steady and noncommital gaze. She hoped she wouldn't have to repeat it, as she wasn't sure she'd remember the details, which included coming to the library in search of something to read and recognizing Brian's handwriting on a corner of the poem that was protruding from the stack of papers. When she finally ran out of things to say, Michele nodded approvingly. "You did exactly right. I should have given it to you myself, but I was afraid it would pain you."

Sally wasn't sure she believed him, either, but she was relieved at being let off the hook. She said, "I don't understand something."

"What?"

"Why did Brian talk to you that night? I mean, tell you all his secrets?"

Michele paused to consider before he said, "Two reasons, I suppose. First, he was desperate and ready to talk. Second, he told me his secrets because I told him mine."

Unaccountably, Sally felt stung. She wondered what Michele had told Brian that he hadn't told her. "Your secrets?"

Michele walked to the French windows and peered up at the sky. "Do you know, I think it will rain," he said.

Sally waited. She wasn't going to discuss the weather. He returned to the chair opposite hers and sat down. "You must understand that I am a lily of the field who neither toils nor spins," he said. "My life is not dull because I know how to amuse myself, and my attention is easily caught. It was caught by Brian."

He settled himself in his chair, seeming to compose his body carefully. "When I saw Brian at the *taverna,* he was the picture of despair. I was intrigued, as I told you. Why should a man so young and beautiful be so dreadfully sad? I tried to talk with him, but he would barely answer me. I suppose he thought I was interested in him in a sexual way.

"You may be too young to have learned this, Sally, but often telling someone your secret will lead that person to tell you his. A confidence will elicit a confidence. I saw that Brain was sad, and if I wanted to know why, I had better be sad myself."

At Michele's last words his face changed, almost miraculously it seemed to Sally. His mouth drooped, his cheeks sagged, even his skin appeared to change color, and when he continued, his voice had a tight, gritty quality. "I began to speak about my beloved wife, Antonia, who has left me. He ignored me at first, but my account of abandonment and despair was irresistible. I was moved by it myself, almost to tears. After I told him my story, he told me his. He had written a poem about Medusa which expressed some of his despair, and he gave it to me. I was very touched."

Michele's face cleared. "That's how it happened."

"But was it a lie? About Antonia?" Sally asked.

Michele frowned. "Certainly not. It was all true."

Then why were you talking aobut it just for fun, just to

186

trick Brian, Sally wanted to ask, but didn't. Wind rattled the windows, and the room darkened a little.

"Antonia doesn't like Venice," Michele said in a soft, absent tone. "She tells me, 'If you love decay so much, why don't you shut yourself up in a shabby, tumbledown room with beautiful, rotting things in it and watch them fall apart around you? That's what living in Venice is like.' "

"Is that why she stays in Milan?"

"She stays in Milan because she loves the future. What future does Venice have? Inundation. One day, waves will break over the domes of the Basilica. Antonia has no use for such melancholy thoughts. She has a design studio in Milan, she has many forward-looking friends. They sit in rooms where everything is white, even the floors, and smoke cigarettes and talk about the future. Antonia doesn't like pattern, complication, intricacy. She thinks Venice is too elaborate to be truly stylish. She's right, of course."

Sally couldn't think of any reply. She wasn't used to this kind of talk.

"I said Antonia doesn't like pattern, complication, and intricacy," Michele went on. "On the other hand, they fascinate me."

"Do you and Antonia agree about anything?"

He smiled ruefully. "Some years ago we agreed to get married. Quite frankly, I thought if she didn't marry me I would die. To spend an hour away from her was torture. She felt the same. Oh, yes, we were in complete agreement then." His shoulders twitched. "But now she is in Milan, and you and I are in Venice, surrounded by as much pattern, complication, and intricacy as we could wish." A slow smile touched his lips. "Imagine how she'll feel when she hears I've solved a murder."

Footsteps sounded in the hall. Maria came in and spoke to Michele in Italian. He seemed surprised, Sally thought, at what she told him. When Maria had left, Michele turned to Sally and said, "Francine is on her way up. She arrived uninvited and asked to see me."

Sally didn't want to see Francine. She had too much to think about, too many things to sort out. She stood up. "Look. Can't I wait in my room until she leaves?"

"Of course, but you'd better hurry if you don't want to meet her."

Sally rushed down the hall and across the landing. As she pulled open the bedroom door she heard Michele's voice greeting Francine.

The door closed behind her, and in the silence she began to consider how she was going to get out of there.

LUNCH
IN THE *CAMPO*

FRANCINE, Tom, and Jean-Pierre huddled over stale sandwiches at a table in the Campo Francesco Morosini, although it was almost too cold now to sit outside. Revelers passing on their way to the Piazza bent into the wind, capes and veils billowing. One among them, a Pierrot, his sad-clown mask framed by an extravagant ruff of black net, escaped the crowd to hover in a nearby doorway. A café employee, looking at the sky, began stacking unoccupied tables.

Francine felt cheated and dissatisfied in the aftermath of her conversation with Michele Zanon. Although the count had been extremely courteous, he had told Francine nothing new, and she had had no chance to look around the palazzo on her own. Neither, to her chagrin, had there been an opportunity to discuss Sartre.

The meeting was hardly worth the difficulty Francine had gone through to get there, which had been considerable. She had despaired of ever being free of Ursula's company again, but eventually even Ursula's inventiveness and capacities had flagged and she'd pronounced herself ready for a siesta. She had insisted that Francine remain with her in the darkened bedroom until she fell asleep. When Ursula was emitting breathy snores, Francine tiptoed out and escaped.

Francine had felt more than ready for a siesta herself. Her head ached, and the bright sunlight and brisk winter breeze seemed unpleasantly harsh as she wound along the route that led to Michele Zanon's palazzo. Ursula had not been particularly willing to divulge the directions, but Francine was not above withholding, or threatening to withhold, skills she now knew appealed to Ursula very much. Ursula finally told her, then clutched Francine and said, "You won't leave me for Michele will you, *cara?*"

"Don't be absurd," said Francine, repeating the directions several times in her head.

Now, her meeting with Michele ended, Francine's headache was worse and she felt hollow inside. This bad feeling came from fear and anger at Sally.

Francine had, she was sure, seen Sally in Michele's palazzo. Sally was wearing her dreadful sweater with the flying geese on it, and she was slipping stealthily into another room as Francine approached. When Francine asked Michele, he blandly denied it, saying Francine must have caught a glimpse of his wife, Antonia, who had arrived from Milan. Antonia apologized, Michele said, for not coming to meet Francine, but she was exhausted from her trip.

Francine wasn't fooled. Sally was staying in the palazzo with Michele, and Michele had deliberately concealed the fact. Thinking of it made Francine wild. It was monstrous that pale, plain Sally was enjoying the company of Michele Zanon, living with him not only shamelessly but in great luxury.

Francine wanted, she needed, Michele as her ally. She couldn't have Sally standing in her way.

The final annoyance had been running into Tom and

Jean-Pierre outside Michele's gate after her unsuccessful visit, where they apparently had just bumped into one another. Michele had seen Tom earlier, and had left a message for Jean-Pierre, and both wanted to speak with him. Although Francine supposed it was reasonable that if Michele had sought her out, he would have visited the others, she wished it weren't true. She wished she had been singled out, unique.

Jean-Pierre seemed to be barely functioning. Tom rubbed his cheeks in a way that drove Francine mad, and treated her warily, as if fearing a repeat of their early-morning quarrel. It was he who suggested the three of them exchange addresses and then go on to lunch together nearby.

Jean-Pierre had eaten nothing, and Tom had two whiskies and a half a sandwich, but Francine was ravenous. She also had an idea. She nodded in the direction of the palazzo and said, "Do you know who's staying there with Count Zanon? Sally."

Tom, frowning, settled his chin deeper into the collar of his coat. "How do you know?"

"I saw her. And let me tell you something else." She leaned over the cold metal table. "The count gave a party last night—a masked ball, and breakfast on Torcello. Count Zanon dressed as Harlequin. He even did acrobatic tricks."

Francine waited for possible comments, then continued. "Sally was there, too. She was dressed as a Spanish señorita in a black-and-white ruffled dress, a gaucho hat, and a red shawl."

Tom looked at Francine as if she were a maniac. "I don't believe it," he said flatly.

Francine looked at him with loathing. "Well, why don't we dispute what I saw with my own eyes? She had on makeup, a great deal of it. And she said to me"—Francine affected a sophisticated air—"'Are you a friend of Michele's?'"

191

Tom stared.

"And if you don't believe me, you can ask Michele Zanon," Francine finished triumphantly.

Neither Tom nor Jean-Pierre said anything. It was difficult to say if Jean-Pierre had heard. His eyes were blank. Tom sat shaking his head. At last he said, "God."

Francine considered this enough encouragement to continue. "We've completely underestimated Sally. If she can go to a fancy dress ball a few hours after her husband's murder, she's capable of anything."

Tom said, "That little pipsqueak couldn't—"

Francine thrust her jaw forward. "She could and she did. And she and her Harlequin, her aristocratic lover, are probably laughing about it now."

This maddening thought inspired her to continue. Her idea was growing, blossoming, like a rare flower that has found the hot, moist dampness it needs. "I think she killed Brian. She wanted to be with Michele. She waited for her opportunity and took it."

Tom was rubbing his face. He shot a look at Jean-Pierre. "Brian didn't want her, anyway. Sally could've been with Count Zanon if she wanted to. She didn't have to kill Brian for that."

Jean-Pierre pushed his chair back and stood. "I must go," he said. Before either of them could protest, he had left, threading his way through the crowded square.

Francine wanted to continue elaborating on her idea, but Tom's responses seemed halfhearted. After a short while he, too, excused himself and left.

Most of the tables were stacked now. The costumed crowds, still hopeful that the weather would hold, jostled toward the Piazza. The Pierrot had disappeared from the doorway. Francine sat alone in the Campo Francesco Morosini, beneath the overcast sky.

BRIAN

SOMETHING COLD and viscous was rising in Brian's throat, something he didn't want to taste. He would taste it soon. It was rising, and there was nothing he could do.

Brian saw through brackish water with pale gobs of matter floating in it. These gobs changed shape, stretched out and folded in as the waves dictated.

Through the polluted water of his eyes, Brian saw drowned towers and domes, underwater bridges, deep-sea divers in bright costumes. The divers swam by him, laughing in their lace and feathers, sequins and gauze, their cloaks flowing, their jewelry glimmering in the marine light.

Choked, Brian could not call out. He could not tell the swimmers what they needed to know. He could not tell them how cold and unclean death was, how soon it came, how long it lasted. They swam strongly while he drifted, but they would drift and dissolve in their turn. If his throat were not filling, he could tell them.

Still they swam by him, dressed in their disguises. With the right disguise, you could conceal shame. With the right disguise, you could even hide death for a little while, and death was the greatest shame of all.

Something was rising in his throat. There wasn't much time.

Death should not have happened to Brian. He wouldn't flow away yet, as much as he might spread and loosen, because he was caught against his rage the way a plastic garbage bag tossed into a canal might be caught in a corner by a bridge, might ride out a tide or two next to this barrier while the garbage inside became more and more foul.

Something was rising in his throat, and he had to hurry. Soon he would be inundated by his body's tides.

IN ANTONIA'S ROOM

SALLY SAT in Antonia's armchair, trying to put her thoughts in order. She had been sitting there a long time. The sun no longer danced on the walls, and the light in the room was a shifting, watery gray.

Michele believed, or said he believed, that Rolf had killed Brian because he thought Brian was Sally. Sally had asked herself if that idea was the least bit plausible, and decided it was. Brian was taller and heavier than she was, but the Medusa's robe and headdress distorted and concealed physical attributes. Plus, Rolf might have been convinced beforehand, for some reason, that the Medusa was Sally and never doubted it.

On the other hand, Sally hadn't seen the mirror-man— Rolf, if that's who it was—attacking Brian, but bending over his body. Sally knew that wasn't proof Rolf had killed him. It was circumstantial evidence. Wasn't it suspicious, then, that Michele seemed so anxious to convince her and the police that Rolf was guilty?

Michele was playing a game of his own. Sally could see how he had capered around her in circles while she'd made herself dizzy spinning to keep up with him. He was exasperating, and frightening, but worst of all he was attractive, too, and he knew it and used it to keep other people in line and get his way. But what, in this case, did "his way" consist of? He could be playing detective to impress Antonia, or he could even have killed Brian and be scrambling now to cover his guilt. His interests and Sally's didn't coincide in either case, but he kept acting as if they were allies and she, in her need not to feel so totally alone, had responded in spite of herself.

She got up, crossed the room, and opened the door a crack. She couldn't hear anything. She assumed Francine had left quite a while ago. She closed the door and leaned against it.

Brian's poem about Medusa was still in the pocket of her jeans. Michele had intended to give it to her—or so he said. But Michele found her in the library. He might have suspected, mightn't he, that she had found the poem already? If that were true, his pretending to search for it to give to her could have been a way to put her on the defensive.

Whatever the truth of any of this, Sally wanted to get out. She wanted to get out, but she was afraid of the ghost-Medusa with hate-filled eyes, who might be waiting for her.

The best thing would be to vanish. Sally wished she had a cloak of invisibility.

Since she couldn't vanish, she thought she'd have a talk with Michele. He might have explanations he could convince her to believe. She wanted to believe, wanted him to still her doubts.

She opened the door again and slipped out into the hall, not sure where to look for him. She walked down the hall and through the hushed dining room toward the salon.

She was almost at the door when she heard Michele's voice and drew back, thinking Francine must still be there. Michele was saying, "—that even the most profound loves have their times of difficulty and upset. Perhaps the greater the love, the greater the difficulty, do you think?"

"I don't know."

The voice that replied was muffled, although clear enough for Sally to know it wasn't Francine's, but a man's. She hesitated, listening.

"This has been terrible for you," Michele continued.

"Yes." The voice sounded hollow, wistful. It went on, "How did you meet Brian?" Sally realized the speaker was Jean-Pierre.

"Just briefly, by chance. He told me of his love and concern for you."

"He did?" Jean-Pierre sounded animated for the first time. Sally leaned her forehead against the door frame and closed her eyes in order to hear better.

"Yes. He loved you very much." Sally could picture Michele's face in an expression of exquisite sadness.

"And I loved him," Jean-Pierre said.

"I hope you were spared seeing his body."

Sally heard Jean-Pierre draw in a breath. "I was. I had followed him from the Piazza because, of course, I recognized him, even in costume. I lost him in the crowd. I never saw him again."

A few moments passed, and then Michele said, "Slime is the agony of water."

Sally's eyes opened. She was staring so intently at the door frame that she could see a tiny, feathery brush stroke in the cream-colored paint. *Slime is the agony of water.* One of the four sentences in the stolen letters. Michele knew about, had read, the letters.

Sally stepped backward. She barely heard Jean-Pierre's choked, guttural sob. She turned and hurried quietly back to Antonia's room.

JEAN-PIERRE
COMFORTED

JEAN-PIERRE heard steps behind him on the gravel garden walk of the palazzo garden. He felt an arm around his shoulders. "My poor friend, I can't possibly let you go like this," Michele said.

Jean-Pierre shook his head. Through his tears he saw wavering gravel.

"I feel dreadful," Michele said. He shook Jean-Pierre gently. "We'll walk awhile, eh?"

They passed through the wrought-iron gate. Jean-Pierre blotted his eyes and saw Michele's hand proffering a crisp handkerchief. He took it and dabbed at his face.

Michele said, "I am so thoughtless, so careless. I wear the costume of Harlequin, you know, and sometimes I act too much like him. Can you forgive me for hurting you?"

Jean-Pierre intended to say, "Please don't mention it." He said only, "Please don't—" before tears choked him again.

They stopped walking. Michele put his arms around Jean-Pierre, and they stood until Jean-Pierre could get his breath. Then Michele said, "You still have the handkerchief? Good. Let's walk on a little."

As they continued, threading through the streets and *campos*, Jean-Pierre began to get hold of himself. He cast sidelong looks at Michele Zanon, the man who claimed to have been a friend of Brian's, the man Francine said was Sally's lover.

"You are feeling better?" Michele said.

"A little. I'm sorry."

They leaned on the railing of a graceful, arched wrought-iron bridge, gazing down a gloomy canal lined by houses with crumbling walls and rusting water gates. A gondola slid silently beneath them, the black-clad gondolier alone in his boat.

Slime is the agony of water. Jean-Pierre swallowed. "I would like to ask you. What made you say—the thing you did?"

Michele sketched a shrug. "I must have read the phrase somewhere, and it entered my mind to say it. Of course it was macabre, awful. I didn't think."

"It's just that—with Brian—"

"Please. You don't have to explain."

Jean-Pierre studied Michele's profile, with its long, straight nose. The face was not interesting at first. The face became interesting after you looked at it for a time. Francine said this man was allied to Sally. Jean-Pierre found the thought intensely disturbing.

Michele turned to Jean-Pierre. "Will you allow me a question?" he said.

"Yes."

"Your face. It looks as if someone hurt you badly."

Jean-Pierre's mouth twisted. "I did it to myself." He remembered the blows falling, the numbing pain.

They continued to gaze at the deep-green canal. The sky was darkening. *Slime is the agony of water*, Jean-Pierre thought.

"I expect that soon the police will arrest the killer," Michele said in a comforting tone.

And what does that matter, Jean-Pierre thought, when the truly guilty still go free?

They walked a little longer, and then Jean-Pierre excused himself, thanking Michele Zanon for his kindness, pardoning him once more for what the count called his unforgivable insensitivity.

As Jean-Pierre watched Michele walk away, he felt certain that the count was not Sally's lover. The real connection had been between Count Zanon and Brian. Jean-Pierre closed his eyes and descended into the familiar blackness.

AN UNEXPECTED
MEETING

ROLF SHRANK back, his gloved hands splayed against the plate glass window of a bakery, as he tried to avoid being pushed toward the Piazza. People thronged the street leading out of the Campo Francesco Morosini. Twenty or so men and women dressed in multicolored ruffles and shaking rattles were trying to squeeze a conga line through. One of the dancers, stalled next to Rolf, smiled and shook her rattles in his face. Automatically, he picked up the game and plucked the rattles out of her hands. She laughed, grasped his black net ruff, and said, loudly and tunelessly:

> *"Au clair de la lune*
> *Mon ami Pierrot—"*

He saw the beaded sweat on her upper lip, smelled the wine on her breath; then the crowd started to surge forward, and she snatched the rattles from him and danced away.

At last he got through the worst of it and emerged in a

wider street. He found a sheltered corner and stopped to adjust his mask and get his bearings.

Earlier, he had seen Francine, Tom, and Jean-Pierre sitting around a table in the *campo*. Everyone was there except Brian, who must have been taking care of arrangements regarding Sally's death. It was curious, Rolf thought, that all of them were here in the neighborhood of Michele Zanon's palazzo. Rolf felt obscurely that they had betrayed him, and the feeling added to his fury.

Filled with loathing, Rolf had stood in the doorway watching them—Francine talking with her mouth full, Tom rubbing his naked chin, Jean-Pierre slumped over like a zombie. Rolf hadn't been able to get close enough to hear their conversation. He was afraid Jean-Pierre might recognize the Pierrot mask and costume, although Jean-Pierre looked incapable of doing so. Besides, with so many Pierrots around, and with Jean-Pierre's believing his disguise was in a pile of garbage, it wasn't likely.

Jean-Pierre was stocky and of medium height and Rolf tall and thin, but Jean-Pierre's costume fit Rolf surprisingly well. The long overblouse and pajama trousers were appropriately loose and floppy, even though Rolf was fully dressed underneath. The arms and legs were too short, but that was all right. Rolf wanted to hide his identity, not win a prize at a masquerade party.

Because of Michele Zanon, Rolf had to leave Rosa and Gianni's, but he was not leaving Venice before he showed Michele Zanon he couldn't fuck around with him. Rolf clenched his fists as he thought about the smug little count who looked as if he wanted to laugh in his face.

Rolf had, by exercising all his skill in Italian, managed to get from Rosa fairly complete directions to the palazzo. She had even drawn a rough map, which Rolf now laboriously extracted from the pocket of the jacket he wore under the white satin blouse. Luckily for Rolf, Rosa was so crazy about him now that she'd do whatever he wanted, as long as he could make her understand what it was.

Rolf consulted the map. He wasn't far away now. He stepped out of his corner and bent into the wind.

The wrought-iron gate leading to the garden of the Zanon palazzo was down an empty little cul-de-sac. The gate stood ajar, but the two ground-floor windows were barred, and the door appeared heavy and was surely locked. As if that weren't enough, Rolf could see someone, probably a doorkeeper, moving behind one of the barred windows.

The street dead-ended at a stone archway through which Rolf could see the cold glimmer of the canal. Exploring, he walked to the archway, then went through it. He was on the edge of the Canal. Seagulls, with their heads tucked down, perched on the wooden mooring poles in front of the palazzo, and the wind chased ripples along the water. Rolf thought the chances of rain were better than fifty-fifty. He looked to make sure of what he already surmised. The only way to approach Count Zanon's house from the front was by boat. He moved back inside the archway.

Rolf was not going to be kept out of this fucking palazzo. Michele Zanon, with his locks and his doorman, thought he was safe from Rolf, but he wasn't. Rolf felt invincible, blazing with determination. He had thought about weapons, but he didn't want a weapon. He walked back to the gate of the palazzo, through the garden, and up to the door.

As soon as he rang the bell, a man wearing a blue smock peered through one of the barred windows at him.

Grinning beneath his mask, Rolf made an elaborate, Pierrot-like bow, bending low with many flourishes.

The man in the blue smock opened the door a tiny crack and said, *"Signor?"*

"I'd like to see Count Zanon," Rolf said.

"Your name?"

Grinning even wider, Rolf gave Tom's name.

The man said, *"Momento."* He was closing the door.

Rolf hurled himself against the door, knocking the man

backward. He rushed inside and, before the man could regain his balance, tripped him so he fell heavily to the floor. The thump the man's body made sounded good to Rolf. He almost shouted with joy as he threw himself on the man, grabbed him around the neck, and gave his head a couple of solid whacks against the marble floor.

Rolf was almost disappointed to feel the man's body go slack. He wished there had been more of a fight. With Count Zanon, he'd make sure it didn't end so quickly.

The man's breathing was labored and noisy. Rolf got up and closed the door to the garden and surveyed the long room with its upright benches along the walls, the upended boat and oars in a corner.

There were three doors in the wall opposite the staircase, one standing ajar. Rolf glanced in and saw a lounge where the doorkeeper must spend his time.

The other two doors led to dark little storage rooms—one with crates and trunks stacked along the walls, the other filled with paint cans, bits of lumber, and—yes—several coils of rope of varying thickness.

Rolf dragged the inert doorkeeper into the lumber room and tied him up. He felt intensely satisfied with the feel of the rope in his hands, the strength and intricacy of the knots he tied. He took a paint-encrusted cloth, gagged the man, and left him behind a pile of cardboard boxes. He closed the door of the room softly when he left. He felt wonderful. He crossed the room to the staircase and began to climb.

So here Rolf was, in the stronghold of Michele Zanon. Michele Zanon had tracked Rolf down, discovered Rolf's secrets. He'd find that Rolf, too, could track people down, breach their security, invade. Rolf longed to see the count's self-satisfied face crumple as he realized what Rolf was going to do to him. Rolf reached the top of the stairs and started down a hall. His senses heightened, he touched the wall, listening to the tiny scratching of his glove against the silk. He passed a closed door and breathed the lemony smell that emanated from the wood. He was strong, at one with the house.

The hall ended at a high-ceilinged dining room. Rolf peered through the doorway at the long table, the bouquet of yellow roses, the chandelier, the windows with flounced white curtains. The room was empty. Rolf entered, moving stealthily through the still air and subdued light. He ran his fingertips over the table and bent to see his Pierrot reflection in its polished top. He thought he saw a sparkle from the tear in the cheek of his mask. He turned toward the door at the opposite end of the room, and was about to take his next step when Sally walked in.

Rolf felt an intense desire to urinate. She had stopped when she saw him, and she stood there, just as always, pale and freckled and scared-looking, wearing her awful sweater with the flying geese on it. Rolf's knees gave, and he supported himself against the table. It was Sally. Sally wasn't dead.

Sally looked startled, too. Even at this distance, he saw —or thought he saw—her lips tremble. She said, hesitantly, "Who are you?"

Rolf didn't speak. He heard her. He saw her. She was there.

She said, "Are you looking for Michele?" Her voice was shaking.

Rolf couldn't move. He couldn't move, then he could. He turned and ran down the hallway, bouncing from wall to wall, desperate to get out.

ROLF'S ESCAPE

SALLY'S VOICE, high and thin, calling "Michele!" reverberated in Rolf's head as he stumbled down the staircase. Perspiration washed over his face under the Pierrot mask. All he knew was that he had to get away.

By the time he reached the bottom of the stairs, he had had a semirational thought: He should get rid of this costume. The doorkeeper had been attacked by Pierrot. Sally had seen Pierrot.

Rolf ducked into the trunk-filled storage room. There was no sound from the next room, where the doorkeeper was probably still unconscious. He tore off the scullcap, mask, satin blouse, and drawstring trousers and left them in a heap on the floor. He opened the door and listened. Nothing. He ran for the garden door and in moments was on the street.

Once in a more populated area, where costumed crowds surged under a darkening sky, he had time to think. Sally was alive. Who, then, was the dead Medusa, the woman whose visage turns others to stone? He had been so sure it was Sally. The words fit her perfectly.

A burst of applause and jangling bells disturbed his thoughts. An acrobat in a jester's costume was performing to an adoring crowd in a corner of a *campo*. Rolf passed by without stopping. In a way, everything made more sense now. He had thought, during the struggle, that Sally was surprisingly strong. But if it hadn't been Sally, who was it?

Brian. Of course. It was surely a member of the group, and Rolf had seen all the rest of them sitting in the *campo*. The Medusa had been Brian, and Sally was alive, and she was staying with Michele Zanon in his fancy palazzo.

At the thought of Michele Zanon, Rolf's anger began to seep back, crowding out the shock and confusion of his unexpected meeting with Sally. The anger was with himself as much as anyone. He had acted like a chickenshit jerk, running as if he'd seen a ghost, which he guessed he'd thought he had. He had let it throw him off, and he'd lost his advantage and knocked out the doorkeeper for nothing. They'd be doubly on guard now, although that wouldn't stop Rolf if—when—he decided to go back.

When he did, nothing would stop him.

He had to make plans, but first he would meet Rosa and get his backpack. He pulled out her map again. He wished he and Rosa could communicate a little better. What he thought he had told her was that he felt uncomfortable staying in her home since they'd started this romance, and he needed another place. What he thought she had told him was that her cousin, or somebody, had a room above a coffee house called the Colombiana. The cousin worked for a family that had gotten out of Venice for the duration of Carnival, so the place was empty, and Rosa had a key. She was meeting him there with his stuff, since he hadn't wanted to carry it with him on his foray to Michele Zanon's.

Having her cooperation was a stroke of luck, but Rolf wasn't sure how well she'd handle it when the police turned up on her doorstep asking about him. Since he was now fairly certain they were going to, her cousin's room could be only a pit stop.

The Colombiana was little more than a smoke-filled hole-in-the-wall with a bar and two tables crowded with people drinking espresso. None of them was wearing a costume. Obviously, this was a working-class hangout where people didn't have time to prance around pretending to be what they weren't. Rolf was doubly glad, now, to have shed the Pierrot disguise.

The stairs were off to one side, through a glass door. They smelled like coffee and smoke. Rolf climbed to the second floor and tapped at a door on the drab little landing. He heard Rosa's voice asking who it was, and he said, "It's me. Let me in."

She was overjoyed to see him, pulling him into the room and embracing him, pushing her body close to his. This was one place, anyway, where he was still in charge. When he kissed her, deeply, she rubbed her thigh against him, making noises of admiration and gratification. Rolf felt good again, powerful again, ready. He walked her over to the bed he had barely glimpsed when he came in, and they collapsed on it.

She was as ready as he was, had probably been thinking about him the whole time they were apart, and she had already contracted, gasping and mumbling in Italian, pulling on handfuls of his hair, when he pulsed and shot, with Sally's scared face wheeling through his mind.

After that, all he could hear was his own hoarse breathing and Rosa's in his ear, and it was a long time before he opened his eyes and saw Rosa's husband Gianni standing in the doorway.

SALLY MAKES
A PLAN

SALLY SAT AT the dressing table, hastily tying on Antonia's gold mask with the black chin-length lace. When the mask was adjusted, she jammed on the black gaucho hat. Antonia's cascading white ruffles tumbled over Sally's lap and the dressing table stool nearly to the floor. The skirt was almost long enough to hide the fact that Sally was wearing her own boots instead of pretty shoes. The señorita had returned.

Sally would not stay here another minute. Her encounter with the Pierrot in the dining room had clinched her determination to leave, no matter what awaited her outside. She had been searching for Michele, ready to confront him about the letters and his talk with Jean-Pierre. *Slime is the agony of water.* She hadn't found him, and then she walked in on the Pierrot. She knew in the first instant that the costumed figure wasn't just a friend of Michele's who had dropped in for a Carnival visit. The most terrifying aspect of the encounter, though, had been how frightened he seemed to be of her.

Michele had told her Jean-Pierre planned to dress as

Pierrot for the game, but the Pierrot she had seen was not Jean-Pierre, Sally felt sure. She didn't think it was Michele, either, although Michele seemed to have disappeared.

Sally had looked for him frantically after the Pierrot encounter, including in the kitchen, where she found Maria sitting in her stocking feet drinking coffee and eating a cookie dusted with confectioners' sugar. In a flurry of embarrassment, brushing sugar from the sides of her mouth, Maria shook her head when Sally tried to ask where Michele was. When Maria shrugged, dots of sugar moved up and down on the front of her black dress.

Sally had wished for a cloak of invisibility, a way to vanish and evade the eyes of the Medusa or whoever else might be looking at her. In her desperation, she realized that she *had* such a cloak—Antonia's costume. Wearing it, once she was out of here, she could go where she wanted and nobody would know who she was. The señorita costume had fooled even Francine. As for the doorman downstairs, she would simply insist that he let her out. He couldn't call and check with Michele, because Michele wasn't there.

Under the black lace, Sally's lips were trembling. She pressed them together, hard. She had never in her life felt so alone.

She had had good friends in Tallahassee, friends she laughed with, studied with, told everything to. She had sat with them at Formica tables in pizza parlors near the campus and talked about professors and boyfriends—although Brian was the only serious boyfriend Sally ever had—and about how much work they had to do. Her friends envied Sally because Brian was so good-looking and was going to law school. She wondered, if she saw them now, whether she would be able to tell them what had happened to her. They were graduate students, or starting in careers, maybe married, or even mothers. She wondered if they could possibly understand.

Why not? her mother said. *They may have had troubles, too. You may have lived in Paris, France, but you're not all that different.*

Outside, the wind was blowing, and it looked like rain. In an agony of haste, she searched Antonia's closet. Among the sequined chiffon blouses, cable-knit sweaters, sleek suits, and soft angora dresses was not one raincoat. There was an umbrella, though, a distinctive green one. Its thin, curving wooden handle ended in the carved claw of a bird, and the claw held a round green stone. She snatched it up to take with her.

Sally wrapped herself in the red shawl and picked up her tapestry handbag. She didn't have time to pack her things. She had to escape—now. Maybe once she was away from here, she could figure out the truth about what had been going on.

The truth shall make you free. Why had she thought of that? Maybe the confectioners' sugar on Maria's dress. She remembered, now, how before dinner one Sunday she had eaten two pieces of divinity—sweet, white, nut-studded— out of her grandmother's candy bowl and then lied about it. As she stubbornly shook her head no, the crumbs on the front of her dress giving contrary evidence, her mother said, "The truth shall make you free, Sally," and thinking that meant she wouldn't get spanked, she confessed. She got spanked, anyway, and afterward, howling with fury, went out in the back yard and sat in a pile of raked pine straw to get over it. There, in her nest of prickly brown needles, Sally realized that the truth would not necessarily help you avoid a whipping, but that taking a whipping might be less painful in the long run than living with lies.

She turned out the light, closed the door behind her, and started down the hall.

EXPLANATIONS

URSULA, wearing a dressing gown of cerise quilted satin, was slumped in a chair, moodily smoking. A yard or so away from her feet in their feathered mules lay two tightly crumpled balls of paper and a yellow rosebud, now wilted to brown. Francine wondered if Ursula would slap or kick her if she tried to pick up the balls that were, she had confirmed in the brief moment when Ursula had shaken the paper under her nose, the two halves of her copy of the Medusa poem. The poem and the rosebud had been in Francine's suitcase. Francine now realized that Ursula considered going through Francine's possessions without her permission to be natural behavior.

Ursula, it seemed, had awakened rather soon after Francine went out. Certainly, by the time Francine returned, she was in a frenzy. She shrieked that Francine had gone to see Michele Zanon. While she, Ursula, slept, the treacherous Francine had slipped away to Michele!

Since this was indeed what Francine had done, although her mission had not really been accomplished, Ursula's accusations grated on Francine's nerves. Francine turned her back on Ursula and said coldly, "I refuse to respond to baseless, ridiculous accusations."

"Baseless!" Ursula bounded in front of Francine. From the pocket of her dressing gown she pulled the limp-looking rosebud. "Who else but your wonderful Michelazzo wears a yellow rose in his lapel every day! You must think I'm the world's biggest idiot."

"Not at all. I think you're the world's biggest sneak!" Francine had intended to maintain icy control, but her voice was rising.

"And this!" Ursula pulled a piece of paper from her other pocket. She unfolded it with trembling fingers and shook it under Francine's nose. "Poems! He sends you poems! That's all the impotent fool is good for!"

Stumbling a little over the English words, Ursula read aloud:

> *The woman whose visage turns others to stone*
> *Changes trusting friends into people alone.*

She stopped and narrowed her eyes at Francine. "The two of you mock me," she hissed. "He sends you poems that make fun of me."

Francine shot Ursula a look meant to convey consummate scorn, marched to the sofa, and sat down. She let her head loll back against the sofa cushions and gazed upward. Carved scrollwork, gracefully curved, divided the ceiling into three concentric areas around the chandelier. The center was painted a rich cream color; the next division was a subtle peach; the outermost, light sea-green. Francine heard a tearing, then a crumpling sound. She heard the scratchy impact of what might have been two wadded-up halves of a poem hitting the carpet. She heard a heavy thump that was probably Ursula dropping disgustedly into a chair. She heard the flicking of a cigarette lighter and smelled smoke.

Francine raised her head. She wondered if she should try for the poem. She would leave the rosebud, which she'd been silly to keep, in any case. She gauged the distance to the balls of paper. If she rushed forward and picked them up, then ran for the door, Ursula might not be able to catch her. Francine could barricade herself in her room and decide what to do next.

Ursula looked at Francine. Her eyes were brimming. "Why do you do this to me, *cara?*" she whimpered.

Francine relaxed a little. Perhaps the worst was over. "If you would only listen to me, my—my *cara,*" she said. The Italian word felt strange on her lips, but Francine couldn't bring herself to use any of her more accustomed endearments.

"You want to betray me every moment. With that awful señorita, with Michele—"

"That isn't true. Let me explain." Francine licked her lips. Ursula looked at her expectantly.

Francine said, "Could you give me a cigarette?"

Ursula could have simply tossed her embroidered cigarette case and gold lighter to Francine. Instead, she got up and crossed the room, put a cigarette between Francine's lips, and lit it, keeping her eyes locked with Francine's all the while.

Francine took a long drag on her cigarette and let the smoke drift slowly out of her nostrils. She said, "In a sense, you are completely correct. I *am* very interested in Michele Zanon."

Seeing Ursula's jaw tighten, Francine continued, "It isn't at all what you think. You have accused me of having romantic feelings for him, but in fact I am pursuing him in the interest of justice."

"Justice?" Ursula's tone implied that Francine was still very much on probation.

"Justice. Do you have a copy of today's newspaper?" Francine knew Ursula did, since she herself had snatched a minute to look at it earlier.

With a resigned look, Ursula got up and brought the paper to Francine. Francine turned to the story about Brian's death, which, perhaps understandably in a tourist-conscious city, had not been given a prominent position or a great deal of space. Handing the paper back to Ursula and pointing, she said, "Read that."

It took Ursula longer to get through the article than even Francine had imagined it would, but at last she looked up and said, "Well?"

"Well. I knew the man who was killed, and I'm investigating his murder. I believe Michele Zanon may have been indirectly involved."

Ursula gave a scoffing laugh, but she looked interested. "Michele Zanon involved in murder!" Ursula jeered. "He may have killed a fly once."

"I didn't say he killed anyone. What I suspect is that he is harboring the murderess—the señorita you remember so clearly, who plays such an important role in your accusations of me." Francine felt, and knew she sounded, triumphant, and she saw that Ursula was impressed.

Skepticism crept back, however, and Ursula said, "Investigation? Are you a member of the police?"

Francine raised her eyebrows. "Hardly. How anxious do you think the police would be to inconvenience Count Zanon?"

Ursula frowned. "Then this investigation of yours—"

"Strictly private."

"The poem? The rose?"

"Clues."

Ursula lit a cigarette and stared at her feathered toes. At last she said, "I don't understand. Why would Michele be —what did you call it—harboring this murderess?"

"You see"—Francine leaned forward—"that's exactly

what I must find out. That's why I must return to the palazzo and continue my inquiries."

Ursula didn't answer. Unbelievable as it seemed, she still looked dubious. Francine thought Ursula would drive her mad, but then an idea came. She said softly, "Actually, I've been thinking. If you're willing, there are ways you can help me."

SALLY FINDS
SHELTER

WET WIND swept the Piazza San Marco. Straw gondoliers' hats hanging on souvenir stands pulled at their cheap elastic straps. Pigeons, feathers ruffled, perched on the edge of the roof of the Procuratie Vecchie, ignoring the damp grain on the pavement. The volume of the recorded music seemed abruptly diminished, the sound carried away by the gusts. Some of the thousands of dancers gave up and left to seek protection. Others danced doggedly on.

Sally watched the scene from the doorway of a closed shop. Behind the iron grille covering the plate glass windows was a display of handmade lace tablecloths from the island of Burano. In another life, Sally might have had a use for a lace tablecloth. She could hardly imagine, now, what such a life would have been like.

Sally had gotten out of the palazzo so easily it worried her. When she left, there was no sign of the doorman, and Michele hadn't turned up, either. On every step of the stairs, through the ground-floor room, out into the garden, she had expected to hear him calling her back, asking where she was going. Only when she was safely out did it occur to her that Michele himself might be in trouble.

True, Michele seemed more like a man who caused trouble than got into it involuntarily. But where was he, then, and where was the doorman, and who was the invading Pierrot? Maybe the Pierrot ran from her because he had just finished hurting Michele, or even killing him, and didn't want to be caught.

The wind tore at Sally's shawl, and she wrapped it more tightly around her. She wished she could make up her mind whether she wanted to escape from Michele or protect him. She would try to call, maybe, once she got situated.

Which brought up another question: Situated where? Her dearest wish had been to get out of the palazzo as fast as possible, and now here she was. She was standing at the Piazza San Marco, waiting for a storm to hit, with nowhere to go and nothing with her except her handbag and a green umbrella.

If she went to the police, they would probably just call Michele and tell him to come get her. The policeman had agreed very earnestly that she should stay at the palazzo. No, what she needed was a place to hide out for tonight. Tomorrow, Carnival would be over, Pierrots and Medusas wouldn't be stalking the streets, and it would be easier to figure everything out.

She had watched for the Medusa since she left, and now she glanced around nervously once again. She hadn't seen it. She didn't see it now.

The cold, hard iron grille dug into her shoulder. She had money enough to go to a hotel. At the thought, objections crowded her mind: She had no luggage. She couldn't speak enough Italian to ask for a room. Everything would be filled, anyway.

On the other hand, she definitely didn't want to spend the night on the pavement, where even now a couple of fat raindrops were making round wet blobs. She took firm hold of Antonia's umbrella and started off to find a hotel.

After the first several tries, she had developed a routine.

Walk in; ask if the person behind the desk speaks English; after the person says—almost always—yes, ask if there is a room; listen to the person say the hotel is full; walk out.

When she had gone through the routine ten times or so, Sally began to get a clutching feeling that this wasn't going to work. Tears of frustration formed in her eyes, and she blinked them back after every defeat.

Depleted and exhausted, she continued automatically until, in a dusty little lobby, she asked the man behind the desk if he spoke English and he replied, "Sure do, honey."

He was bald on top, with a thin fringe of red hair hanging below his earlobes. His eyes were brown and slightly popped. Sally stared at him. At last, she said, "Where are you from?"

He started to smile. "Eufaula, Alabama. You?"

"Tallahassee. Tallahassee, Florida."

He extended his hand. "Well, hey, cousin. My name's Otis Miller."

Sally's tears spilled over. She clung to Otis Miller's hand. "Good to meet you," she said in a quavery voice.

"Tallahassee," the man said. "I had a friend went to the university down there. Before your time, I reckon." He looked at her curiously. "Did you need to sit down or something?"

Sally drew in a hiccuping breath. "I'm looking for a room," she said. She put her hand up to wipe her eyes and remembered her mask. She untied it and took it off, and fumbled in her bag for a tissue.

"I'll tell you. The place is full, but—" A phone at his elbow rang, and Otis Miller picked it up. He said, *"Pronto,"* listened for a moment, and began speaking rapidly in Italian.

Sally felt as surprised as if Otis Miller had suddenly levitated, or turned green. She was amazed at this nice man from Eufaula who could speak both Southern and Italian.

After a brisk conversation, Otis put the receiver down and said, "Where were we?"

219

"You really can speak Italian," Sally said.

"Hell, I've lived here ten years. Came over to paint after I got out of Auburn. Thought my daddy would have a fit." He picked up a pencil and bounced the eraser on the counter. "Now, about a room. Our regular guest rooms are full, but I could put you in Carla's room, over in the annex. They wanted her to be here extra time to help in the kitchen during Carnival, but, instead, she threw a plate of pasta at the cook and went back home to Mestre. It's not good enough for a Tallahassee lassie, but it's the best I can do."

"It sounds just fine."

"Let's go look, then." He glanced around. "Where's your suitcase?"

Sally bit her lip. "I don't have it with me."

A knowing look crept into Otis's protruding eyes. "Had a fuss with your boyfriend? He sure will worry when you don't come back tonight, won't he?"

"Oh—I guess so."

"Sure he will. He'll be real sorry tomorrow. Happens all the time at Carnival."

The annex was behind the hotel, across an alley. Carla's room was tiny, with a sink in the corner and the toilet down a dank, musty-smelling hall. Sally told Otis Miller she would take it, and he left to return to his post. She stood in the doorway and watched until he disappeared down the stairs, and she could no longer hear his footsteps.

ROLF IN FLIGHT

ROLF EXTENDED his head forward cautiously. The wind, whistling down the alley, caught and tossed his hair as he looked around. No sign of Gianni.

Rolf was lucky to be alive, after the rampage that fucking maniac Gianni had gone on after he caught Rolf and Rosa together. No explanation had come out during the brawl, but Rolf assumed Gianni had suspected Rosa of hanky-panky and had followed her to the Colombiana. She hadn't even locked the door. What an idiot she was.

Fortunately for Rolf, Gianni had been interested in roughing up Rosa first. That had given Rolf time to dress. He'd been prepared to leave his backpack behind if he had to, but what with Rosa's sobbing hysterically and Gianni's chasing her around, Rolf had been able to grab it. Since he hadn't planned to stay at the Colombiana, he really hadn't lost anything, provided he could evade Gianni.

Clutching his backpack, Rolf had pounded down the stairs while Gianni, finally realizing Rolf was getting away, followed him, roaring. Rolf hoped Gianni didn't have a lot of pals in the Colombiana to help him search

Rolf out and beat his ass. Evading Gianni had been fairly easy as the two of them dodged through Carnival-crowded streets, because Rolf was fast and in good shape. Gianni was overweight and cutting his wind with all the yelling.

He was around somewhere, though, and Rolf needed to get out of this neighborhood and preferably, since it was starting to rain, off the street for a while. Rolf peered out of the alley again. He didn't see Gianni, but he still didn't feel safe. He'd be better off disguising himself somehow.

At the thought, Rolf nearly laughed aloud. If a disguise was what he wanted, he was in the right place. Diagonally across from where he was standing, in the brightly lighted street his alley opened into, was a store selling masks and costumes. The store was open, still filled with customers on this final night of Carnival. Hanging in the window was a black devil mask with a leering face and curved horns. Rolf remembered that he had originally planned to dress as the Devil, with a branching staff of penises. He checked for Gianni one last time and ran across the street.

By the time he had bought and put on his devil mask and hidden his fair hair under a black knitted cap from his backpack, Rolf had a plan. He set off in the direction of the Accademia Bridge.

The name of Jean-Pierre's hotel, Rolf had learned from the plastic laundry bag in which Jean-Pierre discarded the Pierrot disguise, was the Romanelli. Rolf thought he remembered the street, too. He crossed the bridge and located the place before too long, but when he got there, Jean-Pierre was out. Rolf took off his mask and settled down in the lobby to wait.

Jean-Pierre didn't appear for quite a while, and Rolf was thinking of leaving to have dinner when he finally showed up, carrying a shopping bag. When Rolf hailed him, Jean-Pierre turned and said, "Rolf." Jean-Pierre's face was puffy, and his eyes were weird, glazed,

Rolf said, in a low voice so no one would hear, "Listen, Jean-Pierre. I got kicked out of the place where I was staying. I wondered if I could stay here with you? Sleep on the floor?"

Jean-Pierre blinked. He said, "I can't speak about Brian. I can't."

Rolf held his hands up, palms out. "No problem. Really. I'm really sorry it happened, but—"

"I can't speak about it." Jean-Pierre half turned, as if to leave.

Rolf picked up his backpack. "So it's okay if I come to your room?"

Jean-Pierre frowned. "Come to my room? That's impossible."

"Look, Jean-Pierre—"

"Impossible."

Rolf saw with amazement that the little shit was actually walking toward the door, as if he'd forgotten Rolf was there. Rolf said, "Wait a second!"

Jean-Pierre turned. He said, "I can't. Ask Tom or Francine."

Rolf couldn't believe this. "I don't know where they are!"

Jean-Pierre put down his shopping bag and reached into his pocket. "I'll give you the addresses."

Rolf would get even with Jean-Pierre for this, but now wasn't the time. He snatched the paper Jean-Pierre had scribbled on with a caustic, "Thanks *a lot,*" and headed for the door. Francine would be glad to see him. He'd try her first.

ANOTHER REFUSAL

THE ACCADEMIA BRIDGE was thick with revelers despite the weather. Capes cracked in the wind like flags. An orange plume, escaped from a headdress, flew past Rolf's face, accompanied by the anguished wail of its former owner.

As Rolf retraced his steps on his way to Francine's, he thought about the Medusa at the Rio della Madonna. The Medusa had been crouched beside the canal, the dark blue robe billowing, the red-eyed snakes moving eerily, as if they were alive. Rolf had said, "Hi, Miss Medusa. Changed any faithful lovers to men in despair lately?" He had thought it was funny at first, the way the Medusa— Sally, he believed—lashed out and grabbed the staff. He heard the shattering sound again, the mirror breaking.

How could Rolf have made such an error: He felt outraged, seething with shame. He bit the insides of his cheeks, hard.

At last he found the house where Francine was staying, on a quiet side canal near the Church of Santa Maria del

Giglio. The building had the peeling-plaster shabbiness typical of Venice, but as Rolf had suspected, the interior was more sumptuous than the outside indicated. He climbed to the top-floor flat. The doorbell was answered by a mousy-looking maid who apparently spoke nothing but Italian and who responded to his insistent repeating of Francine's name with gestures indicating that Francine was unavailable.

Rolf didn't intend to leave until he had made arrangements to stay here. He moved over the threshhold, ignoring the maid's startled preventive gesture. "I'll wait."

He surveyed the anteroom with its small chandelier and slippery-looking blue chairs. The maid vanished. Rolf was halfway through a cigarette when a woman in a cerise dressing gown and feathered mules walked in. She had a deep tan and bleached-blond hair. Her arms were crossed, her jaw thrust forward.

Despite her threatening stance, Rolf was relieved. If this was the person who lived in the flat, he'd be in good shape. Rolf rarely had trouble getting women to do what he wanted.

"Who are you?" the woman demanded.

Rolf told her his name and then asked, "What's yours?"

"Ursula," she said, then abruptly demanded what he wanted.

While he was explaining that he was a close, good friend of Francine's, Francine herself, wearing her black dressing gown printed with scarlet poppies, appeared in the doorway. She didn't look pleased to see him. "What in God's name are you doing here?" she asked.

It was a pity Rolf hadn't had a chance to get Ursula on his side before Francine arrived. He reached toward Francine to give her a pat, or perhaps grab her shoulder and dig his fingers in so she'd know he meant business, but she jumped back as if he were poison. "What?" she asked again, her tone scathing.

Rolf explained that, through no fault of his own, he had lost his place to stay, and he was hoping—

"Hoping to impose on my friend?" Francine's voice held out no suggestion that Rolf's hopes would be fulfilled.

"For God's sake, Francine. I'm not asking for any big favors." Rolf didn't understand what was happening here, but he didn't like it.

"You *are* asking for favors. Worse than that, you're intruding. You must leave now."

Rolf was flabbergasted. What the hell was wrong with his sleeping on the floor of this obviously spacious apartment? "Look. I'm just asking—" he began, but Ursula's hand closed on his upper arm in a tight grip.

"You are disturbing my friend," she said, and in an instant had propelled him through the door.

Shock prevented Rolf from reacting until the door was closed, but as soon as he heard the latch click, fury whirled through him. He threw himself against the door, pounding it with his fists and yelling, "Francine! Open up, you fucking whore!" He kicked the door several times, leaving black scuff marks on its white surface. He pounded a few more times, crying, "Let me in!" From behind the door came the sound of a dog's furious barking.

Rolf gave the door one last, reverberating kick and ran downstairs before the neighbors could arrive to investigate. Back outside, he ran until he was on the well-traveled route by the Church of Santa Maria del Giglio. There was a *traghetto* stop down on the Canal, next to the Gritti Palace Hotel. He dropped his backpack there and sat on it, gasping breath after breath of the frigid, damp air. The air tasted like Minnesota. A damp, cold autumn day in Minnesota, where there was a girl he had hurt. He hoped she was hurt. Only hurt. Minnesota felt and tasted like this. Her name was Barbara, and he thought, he was reasonably sure, that she was only hurt.

Eventually, Rolf's breathing became slower. The quality of the air in Venice in February didn't really suggest autumn in Minnesota. It had probably done him good to lose his temper. Worked off tensions. He wouldn't forget it the next time he saw Francine, though. When he felt he could walk easily, calmly, calling no attention to himself, he got up. He'd be at Tom's hotel in five minutes.

ROLF MAKES A
SUGGESTION

ROLF LEANED back and let the drone of Tom's voice hover outside his ears. He had what he wanted: number one, permission to sleep on the floor of Tom's room; number two, everything Tom had heard about Brian's murder. Rolf knew Sally was staying with Count Michele Zanon, and Francine claimed to have seen her, dressed in a señorita costume, at a masked ball just hours after Brian's death.

Rolf took a swallow of beer. He and Tom were in a pizzeria next door to Tom's hotel. Outside the crepe paper streamers the pizzeria had used for decoration were fluttering madly. Rain spattered fitfully against the window.

Tom was talking about May of '68, and how Brian's murder had brought back those days—the sense of danger, the heightened tension. Tom was keeping a journal, he said, and he wanted to ask Rolf some questions. The problem with Tom was that he never shut up. At the next table a woman wearing a beige fur coat and a cat mask made of golden-brown crushed velvet and feathers stretched out long legs in tight brown leather pants. She eyed Rolf over the hulking shoulder of her companion, but Rolf had other

228

things on his mind. *Maybe later, Babe.* He gave her his half smile and watched her smile back, but then he lost interest.

"So I was wondering if you had any idea who killed him?" Tom was asking. Tom's voice sounded hoarse.

"Who knows? Some maniac, probably." Rolf wanted to get off the subject. He turned to Tom and said, "Why did you shave off your beard?"

Tom stopped talking. His hand strayed to his face. "Various reasons," he said tightly.

"Doesn't your face get cold now?"

Tom seemed to cringe before he said, "A little, yeah. A little more than before."

Rolf lit a cigarette, expelled smoke, and looked at Tom. He'd never realized what heavy jowls Tom had. "Was it a self-mutilation thing?"

From the way Tom looked, Rolf could tell he really had him going. "Jesus, Rolf, could we drop it?" Tom said.

Rolf put on an expression of deep sincerity and leaned across the table toward Tom. "I mean it," he said. "You suddenly decide to cut off your beard. That's a serious move. It's got to mean you're not happy with the way you are, doesn't it? Are you mad with yourself about something?" He gave his voice a note of quiet, psychiatric concern.

Tom was rubbing his face. "I said, drop it."

"Yeah, we could drop it, but then it would fester inside you." Rolf leaned even closer. "You know, they say facial hair is connected to your idea of your manhood. If you look at it that way, shaving your beard could be tantamount to—"

"I'm warning you—"

"Castration, couldn't it?"

"God damn it, Rolf!" Tom stood up violently, rocking the little table. Rolf could see him quivering.

Rolf shrugged lazily. "Same old Tom," he said. "You love to dish it out, analyze everybody else's problems, but you sure hate to take it, don't you?"

"That is a fucking unfair, unjust—"

"Give me a break, Tom, all right?" Rolf turned his attention to the end of his cigarette, watching the smoke curl and the ash grow. He'd go back to the palazzo. Now he knew the score, and he'd be prepared. By the time Tom sat back down, Rolf had almost forgotten about him.

"Maybe you've got a point," Tom said in a chastened voice. "Maybe I should talk about it. Maybe—"

Disappointed that Tom hadn't left, Rolf assumed a pontifical mien. "The whole subject hinges on one important question. How's your relationship with—what's her name?"

"Olga."

"Right. Olga. Nice lady, attractive lady."

Tom stared. "Do you really think she's attractive?"

"God, yes." Rolf tried to summon up a picture of Tom's wife. Gray hair, tired-looking. "Hell, I don't know why you're sitting here, when you could be at home banging her."

Tom eyed him. "You're putting me on again, you bastard."

Rolf sat upright, sketched a cross over his heart and then raised his right hand. "I swear. I get turned on every time I see her. That's why I don't visit your place very much."

Tom's face was flushed. "There *is* an unexpected side to her. A kind of tigerish, ferocious side."

"See? I could sense that from just looking at her."

Tom slouched down disconsolately. "You could be right about that self-mutilation stuff," he said.

Rolf was really bored now. If Tom had any pride, he would have stomped off earlier instead of staying around to whine. He glanced at his watch. "You need to get laid," he said briskly. "If it isn't so good with—what's her—Olga right now, well, the world is full of women." He nodded at the cat-lady at the next table. "There's one right there."

"You must be nuts. I couldn't—"

Rolf had a great idea. A true inspiration. "What about Francine, then? Or have you had a thing with her already?"

"No, but—"

"That's the solution. Francine." Rolf finished his beer and stood up. "Can you get the check? I have to go. I'll pay you later."

"Rolf, can't we talk a little—"

Rolf leaned on the back of his chair, bending toward Tom. "Francine. She's hot for you already. She told me."

Tom shook his head. "She hates me."

"Not at all." Rolf moved backward a step. "She just puts that on because she thinks you don't like *her*." He raised a hand in farewell. "Ciao."

Tom's hurt, baffled face receded quickly from Rolf's consciousness. God, people always wanted to waste your time. He walked along briskly, stretching his legs. Now at last he could give his attention to the subject that had been gnawing at him.

To find out that Sally wasn't the simple, unsophisticated girl she seemed should've spoiled her for Rolf. What had excited him, after all, was the dumb timidity, the uncertainty verging on fear, that she exuded. Lose that and, theoretically, her attraction was gone.

It wasn't working that way. That Sally could be simple Sally and at the same time a person who could dress up in a mask and ruffles hours after her husband's murder—the thought hit Rolf in his solar plexus and he could scarcely breathe. He wanted to stretch her out, examine her, see how much she was one thing and how much the other, find out what her breaking point might be.

None of this was like Minnesota. The rain started coming down harder, and Rolf picked up his pace.

TOM'S FANTASIES

TOM WISHED ROLF hadn't left like that, without giving Tom a chance to explore his emotions. They had been getting to something. Tom could feel it welling up. Now he tried to swallow it with the last of his beer.

Rolf had given Tom a few things to think about, anyway. The self-mutilation, castration business, for instance. At the thought, his scrotum pulled up a little, looking for someplace to hide. Jesus. Why would he want to castrate himself? He was sure he didn't. He wanted to shave off his beard, for reasons he didn't care to explain to Rolf, and he shaved off his beard. It would grow back. It felt as if it had started to grow already, the bristles longer than they had been even an hour ago.

And the other stuff—about Olga, and Francine, and getting laid.

It was easy for Rolf. Tom remembered the careless way Rolf asked if Tom had already had a thing with Francine, the way he suggested Tom get involved with the attractive cat-woman at the next table.

Tom gazed at the woman, with her leather pants and fur

coat. Her gold-feathered cat mask covered only the top half of her face. She was drinking Campari. She wore several gold bracelets and a couple of heavy gold rings.

If Rolf wanted that woman, he'd have her—despite the fact that he'd never seen her before, despite the fact that she was sitting with a burly man who looked capable of throwing any intruder through the window. How would Rolf do it? Wiggle his eyebrows at her? Drop a note on the table giving her his phone number? If Tom tried that, the cat-woman would scream for help.

Glumly, Tom watched her finish her drink, shake back her hair as the man paid the bill, and stroll off with him, arm in arm. She was so intriguing, so sexy. If Tom were Rolf, he'd be screwing her by tonight.

Which brought up the idea that there *was* a woman he could be screwing by tonight if he felt like it, and that was Olga. Rolf had said he found Olga attractive; he'd even stayed away from Tom's place because she turned him on. Tom wondered. He couldn't remember any specific times Rolf had refused to come over, and usually Olga wasn't there, anyway.

It could be true, though. Tom himself had found Olga terribly attractive at one time, although now the specific reasons were difficult to recall. He could check out of his hotel and get a plane to Paris, be there for a late supper. And Stefan would be slouching around studying, looking at Tom as if he didn't care whether Tom came back or not, and Olga would be cheery and wanting to know all about Venice.

He could be screwing her tonight, but he'd just as soon skip it.

That left Francine. At times, especially when she was trying to get him to reminisce about his supposed acquaintance with Sartre, Tom had thought Francine was attracted to him. Lately, though, she'd treated him very badly, even considering they were all under a strain.

Yet maybe she *was* attracted, and the hostility and hate-

233

fulness were the other side of the coin. If that were so, judging from how hateful she had been, the attraction would have to be pretty strong, too.

Later, he might go to the place where Francine was staying and talk with her. He needed to do that, anyway, for his research, which was going more slowly than he'd hoped. While they were talking, he could reach over and touch her. He would put his hand on her hair or her shoulder. When he did that, he'd watch to see how she took it, whether she moved away or let it happen. After he saw, he'd know what to do next.

Lulled in his fantasy, Tom felt almost happy. He almost felt Francine's fingers brush the back of his hand, almost heard her voice, miraculously soft, no hint of how strident she could be, murmuring in her pretty accent.

Because Tom was momentarily soothed, the shock of seeing two policemen walk purposefully past the pizzeria window and turn into the door of his hotel was doubly unnerving. Tom sat forward. They *had* gone into his hotel. And they looked as if they weren't just strolling around keeping the peace. Tom pulled a handful of lire out of his pocket and dropped the notes on the table.

Outside, he peered through the glass door of the hotel. He could see the broad, uniformed back of one of the policemen. He pushed the door open slightly. A brisk Italian conversation was taking place between, Tom guessed, the policemen and the desk clerk. Tom heard an Italianized version of his name. He let the door close softly and moved away from it.

So it had happened. Running away from the hotel, losing himself in the darkening, rainswept streets of Venice, Tom could have shouted for joy. It was May of '68 again, and he was one step ahead of the cops. He was a fugitive, an outlaw. He was free.

234

URSULA WRITES
A LETTER

URSULA'S REACTIONS, Francine had now realized, were consistent only in their unpredictability. When Rolf had shouted his last insult and kicked his last kick, when the neighbors had been apologized to and the dog quieted, Francine fully expected a scene of unparalleled jealousy and accusation. She had imagined herself running through the streets of Venice barefoot, in her dressing gown, and stumbling, drenched and half-frozen, up to Michele Zanon's palazzo and into his arms. The vision had been so appealing that although she was sure she was going to be thrown out, she hadn't bothered to get dressed.

But instead of evicting her, Ursula, once all was restored to normal, had regarded Francine with admiration that seemed to border on awe. "What a handsome, cruel-looking lover you have," she breathed. "He must love you fantastically, tremendously, to be so angry. And you sent him away because of me!"

"Of course. He is nothing to me," Francine said smugly.

"He will beat you bloody when he sees you again." Ursula sounded excited at the thought.

"Ha."

"Oh, *cara,* you *are* wonderful!"

Ursula had been so stimulated by Rolf's visit that it had been nearly impossible to persuade her to return to the task at hand, and only after much cajoling did Francine persuade her to seat herself at her desk and pick up her pen.

"Where was I?" Francine asked.

Ursula bent over the scribbled sheet in front of her, running her finger down the much-corrected lines. At last she read, haltingly, "Point two. On the evening of the day her husband was murdered, this woman was observed in attendance at a fancy dress ball. She may have believed that her mask and costume concealed her identity, but—" She looked up at Francine.

"Very well," Francine said. "—concealed her identity, but in fact she was noticed and identified. Point three. The woman is currently living at—no, make that living in great luxury at—"

"For God's sake, go more slowly!" Ursula protested. "I'm not just writing it down, you know. I have to put it in Italian, too."

Francine watched Ursula's bent head with a sense of déjà vu. She wondered if Sartre had ever been forced to resort to measures such as this, and if he had, whether he had found them as frustrating as she did.

"I want some wine. Let's finish tomorrow," Ursula said.

Francine made herself respond with angelic patience. "But we agreed to do it now. There's only a little more."

They finished the first draft at last, but Ursula's constant whimpering broke into a crescendo when Francine told her that the document must now be recopied. "No!" she wailed. "It's too difficult! You do it!"

"As you like," said Francine coldly. "You said you wanted to help. Now I see how mistaken I was to believe you." She picked up the paper and started toward the door.

"Stop! I'll do it!" Ursula cried.

As the chastened Ursula continued to work, Francine

stretched out on the sofa, hands clasped behind her head. This would give the police something to think about. In the meantime, she herself had to get back to the palazzo as soon as possible.

It seemed hours before Ursula put her pen down and said, triumphantly, "It's done."

Francine studied the letter. Ursula's unformed hand slanted across the plain white paper. Francine hoped Ursula hadn't made any stupid mistakes in translation, or in Italian spelling or grammar, but there was no way to check. "Wonderful," she said, folding the document and putting it into a plain envelope. "Now, we must get dressed."

Fully prepared for Ursula's howl of protest, Francine explained that the entire point of finishing the letter immediately was to insure that it be delivered as soon as possible, and that, therefore, Ursula should dress herself in disguise and get ready to carry out the next part of the plan.

"Me? I must disguise myself and take it to the police? But why can't—"

"Because I must continue the investigation at the Zanon palazzo," said Francine.

Ursula eyed Francine. "This isn't all a trick, is it, *cara?* You aren't trying to fool me about you and Michele?"

"This matter is too serious for that," said Francine. "Come along. We should be on our way."

IN JEAN-PIERRE'S ROOM

JEAN-PIERRE was almost ready to leave, but he would rest five minutes first. He stretched out on the bed, and when he did he thought of the Jester.

Although the Jester had stolen his money, Jean-Pierre was able to get more, since the automatic tellers in Venice would take his French plastic *Carte Bleue*. Jean-Pierre was a fairly wealthy young man, but he rarely divulged this fact. He had never even told Brian. He had often tortured himself by wondering if Brian would have loved him better if he had known.

He didn't have to wonder if it would have made a difference to the Jester. Had the Jester known, he would never have left Jean-Pierre so quickly, taking so little. He would be here with Jean-Pierre now.

The Jester slid out of Jean-Pierre's thoughts and joined in oblivion the other things for which Jean-Pierre had no time: a message to call the police as soon as possible; a visit from Rolf, asking for a place to stay. These did not have the power to hold Jean-Pierre's attention.

Jean-Pierre was thinking of Sally, and of Count Michele

Zanon. The two of them had conspired to take Brian away from him. Now that Jean-Pierre had met Count Zanon, he understood much better.

Brian and Count Zanon must have met somehow in Paris, in the weeks before Carnival, and it was the progression of their secret relationship that had made Brian so jumpy, accusatory, and distant. Although Brian had said that he felt stifled by Jean-Pierre's possessiveness, it was now clear that the truth was completely otherwise.

Jean-Pierre hadn't been possessive of Brian. He had wanted only to cherish him at all times, always.

Jean-Pierre remembered very well the day Brian had said tiredly, "It won't do you any good to try to scare me, Jean-Pierre," and when Jean-Pierre asked Brian to explain, Brian said, "Come on. Desire is defined as trouble. Slime is the agony of water."

Jean-Pierre had been baffled. He felt the gnawing in his gut that had started to accompany all their conversations. "What are you talking about?"

Brian looked at him with a stinging disbelief and said, "Oh, nothing. Forget it."

Now, Jean-Pierre had heard Count Zanon say the same ugly words—"Slime is the agony of water." The connection was established.

Sally must have abetted them. She didn't want Brian for herself, as Jean-Pierre had thought, but preferred that he be with Michele Zanon. Now the count returned the favor by taking care of her, Brian's widow.

Yes, it must have started in Paris. No doubt the count visited Paris from time to time. That explained, too, why Brian had been so anxious to come to Venice. And on the day of his death, when Brian left the Piazza, it must have been at Michele's behest. Brian, rushing to meet Michele, had tried to be sure he wasn't followed, but he hadn't counted on Jean-Pierre's desperation.

Jean-Pierre sat up. He looked out his window onto a world of rushing rain. Rain blurred the window glass, made the ivy climbing the wall sway and nod, spattered in the courtyard below. Jean-Pierre knew that he couldn't hate Michele Zanon. The count had betrayed him, but Count Zanon and Jean-Pierre were connected, irrevocably, through their mutual love for Brian. Jean-Pierre remembered the warm pressure of the count's arm around his shoulders. The thought brought tears to his eyes.

Jean-Pierre had only a few preparations left to make, and then he would go.

TOM AND URSULA

TOM'S POUNDING exhilaration carried him along. He barely felt the rain on his naked, now bristly, face, was barely aware of the droplets accumulating in the turned-up collar of his plastic raincoat and sliding down his neck. He was back in Paris, young again, lobbing paving stones at the cops.

His photograph had been taken doing just that. He was behind a barricade, smoke or something was drifting around, and his arm was cocked ready to throw. Other people were in the picture, too, but Tom was the focus. He'd had a look of intense excitement on his face. The picture became symbolic. It was reproduced everywhere, including on the covers of both the English and French editions of Tom's book, *From the Barricades*. Not long ago, Tom had seen it in a French history text, but the text hadn't mentioned Tom's name.

Tom slowed his pace. He noticed for the first time how wet he was getting. In those days, he hadn't cared about being wet or dry, hungry or fed. He'd sleep on somebody's floor, spend the night in a café talking. At odd times, he wrote everything down in his journal—what people said, how they looked, how he felt, what he ate. That's what everyone had liked about *From the Barricades*. It wasn't philosophical, just gritty and real.

He had a chance to do it again. If he didn't do it now— he had to do it now.

Tom had put a significant distance between himself and the cops at his hotel, but he wasn't sure exactly where he was. Despite the steadily falling rain, the streets were clogged. He traversed a *campo* where a band played gamely on for dripping, persistent dancers.

He had to do it again. The necessity was clear, so why hadn't he gotten down to it? He'd barely even taken notes yet. He sneezed. Water dribbled out of his soaking hair and trickled off his bristly chin. Maybe it was time to look for shelter.

He was considering what to do when he saw the notebooks. They lay, confetti-sprinkled and surrounded by long curls of paper tape, in the lighted window of a small stationery shop. They were bound in magnificently colored marbleized paper, and their pages were thick, creamy, and inviting. With one of those notebooks, writing would be easy. The shop, he saw, was still open.

He emerged some time later with renewed determination and a carefully wrapped, angular package under his raincoat. The notebook he had selected, in tones of dark blue and gold with a few flecks of red, was the final impetus he needed to get started. He could hardly wait to begin.

And he couldn't think of a better place to begin than Francine. He had decided to visit her, anyway, both for his project and to test what Rolf had said about her attraction to him. He dug in his pocket, looking for the piece of paper where he'd written her address.

Finding the place in the rain, even with his map, wasn't easy, but Tom managed. When he rang the bell, though, a frightened-looking maid opened the door only a crack. Although he said Francine's name several times, she refused to let him in, repeating in a hysterical tone words Tom took to mean that Francine wasn't there. Tom said, "Can I wait?" and moved forward, but the maid gave a little shriek and closed the door in his face.

Tom stood uncertainly on the landing. He wondered if Francine were really there, hiding out. He had no desire to plunge back into the storm. He'd wait awhile and see what happened. He got out his notebook and settled down on the top step of the staircase. He could get started right now. He opened the notebook and, on the inside cover, wrote his name and address, his pen gliding smoothly over the un-blemished surface. He turned to the first page.

He looked at the page for a considerable time. He couldn't think of anything worthy to write down and spoil its virgin beauty. He should write about Brian. His feelings about Brian. His resentment when Jean-Pierre insisted that Brian, and by extension Sally, be part of Tom's group. Brian's indifference to everything Tom had been and stood for. Tom's pen was poised, but the thought came to him that putting such things on paper could be highly incriminating. He re-capped his pen and was still staring at the creamy blankness when he heard someone coming up the stairs.

Looking down through the banisters, Tom saw a nun wearing a long black habit and wimple and a semicircular white collar. Tom wondered if she were doing door-to-door canvassing for charity. He stood as she approached, and when she glanced up, he saw that she was wearing a mask.

It wasn't a pious, nunlike mask, either, but a tarty, lascivious woman's face with red cheeks, a curling, Cupid's bow mouth, and exaggerated eyelashes. Even Tom, who wasn't at all religious and certainly not a Catholic, felt uncomfortable. Was this a real nun having a weird joke, or what?

He was still trying to decide when she spoke to him in Italian. He said, "I don't—*Non parlo*—"

"Of course not. Who does?" said the nun. "We'll speak

English." Her voice, with its fed-up, irritated tone, seemed strange issuing through the mask's cheerful cherry-red grin.

The nun had reached the landing. She stood with her hands on her hips, looking at Tom. "Who are you?"

When Tom said, "A friend of Francine's," the nun's eyes rolled upward. She pulled a key from the pocket of her habit, unlocked the door, and said, over her shoulder, "Come in."

As they walked through a luxurious anteroom into an even more luxurious living room, a greyhound bounded from somewhere and hurled himself at the nun. She caressed the dog. Tom, making conversation to cover the awkwardness he felt, said, "That's a beautiful animal."

The nun shot him a keen look. "At least *he* is faithful," she said.

Tom decided to shut up. The nun called out sharply, and the maid appeared and, after a couple of quick commands from the nun, disappeared again. The nun took a poker and jabbed at a fire that was already burning briskly. Finally, she removed her mask and wimple, tossed them on a chair, and sat down in another chair saying, "My God, how do they stand the discomfort?"

She was a tanned woman with strong features and bleached hair. She wore bright lipstick and a lot of black eyeliner. Tom made his final decision that she wasn't a real nun, which coincided with her saying her name was Ursula and asking him his.

Tom told her and then asked nervously if it would be possible for him to see Francine.

Ursula shook her head. "She isn't here."

Tom was disappointed. He had worked himself up to this, and he didn't want it to be for nothing. Besides, it was storming outside, and the maid was just coming in with what looked like brandy and little glasses on a tray. "Do you know when she'll be back? I really wanted to see her."

"No doubt." Tom caught a hint of sarcasm, he thought,

in the two words, but Ursula went on amiably enough, "I don't know when she'll be back. She had important business to attend to."

Tom took a brandy. It tasted wonderful. He wondered what sort of business Francine had, and where she had it, but before he could ask, Ursula said, "You are a friend of hers?"

She seemed to be studying Tom intently, and that plus the nun's habit was throwing him off. "Yeah. Yes, I am."

"From Paris?"

"Right, right."

"You are her *close* friend?"

Tom was picking up an innuendo here, but he felt reckless. It would probably be true soon enough, anyway. He gave Ursula a slow, heavy-lidded smile and said, "Sure. Close and good friend."

"I see," Ursula said.

Tom finished his brandy and poured another. He was starting to feel warm and cozy. On the table beside him his beautiful notebook gleamed with promise in the firelight.

"In that case, perhaps you would like to know where she is," said Ursula silkily. "She tells me she is in the midst of conducting a murder investigation."

Tom sat up sharply, with a lurch of fear and resentment. What did Francine think she was doing? Brian's murder was *his* business. Francine would spoil everything. *"What?"* he said.

Ursula nodded. "A murder investigation. At the moment she is pursuing it at the palazzo of Count Michele Zanon."

Tom was furious. He himself had intended to visit Count Zanon and discuss the murder. The thought of what Michele might be telling Francine made him sick. "That's bullshit! She's no investigator!" he cried. "She's just trying to get close to Count Zanon!"

Ursula jumped to her feet. "Exactly! The lying bitch!" she screamed.

Amazed at this reaction, Tom said, "Hey, wait—"

"This moment, this very moment, your lover is betraying you with Michele Zanon!"

"Listen—"

Skirts swirling, Ursula strode to stand in front of Tom's chair. She bent over and prodded his chest with a red fingernail. "You're as big a fool as I am! We are fools together!"

"Maybe you should—"

She put her face close to Tom's. "Fool!" she shrieked. She whirled and ran from the room. Tom heard the dog start barking maniacally.

Tom's ears were ringing. He was shaking all over. Fortunately, the brandy was close by. He poured himself another glass.

BRIAN

BRIAN GLIDES through the streets of Venice. The spongy, slick remnants of what he was, coalesced and held by rage, carry him as if he were alive.

In Venice, night is coming on and the rain has started. The souvenir vendors under the arcade of the Doges' Palace, wearing high boots of dull-green rubber, pack up, muttering invocations to God to condemn and destroy this weather. They futilely try to light cigarettes and call on God again. On the Molo, the prows of docked gondolas rear and pull like tethered ponies, and waves slop across the pavement. Long lace petticoats, satin shoes with sparkling buckles, are dampened and drenched. The sea is encroaching to drown the revels. By morning, perhaps, the tide will bring *acqua alta* and the Piazza will be a lake, a reflecting pool for the doomed beauties of Venice.

None of this concerns Brian. What does high tide matter to the drowned? What is a damp chill to one whom cold has invaded forever? In Brian's vision, the rain has cast over Venice a net of silver filaments. All those caught within—souvenir vendors, dripping maskers—struggle to escape. All except Brian, who is in his proper element.

The water rises, Carnival continues. Musicians pin their sheets of music to wire stands with clothespins and go on playing. A jester spins and somersaults to the applause of a shivering crowd. A drunken gladiator gags in a dim corner of the Procuratie Nuove not far from a mask seller whose wares are spread on a blanket weighted at the corners with bricks.

Carnival continues, Brian continues. His repulsive, loosening, decaying self can still give the illusion of life. For a while longer, he will be able to act.

ROLF KEEPS WATCH

FROM HIS SHELTER in the potting shed, Rolf watched the Zanon palazzo. Rain poured from the shed's red-tiled roof. The walls were runny and damp, the air musty. Rolf sat on a bag of fertilizer and looked through the barely open door. He was wearing his devil mask, knit cap, and black gloves, and it would be hard to spot him here even if someone were looking. Rolf was unaware of the chill, almost unaware of the rain. Excitement was crackling, sparking, and connecting beneath his skin.

He thought it was almost time to move, but he wanted to be sure. He had watched long enough to see that Count Zanon had gotten another doorman, this one a kid who looked seventeen or so. Rolf had glimpsed him moving around inside and seen him again when the kid turned Francine away a short while ago.

No doubt Francine had come to visit the count, but the count had left, in what looked like a big hurry, not long before Francine arrived. Rolf didn't know whether Sally was in the palazzo right now or not, but once he was inside, he was willing to wait. When he felt like this, so alive and sure of himself, he could wait a long time.

Rolf had no doubt he could knock the crap out of this doorman, just as he had the old one, but he had decided to do it differently this time. An incapacitated doorman would be a warning to Count Zanon when he returned, and Rolf preferred to take the count and Sally by surprise. It was Sally he wanted, really. The resurrected Sally, all dressed up in her ruffles. Drops of perspiration formed a line across his forehead, under his mask.

In Minnesota, things had gotten out of hand. The girl, Barbara, the one he had hurt—her fear had made him feel too strong. That moment, the moment she got truly terrified, had been too rich and overpowering, like a flash of lightning, or an ocean wave.

He remembered, all at once, being taken to the seashore when he was small, and being knocked down by a wave like that, tumbling, struggling, spinning, choking, until his older sister, who thought it was funny, pulled him out. He remembered clinging to her sunburned leg, water running from his nose and mouth, her laughter reverberating in his ears. Even now, he felt his face grow hot with shame.

Venice wasn't Minnesota. Sally wasn't Barbara, although she had the same freckles, brown hair, scared look. Rolf would handle it differently this time. Against his will, he saw Barbara. Dead leaves stuck to her brown hair, and there was a wet, red smear under her nose. Her freckles were drowned in the pallor of her skin, and her short, sparse eyelashes looked like tiny needles sticking out of her closed eyelids.

He blinked the thought away and stood up. This was as good a time as any to get started.

The garden was dark, with only a pool of yellow light from a lamp outside the back door of the palazzo and a tiny bit of illumination from the street. If Rolf were careful and nobody showed up, he'd be fine. He pushed the shed door open a little wider and slipped out into the downpour.

Keeping his eye on the ground-floor windows so he could stop dead if the doorman looked out, Rolf moved from the potting shed to the ivy-covered garden wall. The rain, drumming on gravel and leaves, bouncing off the top of the wellhead, was loud enough to cover any sounds he made. He slid along the wall toward the palazzo, wet ivy leaves dragging along his back, tickling his neck, depositing moisture on his earlobes.

When he had nearly reached the palazzo, it was time to begin the hard part. Rolf turned to the wall and gauged the distance. He'd prefer to have a running start, but that was impossible. He took as deep a breath as he could with his mask on, flexed his knees, and jumped.

He got hold of the top of the wall easily and clung to it until his feet found a purchase in the ivy and he could climb up. He sat on the top of the wall, panting, anticipating the next step. This was where the rain would work to his disadvantage, because the iron balcony would be slippery, but Rolf had no doubt he would pull it off.

The wall was fairly broad, and when Rolf had caught his breath he worked his way along it until he reached the point closest to the balcony. Here, he spent some time in contemplation. It wasn't a long leap, but he'd only get one chance. Water streamed from the balcony and glittered in the pool of light below. Watching it, Rolf felt almost hypnotized.

Then the right time came, and he got to his feet and leapt. His gloved fingers slipped and clung to the balcony's wrought-iron supports. He let himself be sure of his grip, then swung his feet once, twice, and on the third try got his toe between the supports. Laboriously, he dragged his body upward, but he knew he'd make it. He climbed over the rail and collapsed on the balcony floor, drenched and gasping.

Eventually, he dragged himself up and crouched next to the door. It was locked, of course, but Rolf had a knife and a screwdriver in his pocket. The job wouldn't be done elegantly, but it would be done. In a short while, sooner than he would have predicted, the door was open, and Rolf was dripping rainwater onto the floor of Michele Zanon's library.

THE MEDUSA
RETURNS

SALLY HAD DINNER with Otis Miller. After sitting in her drab room tormented by nerves, and creeping down the hall to the depressing bathroom quite a few times, shaking like a leaf every time, she had had enough. She realized she might feel better if she ate something and went in search of the hotel dining room. She also went, she had to admit, a little bit in search of Otis Miller.

"I'm afraid we don't serve grits, young lady," Otis said, and then recommended a dish called *seppie con polenta,* a Venetian specialty. Sally agreed, but when her order came, it was a plateful of tentacled black goo, along with a couple of pale yellow squares that looked like fallen cornbread.

Otis chuckled. "It's supposed to look like that. Squid cooked in its own ink. Try it, Miss Sally."

Sally didn't want to hurt Otis's feelings. She took a small bite of *seppie con polenta*. It didn't taste as horrible as it looked. She could get through a few bites for the sake of politeness, she thought, but what with drinking wine and laughing at Otis's stories about his growing up in Eufaula, Alabama, she finished it all.

Otis had been a misfit in Eufaula, he claimed, because he hated to hunt and fish. When he came to Italy, he felt at home for the first time.

Sally wasn't surprised. "But you seem"—she wasn't sure how to put it—"you seem so much like Eufaula."

"Well, sure. I'm from Eufaula. I wasn't raised on some Tuscan hillside, and there's no point in pretending I was." Otis looked as if the point meant a lot to him. His eyes bulged even more than usual, and his face was flushed. Then he relaxed and said, "What about you?"

Sally bit her lip. She wished she could tell Otis everything, but she was afraid to. It had been a long time since she'd felt she could trust anybody. "I'm in trouble," she said. "It's bad, but I can't talk about it."

Otis nodded as if he had known. "Anything I can do?"

Sally couldn't get over her nagging worry about Michele. It had hovered just outside her consciousness during dinner, and now it descended again. She had considered calling, but her little room in the annex had no telephone. "Could I make a phone call?"

"Sure thing," Otis said, and when she got out money to pay for dinner, he waved it away, saying it was on the house.

Back in the lobby, Otis pushed the telephone across the counter and handed her the phone book. Now that she was about to call, Sally's anxiety returned. She looked up Michele's number and tried to dial it, but the numerals kept slipping from her mind. After a couple of tries she wrote it on a pad, and after that she got through.

Maria answered. Her voice sounded tense, high-pitched. Sally's words stuck in her throat. Maria kept talking, asking who was there, Sally guessed. Sally hung up.

"Nobody home?" Otis asked.

She shook her head. "Thanks, anyway."

In her room once more, Sally was restless. She was hid-

254

ing out, acting like a scared rabbit, instead of going to the police, putting the situation in front of them, and letting them take care of it. Michele could be in trouble, and time might be important. She had her disguise, Antonia's costume, so she wouldn't be recognized. She should go now. She tied on her mask, rearranged her hat, and started out.

Antonia's green umbrella provided some protection against the downpour, but the red shawl wasn't warm enough, and she soon felt damp to the skin. She thought she could find the police station where she'd been with Michele, and if she didn't find that one, there had to be others.

She turned into a little *campo*. A small bandstand there was empty, its bunting sagging, but underneath a low, covered passage leading through to another street huddled several musicians, blasting away at a tune that sounded like "Yankee Doodle" but probably wasn't. In the middle of the *campo* a dozen or so people were dancing in the rain. They were laughing with the abandon of those who can't possibly get wetter, their hair plastered down, skirts and cloaks dragging, feathers and ruffs limp. As Sally tried to edge past them, a man wearing a waterlogged Renaissance cloak caught her hands and swung her around, the two of them slipping over the paving stones, Antonia's ruffled skirt flying out like foam, the green umbrella bouncing over their heads.

When he released her, she saw the Medusa. The white figure hovered in the shadows where the street she'd just left joined the *campo*. She couldn't possibly mistake the waving headdress, the blank white mask. She stumbled backward, turned and fled.

As she pushed past other umbrellas, other costumed figures, her heart lurching, Sally tried to figure out how this had happened. She had checked, as carefully as she knew how, to see if the Medusa were lurking around the palazzo when she left. She had seen nothing. Furthermore, she was wearing Antonia's costume, her cloak of invisibility. Nobody was supposed to know that the masked and ruffled señorita was Sally.

Michele would know. Of course Michele would know.

Sally shook her head. She had seen Michele and the Medusa together, when Michele frightened the Medusa away, so Michele couldn't be the Medusa. Or he couldn't have been that time.

At last she found the nerve to slow down and look behind her. She was in a well-populated street lined with packed trattorias, souvenir shops doing the evening's final business, bars loud with commotion. The Medusa was gone.

Now she was so rattled and disoriented, she wasn't sure of her directions anymore. She'd have to ask.

She entered a bar, clutching the dripping umbrella, and yelled at the bartender that she wanted to find the police station.

The bartender spoke English, after a fashion, and he was eager to help. He explained in detail where the police station was. Sally listened, but she was having trouble concentrating, and his accent was difficult to understand. The bartender kept waving his arm. She thought he was saying straight for a while, then turn left, then the station was close by. She could remember that much, at least.

She thanked the bartender several times, but after that there was no excuse for waiting.

Straight for a while, then left. No sign of the Medusa. She wished she had been able to understand exactly when the turn should come. She walked for a reasonable distance, then veered left. What had seemed a well-lighted and well-traveled street rapidly became dim, small and deserted. The wares in the windows of the darkened shops looked a hundred years old. The only sounds were Sally's feet and the pounding rain. She started across an arched stone bridge and saw raindrops, millions of them, dimpling the black canal below. On the other side of the bridge was darkness, punctuated by one or two bulbs over doorways.

This couldn't be the right way.

Abruptly, in the middle of the bridge, she stopped. She had to go back, try again. She turned to retrace her steps. At the foot of the bridge, a white figure stepped to one side, out of the light.

It was the Medusa. Sally whirled and ran for the darkness on the other side.

SALLY PURSUED

SALLY LOOKED BACK at the bridge through the columns of a portico bordering the canal. She was crouched in a corner against a damp stone wall, surrounded by the odors of garbage and urine. She thought she might pass out.

She was sure the Medusa hadn't had time to cross. The bridge had only been out of her sight for the few moments it took her to careen down a street she had hoped would lead far away. The street curved back treacherously, as Venetian streets so often did, and deposited her on the edge of the canal not far from the bridge. To go back was to risk coming face to face with her pursuer. To stay here was to risk being trapped. As a hunted creature will, she hunkered down to watch.

A flat-bottomed boat, loosely covered with a tarpaulin, was moored in front of her. She heard the faint groaning of the ropes as it was pulled by wind or current, followed by a bump as it nudged the side of the canal.

Then came another sound—a rustling or scrabbling. It stopped, but soon started again, louder. Let it be cats, Sally prayed. Let it be cats. Not rats. Please. The *seppie con polenta* she had eaten with such gusto threatened to come up, but she closed her throat in time.

In a building across the canal was a lighted window with a lace curtain hanging over it. Behind the curtain, a woman moved to and fro. The woman had dark hair, and in her hair, over one ear, was something red—a flower or a ribbon. Sally stared at the woman, lost in painful envy, until the Medusa started across the bridge.

Then Sally realized how much she had hoped the white figure wasn't the Medusa, that the whole thing had been her imagination, after all. The Medusa stopped at the top of the bridge, as she had. It looked her way, but she knew she couldn't be seen. Not yet. Not from there. The Medusa continued. Sally was close enough to hear its footsteps.

If the Medusa came the way she had, Sally would be trapped, with no alternative but to jump into the canal.

Quickly, ratlike herself, she scuttled across the portico to the canal's edge. A few feet below was the tarpaulin-covered boat. As silently as she could, she let herself down into it. The ropes groaned as the boat moved, but only a little. She picked up the edge of the tarpaulin, crawled underneath, and pulled it over her. She lay curled up, motionless on the slatted bottom of the boat.

Her hat was wildly askew, the chin strap nearly choking her, but she didn't dare move to loosen it. She had a moment of panic, thinking she'd left the green umbrella, then realized that her hand was fastened tightly around it.

She could hear nothing but the rain pounding the tarpaulin and the occasional groan of the ropes. She would have no clues like footsteps to tell her if the Medusa had come and gone. She could only lie and wait.

She waited. The air was suffocatingly close. After a long while she reached up slowly and loosened the chin strap of her hat. When she did so, sweat broke out on her scalp, and she began to tremble, her legs wanting to jerk until she managed to force them to be still.

Although she could see nothing, she couldn't close her

eyes. Surrounded by the sound of the rain, she stared wide-eyed into the blackness.

When she couldn't stand it any longer, she crawled out from under the tarpaulin and stood up, filling her lungs with cold, wet air. She climbed up onto the pavement and again took shelter under the portico. She didn't see or hear anybody. Across the canal, the lace-curtained window was dark.

She retraced her steps. Peering around for her pursuer, she found her way back to the street from which she'd taken the wrong turn. Despite the rain it was filled with people, many of them in evening dress or elaborate costume. Raindrops bounced off their umbrellas, glistened on the women's fur coats. Sally moved into the flow.

The neighborhood began to look familiar. She realized that the hotel where she and Brian had stayed was nearby. The crowd must be moving toward the Fenice opera house. Across a bridge she saw bright lights through the rain.

People thronged the steps of the Fenice, spilling down into the square. Umbrellas knocked into one another. Gawkers, photographers, and a television crew competed for space. A man and woman halfway up the steps, illuminated by television lights and flashbulbs, waved to the crowd. Sally didn't recognize them. Maybe they were Italian movie stars.

Sally turned her head and saw the Medusa.

It was standing about ten feet away, eyes fixed on her. Rain made the snakes in its headdress bobble and bounce. Sally felt the last of her energy drain away. She stood still, the green umbrella tilted back, Antonia's wet red shawl around her shoulders giving no protection to Antonia's beautiful, bedraggled dress.

A female voice screamed, "Antonia!"

Sally looked toward the sound. A woman halfway up the packed steps was waving frantically. The woman had blue-black hair and wore a white sequined evening gown and a white fur stole. The top half of her face was covered by a silver mask adorned with white ostrich feathers drooping from the damp. A man in a tuxedo held an umbrella over her head. "Antonia! Antonia!" she called again, and the heads of people near the woman turned toward Sally.

Sally made no conscious decision to wave and only realized she was doing it when she felt the air moving against her hand.

Heedless of the rain, the woman in white pushed down through the packed crowd. She grasped Sally's hand in a grip made excruciatingly painful by a huge ring she wore on her white-gloved hand and, determinedly, dragged Sally up the steps behind her.

Several people nodded at Sally and said, "Ciao, Antonia," but in the hubbub it didn't matter if Sally said anything or not. Sally looked back. The Medusa stood at the edge of the crowd and didn't seem about to follow.

The crowd inched forward. The woman in white was still clutching Sally's hand painfully. Sally didn't have a ticket to the performance, but she would worry about that —as she would worry about not being Antonia—when the time came.

The ticket problem never arose. Someone had a sheaf of them, and Sally, still in tow, squeezed through the door with the others. Inside the lobby, the noise level intensified. Sally was pulled toward the coat-check desk, where the woman in white slipped out of her stole, and Sally felt Antonia's umbrella being removed from her hand and Antonia's shawl plucked from her shoulders by one of the men in the party. He handed shawl and umbrella to the girl behind the counter and put the claim ticket in the pocket of his tuxedo.

Sally noticed that the woman in white was no longer holding her hand. She slipped back into the crowd. Pushing through the lobby, she found a flight of stairs. From the mezzanine, she looked down on the woman and her friends. She couldn't tell if they had missed Antonia.

A bell began to ring. Sally moved away from the railing

and found a door on which was written *Damas*. Inside, the ladies' room was the scene of frantic last-minute powdering and combing, but nobody was sitting on a little upholstered bench in the anteroom. Sally sank down on it, leaned against the wall, and closed her eyes.

IN THE TRATTORIA

THE KITCHEN DOOR of the trattoria flew open every few seconds and waiters burst out carrying platters and bowls: pizza with mussels, roasted peppers swimming in oil, bean-and-rice soup. Pitchers of red wine left rings on paper table covers. Music from stereo speakers mounted high on the walls was intermittently audible over the babble of voices. The music and conversation effectively drowned out any noise from the storm, although Francine, sitting at a tiny table next to the kitchen door, could see that the rain was still pelting down, each drop a miniature meteor in the light from the front window.

Francine rarely looked up, however. She was reading *Being and Nothingness*. "There is no one who has not at some time been surprised in an attitude which was guilty or simply ridiculous," she read. Francine's lips twisted. Sartre was so wise. She wondered what he had done when he was surprised in a guilty or ridiculous attitude.

Although Michele had not been in when she called, Francine had decided to wait and try again after dinner rather than return to Ursula's apartment. It was a relief to be rid of Ursula for a while. Ursula meant well, but being around her was a strain on the nerves. Also, Francine wasn't sure how completely Ursula had accepted her story that she was conducting a murder investigation, and she was weary of thinking of excuses to return to the palazzo. At least Ursula had been of some use in writing the letter to the police, and Francine trusted she had delivered it without incident.

Francine pushed her hair out of her eyes and tried to focus on the page in front of her. What a ludicrous situation. If only Brian hadn't ridiculed her. The antagonism between them had been palpable from the beginning, when Jean-Pierre, bursting with pride, brought Brian to the Café du Coin and introduced him. Brian had stood there, in all his beauty, like a prince awaiting homage, and at that moment Francine had determined that he would get no homage from her. She had given him a brief glance and a cursory greeting, treatment he was surely not accustomed to receiving from anyone—lovely, truly lovely, as he was.

Unaccountably, Francine's eyes filled with tears. Sartre's words swam on the page. What could she be expected to do? Submit without comment to Brian's teasing and denigration, his ignorant attacks on her passion for Sartre? Surely she could be excused for defending herself, since no one else would. When Brian made outrageous statements, Jean-Pierre sat by dotingly, Rolf was indifferent, and Tom ignored him and went on to another subject. Francine couldn't ignore him. He was like a dark angel, whispering in her ear that she was absurd. How she had longed to be free of his galling mockery!

Francine dug the heels of her hands into her eyes. She would get out of this. She would. The next step was to go back to the palazzo.

She turned to her book once more, but shouts of laughter at the next table disturbed her concentration. She tried again, and read, "But I know neither what I am nor what is my place in the world, nor what face this world in which I am turns toward the Other."

Outside, it was still pouring. Francine closed her book and reached for her coat.

WATCHING THE FIRE

TOM LEANED AGAINST the sofa cushions, sipping his brandy and watching the fire. Ursula hadn't returned after her stormy exit scene, and he felt no inclination to go after her.

Ursula's assertions that Francine was investigating Brian's murder and (or) having an affair with Count Zanon had disturbed him badly and made it even more imperative that he see Francine as soon as possible. He couldn't, he could not, let her muck around in this. As for Ursula's violent accusations of betrayal—Tom could only conclude that Ursula was the wronged lover of Michele Zanon.

If that were the case, Tom admitted feeling a kinship with Ursula, strange as she was, because Tom felt wronged also—by Francine.

It wasn't rational. His romance with Francine had so far taken place in his fantasies. She was free to have affairs with twenty Italian counts, if that's what she wanted.

And yet—the fantasy had been so real, so sweet. Tom and Francine had talked, in quiet voices, about their deepest thoughts. Tom had reached over and stroked Francine's hair, or touched her shoulder, and she had responded. Maybe she bent her head against his hand, and through the cushion of her hair he felt the skull beneath. The moment took his breath away, even now.

He sensed a presence, and looked up to see Ursula glowering in the doorway. She was still wearing the nun's habit. She crossed to the brandy, poured herself a glass, and slumped into a chair next to the fire. She stared at the flames with a brooding expression, rolling her glass between her hands. Tom's best course, he thought, was to keep quiet.

"So. We are both fools." Ursula's voice was constricted.

"I guess we are." Even as he assented, Tom felt uncomfortable. He had been called a fool more than once lately, and he hadn't liked it. His hand strayed to his face. Under his fingertips he felt bristles. Long ones. "Actually, I don't know why you say that," he amended.

"Betrayed, abandoned—" Ursula stretched out her arms in a gesture of hopelessness, then tossed back her brandy and put down the glass.

"Maybe it isn't as bad as all that," Tom ventured. "Maybe the thing between Francine and Count Zanon isn't serious."

"Ha! Of course it isn't. Michele Zanon was never serious about anything in his life."

Tom wondered why, if Ursula knew Michele Zanon was never serious, she hadn't been better prepared for his betrayal. "Is Count Zanon married?" he asked.

Ursula's answer was more than Tom had bargained for. She stood up, buried her hands in her hair, and let out a piercing howl. "My God, how many times must I answer that question!" she shrieked. "Yes! Yes! Yes! He is married! Do you, too, want to try to cure his impotence?"

In the silence that followed Tom heard the door behind him open and, a few seconds later, close. He presumed the maid was looking in to make sure Ursula wasn't being murdered. Or maybe the maid was used to these outbursts and just wanted to see how the brandy was holding out.

"I'd better go," Tom said.

He was interested in the sexual aspersion Ursula had cast on Count Zanon, but her decibel level was getting to him. Besides, he needed to find out what was happening with Francine. He poured himself a splash of brandy for the road.

As he drank it down, matters took another turn. "What am I saying?" Ursula breathed. "You are suffering as much as I am. Forgive me." She knelt in front of Tom and rested her forehead on his knee.

"Jesus. Get up," Tom said.

"Do you forgive me?"

"Sure. I mean—sure."

She raised her head, but moved aside only slightly to sit on the floor next to his chair. Nobody had ever knelt in front of Tom and begged his forgiveness before. Clumsily, he patted Ursula's disheveled hair, and through the cushion of her hair he felt her skull.

IN THE LADIES' ROOM

SALLY HAD BEEN in the ladies' room of the Fenice for an hour and a half. She had patted her stomach and said, "Sick," several times to the pink-clad attendant, and the woman seemed to understand. After the crowd cleared, the attendant sat on a chair in a corner of the anteroom knitting something out of fluffy yellow wool. She paid no attention to Sally, who took off her hat, mask, and boots and lay down on the upholstered bench. The anteroom was warm to the point of stuffiness and smelled of stale perfume. Sally closed her eyes.

Her parents would come, tomorrow maybe, and she would go home with them. Sally saw the sun sifting through Spanish moss, bursts of azaleas, a red-winged blackbird on a live oak branch. Her room would be the same as always, except that on the dresser Sally's mother would have put an elaborately framed wedding picture of Sally and Brian. Sally would ask her mother to take it away before she moved back in.

Sally was under the carport, kneeling by a trunk filled with her old dolls. Their eyes wouldn't close, and she

269

shrank from their rigid faces. In the woods behind the house a tomcat, his belly low to the ground, stalked the red-winged blackbird.

She shuddered and woke. The attendant, fingers stilled, was looking at her with mild apprehension.

Sally shook her head. "It's okay. Okay." She rubbed her hands over her sweating face.

The woman dropped her eyes to her work again. Sally tried to think rationally. Considering everything, she had ended up in a pretty good position. The Medusa probably didn't have a ticket to the performance, so it wouldn't be able to come in to search for her. What it would do this time, probably, was what it had done before—wait in hiding until she emerged. Which meant she wouldn't emerge just yet.

She turned on her side. The bench felt lumpy, the buttons in the gold plush upholstery making uncomfortable valleys.

She wouldn't leave yet, but she couldn't spend the night in the ladies' room. If she tried to hide in here, she'd probably be discovered and ejected. And if she were able to stay, suppose the Medusa found a way to slip in after the performance, when the place was deserted?

Sally thought she'd better remain Antonia a little longer.

She sat up. In the mirror on the wall of the anteroom, she saw that her topknot was listing to one side, and a lot of hair had escaped from it. Her face was a milky blob punctuated by shocked-looking eyes with deep circles under them, but her face didn't matter. If anybody saw it, the whole plan would be ruined anyway.

She was still gazing at her reflection when the outer door burst open and a group of laughing women entered. Her stomach turned over. Intermission. The woman in white could walk in at any minute. She grabbed up her things and rushed to lock herself in a toilet stall. She put down the toilet lid and sat on it. She'd have to wait until everybody left.

Intermission lasted a long time. Sitting in the stall, Sally listened to the swirling chatter. She was afraid someone would make a fuss about her staying in the stall so long, but there were no knocks on the door, no murmured questions.

When everyone had gone, she emerged. She had to work on her appearance. Antonia would never go around looking like a mess, Sally was sure. She splashed water on her face and washed her hands, then extracted the pins from her hair, combed it thoroughly and put it up again. She fluffed and straightened Antonia's dress, which looked wilted, but that wasn't unusual, considering the rain.

When she thought the performance must be drawing to a close, she donned her mask and hat and pulled on her clammy boots. The attendant continued to knit. Sally felt a pang at the thought of leaving this haven and the woman who had been so conveniently and quietly indifferent.

Although the attendant wasn't looking at her, Sally waved. She said, "'Bye," and left her sanctuary.

A MASKED BALL

AT THE EDGE of the shoving, babbling crowd around the coat-check stand, Sally stood on tiptoe and craned her neck. The performance had been over for ten minutes, and there was no sign of the woman in white or the man who checked Sally's umbrella and shawl. If they didn't show up soon, the crush might have thinned enough so conversation would be possible, and that would be a disaster.

Meanwhile, Sally wasn't poor little Sally, her husband murdered, pursued by a Medusa. She was Antonia—Michele's beautiful, lost Antonia.

The thought made her feel stronger. A few seconds later she saw the woman in white in her ostrich-feather mask and waved energetically, the way she thought Antonia would. As she pushed toward the woman and her friends, she made the lavish shrugging gestures with which Antonia might indicate amused dismay at their separation during the performance.

An unexpected charge of energy hit her, burning away her enshrouding fear. The confident, carefree gestures she was making seemed to have unlocked reserves of daring and panache. Had Sally actually absorbed Antonia's spirit by sleeping in her room and wearing her clothes? Or had this lively creature been inside Sally all the time, waiting to be called on to show what she could do?

As they were jostled from all sides, the woman grasped Sally by the shoulders and bawled something. Sally gestured airily at her ear and shook her head. She felt completely in command, as Antonia would have been—Antonia, who was vivacious and had friends who were always happy to see her.

A minute or two later, the man in the tuxedo was helping Sally with her shawl and handing her the green umbrella, and soon the party was once again on the steps of the Fenice. The rain hadn't stopped, which meant they'd be walking fast, and since Sally had her own umbrella she needn't be too close to anybody. Walking with the laughing, chattering group, Sally looked around for the Medusa. She didn't see it, but it could be hiding in any of these dark side streets.

As they walked, the woman in white, who had been talking animatedly, began to sing. There were calls of "Brava! Brava!" and others joined in. Everybody seemed to know the words. Sally felt almost as if she too knew the words, and she hummed along with the vigorous chorus.

The song ended. They began another and were still singing when they turned down a passage onto which, a moment later, a door was flung open, pouring out light and the sound of an orchestra. Sally would go in with them. She nearly belonged there, now.

Inside, she again surrendered her shawl and umbrella, this time to a man wearing an embroidered waistcoat and white gloves. With the others, she climbed a marble staircase, passed through a room filled with orchids, and entered double doors into a ballroom.

People in masks, wearing costumes or evening dress, danced under huge, glittering chandeliers. Painted on the ceiling was a scene of people riding through the sky in a chariot. Cupids, thick as a swarm of bees, flew toward the chariot from the ceiling's four corners. Cupids carrying flags, cupids carrying garlands, cupids carrying bows and arrows tumbled through the sky. They held out chubby hands to steady themselves, and in a corner one of them had slipped down so far that his dimpled knee and foot seemed to cast a shadow against the wall.

Sally forced herself to stop gawking. Antonia wouldn't gawk, because she'd been places and seen things. Antonia would know how to enjoy this occasion.

A couple of people nodded and said, "Ciao," and Sally nodded back. The woman in white and her party had melted into the crowd. Sally wandered to the buffet. She ate lobster salad and small, frosted cookies and drank champagne, thankful that she could eat without taking off her lace-hung mask. Later, dizzy from the champagne, she sat on a spindly chair of gold-painted wood and watched the dancers—fairy princesses, vampires, Egyptian pharaohs, Greek goddesses—whirling under the painted cupids. Soon, she would have to decide what to do next, but not yet.

There was a flurry at the door, not far from where she sat. She looked up and saw Michele.

He was dressed once again as the Harlequin, in his costume of pale silk lozenges and lace, bicorne hat, and black mask, the wooden baton at his belt. He surveyed the room from just inside the doorway, ignoring the greetings of the people near him.

Sally stood up as his eyes found her. When they were face to face he said, "Antonia. *Carissima.*" The next moment they were dancing.

PART FOUR

INTERLUDE

TONIGHT, there are masked balls all over Venice. In a palazzo, dancers whirl beneath the painted antics of cupids celebrating a wedding. Across town, on the basketball court of a high school gymnasium, teenagers in Halloween masks contort their bodies to deafening music. Revelers who are too drunk, too carefree, or too wet already to mind the rain, dance in the Piazza, where the streaming domes of San Marco loom over all.

On this night, St. George and the dragon may join hands and waltz, a priest and the devil drink each other's health, a lion and a lamb embrace, full of the fevered knowledge that they will lie down together.

During it all, the tide is rising. Parts of the Riva degli Schiavoni have been washed by occasional waves for some time now. Across the Bacino, water slops against the steps leading to San Giorgio Maggiore. It threatens the *fondamenta* of the Giudecca. The Venetians who have not joined the tourists in dancing, drinking, falling in love, and making mistakes they will repent for the coming year and perhaps longer, turn on the weather report. Yes, the Adriatic tide is *molto sostenuto*. They dial a telephone number to hear the same news: The tide is high; by tomorrow, there may be *acqua alta*.

The Venetians are accustomed to this by now. In the closet are their high wading boots of sturdy, olive-green rubber. Platforms for those without wading boots stand ready to be assembled. If there is indeed *acqua alta,* everyone will know when the sirens go off.

In the lobbies of chic hotels, preparations for the high tide are under way. Staff members roll up carpets, leaving the terrazzo floors bare. They ready planks to be put down for guests to walk on if the Grand Canal, which is now licking at, even encroaching on, the landing stage outside, should slide inexorably under the doors and spread across the terrazzo, creating a treacherously slippery pool, washing against the lowest step of the wooden staircase where former tides already have left a high-water mark. Curtains must be tied up, antique tables and chairs moved to safety, signs put out saying *Attenzione*.

It is all routine. Tomorrow, cold Adriatic water may flow through the streets, stand in the Piazza and the *campos*. A few hours later, it will be gone. The inlaid patterns on the Basilica floor will dry. Venice will not sink under the waves before the end of Carnival.

IN THE BALLROOM

BECAUSE SHE WAS Antonia, Sally was able to dance, her feet in the damp, clumsy boots as nimble as if she were wearing satin slippers. Michele's hand barely touched her back, and his grasp on her fingers was so light she was hardly aware of it. Together, yet barely connected, the two of them moved across the floor. Drops of rain shimmered on the delicate leaves and flowers of the Harlequin's lace collar. The drops spread out and turned warm under Sally's hand.

Sally's joy at seeing Michele alive and unhurt overwhelmed and disturbed her. Nothing had changed, nothing at all. She was bereft, in danger, alone. And yet she felt, clearly and irrationally, that this was a moment of magical suspension. To be here dancing with Michele, breathing the music like air, to be Antonia, dancing in this Venetian ballroom, was some compensation for her grief and upset.

Sally felt she could apprehend the world. She could smell the perfume and perspiration in this room, the food and wine, the wax on the floor. Beyond that, the sea and the fumes from the mainland factories, and far beyond that, the hint of gardenias that would bloom next spring in Tallahassee. She could see past the cupids on the ceiling to the wet, red-tiled roofs of Venice and above the roofs and the rain, the massed storm clouds, and above the storm clouds the stars.

Then, like sparks of light from a fireworks display, sliding down the sky and going out, the euphoria started to fade. She had enemies, and possibly one of them was holding her, spinning around with her now. It was crazy to long for a man so wrapped up in his own crazed longings, and yet for just a second or two more she wouldn't worry about it, but would let her fingers tighten on his shoulder and would move with him as if the warm space between them was only an extension of their one self. Under the lace of her mask she was smiling, almost laughing, and she knew he knew it, although he couldn't see her face.

They danced without speaking until the music ended. When Michele had bowed an elaborate bow, almost a parody of courtliness, he said, "They called and told me you were here."

He had spoken in English, so he didn't think she was Antonia after all. She wondered, bleakly, if she had actually fooled anybody—except herself. "Who called?"

"My friends who met you at the Fenice."

"What did they say?"

Michele smiled. "They said Antonia was here, but she seemed too quiet and sad. They urged me to come dance with her and cheer her up."

So she had pulled it off. She had been Antonia. "What did you think?"

"Why, of course, I thought Antonia had come back to me," he said in a mocking tone.

The music began again. Michele kissed Sally's knuckles. "We must go," he said.

She followed him through the crowd and at the door took a last look at the dancers under the cupid-crowded sky. She wanted to stay, to be the one Michele had hoped to find here. She turned away, and let him lead her down the marble staircase.

"I was sure you had been abducted," said Michele as they redeemed his coat and her shawl and umbrella. "I had gone out unexpectedly, and when I returned, both you and Sandro, the doorman, had disappeared. I was frantic and became even more so when I found Sandro in a storeroom, bound and gagged. He said he had been attacked by your friend Tom, who was dressed in a Pierrot costume."

"Tom?"

"The Pierrot gave Tom's name. Do you think Tom is capable of that sort of violence?"

Sally wondered. "I guess he is," she said slowly, "But I saw the Pierrot in your dining room, and I don't think it was Tom. He was too—I don't know—too quick."

Michele took the red shawl and wrapped it snugly around Sally's shoulders, the way he must have done with Antonia. They were ready to leave. Sally looked with foreboding at the massive front door, which a man stood waiting to open for them. "The Medusa came back," she said.

Once she had started, the story tumbled out—leaving her room at the hotel, hiding in the boat, being saved at the Fenice by the woman in white. Michele's eyes, behind the black Harlequin mask, were attentive. When she finished, he said, "He followed you even though you were wearing Antonia's disguise. That's very strange."

"Yes. I had the mask on and everything."

After a moment of thoughtfulness, Michele gave her a hearty clap on the back. "We shall defy the Medusa, and walk home together with stout hearts," he said. "No monster would dare attack the two of us."

Sally wanted to tell him it wasn't a joke, but at the same time she felt cheered by his mock courage. She took his arm, and they emerged into the rainy night.

There was no sign of the Medusa. As they walked, Michele said, "I have a question to ask you."

"What?"

"If you weren't abducted, why did you leave?"

Why had she left? At first, Sally could barely remember. She had left because she thought Michele had stolen Brian's letters. She had heard him quoting one of them to Jean-Pierre. Then the Pierrot had terrified her. For now, she limited herself to saying, "I was scared when I saw the Pierrot. I didn't know what was going on, so I wanted to get out."

"How could anyone blame you?" Michele said. "And yet, Sally, I must tell you that you were not wise. I thought you had been kidnapped, and notified the police. The police, instead of taking my view, became suspicious that you had run away out of guilt—possibly with the help of the Pierrot who attacked Sandro. That was bad enough. Now, things are worse. I heard only a short while ago that they have received a letter accusing you of Brian's murder."

FRANCINE WAITS

SEETHING WITH frustration, Francine lit another cigarette. On the murmuring black-and-white screen, a fashionably dressed man and woman spoke intently to one another. The man gave the woman a bouquet of roses, and the woman's eyes brimmed with tears.

The young man in the blue smock shifted in his chair, his eyes focused on the television set. The older man with the bandaged head snored on the sofa. Francine was tempted to get up and run out of the room and up the stairs, but she restrained herself. On the screen, the woman flung the bouquet down and turned her back on the man.

Seeing Michele Zanon had become a project infinitely more difficult than Francine had anticipated. First, he was out. Second, he was out. Third, he had returned, but was about to go out. On that occasion, she had actually managed to see him briefly as he rushed through the ground-floor room in his Harlequin costume, an overcoat thrown over his shoulders. He had greeted her warmly, but seemed distracted.

"I heard you were asking for me," he said. "Certainly

we must talk, but at the moment—"

"It is important."

"Yes, of course." He glanced around. "Could you possibly wait here? You'll be warm and dry at least, and Sandro and his son will entertain you. I'll be back as soon as possible."

Francine had wondered why she couldn't wait upstairs, which would have suited her intentions perfectly, and she cursed herself for not asking. As it was, she had now spent a considerable part of the evening in the doorkeeper's lounge, watching Italian television. Far from entertaining her, neither of her companions spoke either English or French. She couldn't have sworn they spoke anything, judging from the extremely few words they had exchanged.

Francine thought of Ursula and gritted her teeth. Ursula would never believe Michele had been out. She would be convinced that Francine and Michele had spent the evening in passionate embraces, and there would be another tiresome, dreadful scene. Perhaps it was time for Francine's association with Ursula to end. Francine wondered if she could get her things out of Ursula's apartment without having to see her.

On the screen, the woman was sitting on a balcony overlooking the sea. She looked melancholy. Francine detested the woman, just as she detested this room and the two men in it, and the foul-tasting cigarette she was smoking. If only the young man would go to sleep, as his father so noisily had, Francine could slip out the door and up the stairs. She glanced at the young man again. He was riveted to this idiotic program and obviously in no danger of nodding off.

Francine was fed up. She ground out her cigarette and stood. Then she heard the outside door open.

The young doorman left the lounge swiftly, and the older one groaned and sat up, putting his hand to his head. Francine moved to the door and peered out. Michele had come

284

in, and with him was the señorita—Sally. Sally was looking around in an apprehensive way. Francine didn't want to meet Sally, especially now, and she hoped Michele wouldn't call her to join them.

He didn't. He had a short conversation with the doorman, and then he and Sally started up the stairs. The young man reentered the lounge and nodded at Francine. He pointed upward and said, *"Momento.* Okay, *Signorina?"*

Fine. Francine would have preferred a different scenario, but she would carry on. On the screen, the man and woman were locked in a passionate embrace. Francine watched as she stood waiting for the summons to ascend.

ROLF IN HIDING

ROLF CROUCHED at the top of the narrow, barrel-vaulted staircase, away from the faint illumination from the floor below. He heard Count Zanon's voice. When another, fainter, voice made a soft reply, his stomach lurched. Sally, at last.

He had been almost ready to give up. The dizzying charge he had felt from getting inside, being able to wander around stealthily like a menacing and silent animal, lasted for a while. Pulse racing, he had moved from room to room—listening, smelling, exploring. He had located a woman, the housekeeper he presumed, in the kitchen and had smelled the coffee she was making, heard her sigh as she sat down to drink a cup. She had never glanced toward the pantry doorway where Rolf, in his devil mask, stood motionless, indistinguishable from the shadows. Rolf had left her drinking coffee, still unaware, and continued his exploration. He had found the salon, with its paintings and silk-covered furniture and wall of bull's-eye glass, and from there he moved to the dining room, where he had seen Sally earlier. He had been tingling, thinking at any time he could see her again, but except for the housekeeper and the doorman below, the palazzo seemed deserted. He drifted on through the half-light cast by small lamps in corners.

He did find Sally's room. At first he hadn't believed it was hers because the closet was filled with obviously expensive clothes Sally would never have worn, but then he spotted, on a hanger, her awful sweater with the geese flying in front of the moon. Rolf ran his hands over the sweater, and his breath came faster. He took handfuls of it and squeezed hard, biting his lip.

Now he knew where to find her when she came back, when the time was right. He had been moving down the hall again when he heard footsteps coming up the stairs.

That time, Count Zanon had returned alone. Luckily, Rolf had already located this secondary staircase leading to a more modest higher floor. He climbed, and heard Michele calling, "Maria!"

The count was back, but where was Sally? Rolf had waited at the top of the stairs, heard the count talking with Maria, heard the telephone ring several times. Rolf couldn't understand what Michele was saying, but he thought he heard a note of consternation in Michele's voice. Rolf could now, if he wanted, confront Michele, have it out with him, make him sorry he'd been so cavalier. He could, but he didn't want to move too soon. Sally was the one he wanted. He'd wait for Sally.

Eventually, Michele had gone out again, and Rolf began to wonder whether something had gone awry, if Sally were staying elsewhere. Then he reminded himself that her clothes were still in the room below and told himself to be patient.

He had been patient, and now she'd arrived. Rolf strained to catch a glimpse of her and couldn't, but he heard her footsteps. He had noted, when he was in her bedroom, that the door couldn't be locked. His energy came flooding back. Now it wouldn't be long at all.

TWO NUNS

THE HEM of the nun's habit was heavy with water, and when Tom walked, it dragged against his pants legs. He couldn't believe he had left brandy and a roaring fire for this. He hadn't had to do it. He had been more than kind to Ursula already. But if he'd said no, he knew Ursula would come by herself. Since, for his own reasons, he wanted to visit the palazzo, it had seemed easier to go along with her plan.

Ursula was setting quite a pace. She was better able to handle these damn skirts. Every time she got several steps ahead, she turned around to see where Tom was, as if she were afraid he'd duck into an alley and take off, which maybe he should.

She turned now, her wimple fluttering, her whorish mask gleaming at him through the rain. Tom hoped he didn't look as ridiculous as she did, but he knew the hope was vain, since his costume was the twin of hers. What in hell would Count Zanon think of him, showing up at this time of night in this garb? Tom's head throbbed and he regretted, not for the first time, the brandy that had gotten him into this.

Ursula, her spirits apparently restored, had presented the idea as a bit of a lark. Tom had protested, he knew he had. "Why do *I* have to be a nun?" he remembered asking.

"It's the only costume I have that will fit you. You can wear it over your clothes," Ursula wheedled. "A friend and I wore them last year. It's funny. A funny joke."

Hilarious. Tom stumbled as the wet skirts tangled with his pants leg. He thought of Stefan. If Stefan ever heard about his father dressing up as a nun, Tom would die. The only saving grace was this: Zipped up in Tom's jacket, below the nun's habit, was his beautiful notebook. Every time its corner dug into his rib cage, he was reminded of the work he was about to undertake.

The closer they got to the palazzo, the deeper was Tom's disquiet. He wondered if the count would be angry at their disturbing his romantic interlude with Francine—if, indeed, that's what was going on. When Tom had broached this subject before they left Ursula's she shrugged airily and said, "He'll be delighted to see us. Michele loves to laugh and play. He loves Carnival. He dresses as Harlequin and plays jokes. He gets bored if things are slow."

She could be right, but in that case, why was she insisting that Tom ask to see the count, while she herself remained incognito? This part of the plan worried Tom most, but Ursula had steam-rollered his objections: "We are going to see what is happening and to make a surprise. I will be the surprise. It will be funny. You'll see."

Only an urgent need to talk with Francine and Count Zanon would have made Tom consent. He hoped he'd get a chance and not be pitched out on his ear. Ursula was beckoning. He picked up his skirts so he could walk faster.

A WATCHER AT THE ARCHWAY

JEAN-PIERRE stood at the edge of the Grand Canal, watching the gate of the Zanon palazzo through a stone archway. He saw two nuns approach the gate, then realized they weren't nuns at all, but revelers in nuns' costumes, wearing lascivious-looking masks. Jean-Pierre's lips stretched in a thin smile. Perhaps Count Zanon was giving a party. Jean-Pierre had seen him return not long before, dressed as Harlequin, accompanied by Sally in señorita costume. In the few moments he could see them, Jean-Pierre had leaned forward avidly, wishing he could touch them— touch Michele Zanon, the beloved of Jean-Pierre's beloved.

Jean-Pierre barely felt the rain, barely felt the hard, damp stone under his gloved hand. Behind him, the canal glimmered, lights from the palazzos reflected in the dark water. Occasionally, a vaporetto droned by. For the most part, the only sounds were of wind and water. *Slime is the agony of water. Desire is defined as trouble.* Jean-Pierre didn't feel tired, or cold, or hungry. He felt light, unmoored, as if he might float away.

To anchor himself, he fastened on memory. He wanted to think about Brian, but Brian's face kept remolding itself, becoming first Michele Zanon's, then Sally's, then Michele's again. Then it shimmered and became the face of Jean-Pierre's beloved dog, Hercule, killed by an automobile when Jean-Pierre was a child. Jean-Pierre stood in the window of the country house, looking at Hercule's fresh grave in the sunny garden below. The shutters were open, and bees tumbled in the trumpetvine flowers overhanging the window. Jean-Pierre looked down on the green tops of trees, tossing hypnotically in the light wind. He teetered forward and back, forward and back, and then there was a rushing sound, and his mother caught him around the waist and, crying his name in fear and anguish, pulled him from the ledge.

If Jean-Pierre had succeeded, he and Hercule could have rested in the garden together. Jean-Pierre would not have had to learn more about death. He leaned in the archway and watched the gate.

A TALK WITH
MICHELE

SALLY STOOD in the doorway of Antonia's room. She was cold. She had never felt so cold in her life, yet at the same time she thought she would suffocate. The thought that someone had written to the police accusing her of Brian's murder filled her with dread. How could she defend herself? Michele had found her next to Brian's body. She had dressed up and gone to Torcello hours after the murder. And, as Michele had pointed out, her leaving the palazzo tonight might be construed as running away. She looked guilty. She felt guilty, too, sick and heavy with guilt for everything wrong she'd ever done.

But not for killing Brian.

Sally didn't see what she could do to get out of this. She knew, though, of one necessary step she could take, and that was to have a serious talk with Michele. By allowing him to frighten and charm her, she had left too many questions unasked. She would ask them now.

She thought immediately of the baton at his belt, and wondered if he would hurt her if she pushed him. She wished she had a weapon in case he threatened her. She thought of Antonia's green umbrella. If it wasn't as good a weapon as Michele's baton, it was at least something to hold on to. She smiled grimly, thinking of the two of them bashing at each other with baton and umbrella. I won't go down without a fight, Mama.

Sally had seen Michele put the umbrella in a closet on the landing. She looked for it, but didn't find it at once. As she spotted it leaning in a corner, she also saw, behind a pair of sturdy wading boots, a limp bundle of white satin and black net. She had seen it before, knew what it was even as she fished it from the bottom of the closet. She unfolded the bundle and saw the mask and skullcap, the long, extravagant ruff and the white satin blouse and trousers of a Pierrot costume. She had no doubt this was the disguise worn by the Pierrot she had seen in the dining room this afternoon. Had it been Michele after all?

Sally rebundled the costume, picked up the umbrella, and went to find Michele.

He was in the salon. A glass of red wine on a table beside him glowed richly in the lamplight. He had taken off his mask and hat, and his hair was ruffled. "There you are," he said. "We must discuss what to do. It's a nuisance, but Francine is downstairs, waiting to see me, and—"

"I don't care about Francine," Sally said. She tossed the satin-and-net bundle in a chair. "Where did this come from?"

Michele raised his eyebrows. "Exactly where it came from I don't know, but I suspect it belonged to Jean-Pierre originally. It turned up in a storeroom on the ground floor. Our intruder must have left it there after attacking Sandro and frightening—and being frightened by—you. We didn't find it until after I talked with the police, so I put it in the closet to give to them."

He looked at her expectantly, as if waiting to see if his explanation met with her approval. He's having a good time, Sally thought. The Harlequin is in his element. She gripped the umbrella. "What did you do with the letters, Michele?" she said.

293

Did his face flush? In the lamplight it was difficult to tell. "Letters?"

"Letters Brian got. 'Desire is defined as trouble. Slime is the agony of water.' Something about fear and death. I found them, but the Medusa came after me and I dropped my bag. When you brought it to me, they were gone."

"So instead of blaming the Medusa, your obvious enemy, you blame me."

"You read them. I heard you say 'Slime is the agony of water' to Jean-Pierre."

He hesitated, then nodded approvingly. "Very good. You're right. I took them."

Sally's legs felt weak. She sat on the edge of the sofa, still clutching the umbrella. "But why?"

"Clues. I only glanced into your bag quickly, after I lost the Medusa, but they were so obviously clues, I thought I'd better take them." He sipped his wine and said, "My God, I forgot to offer you wine. Would you like some?"

Sally shook her head. She found it difficult to stop shaking her head. "What did you need with clues?" she said at last. "You aren't a policeman, are you?"

"No. Although I think I would have been a good one. I discovered that Rolf was wearing the mirror disguise. I found out, too, that Tom was ordered out of your hotel the night before the murder because he was acting suspiciously. And Francine—"

Sally wanted to cry. She put her hand to her face, and realized she was still wearing her mask. Wearily, she loosened it and took it off. "It isn't a game, Michele. It isn't something for you to play around with and impress Antonia."

Michele looked contrite, but Sally knew by now Michele could look any way he wanted to. "You're right," he said. He shifted in his chair. "I had another reason. I hope you won't hate me if I tell you the part I played in Brian's death."

THE MEDUSA POEM

SALLY SAT STILL. Michele looked spent, his face yellow-ish, his body shrunken beneath his exquisite costume. When he began to speak again, his voice was measured.

"You don't know how many times I've relived that evening with Brian in the *taverna,* wishing I had let it be," he said. "We had told our secrets to one another. He copied his poem about Medusa and gave it to me. We could have remembered each other always with warmth. That wasn't enough for me."

Suddenly, his face was flooded with color. "I wanted to be part of it!" he burst out. "I couldn't let something so interesting slip away. Can you understand me if I say it seemed too good to waste? I can sum it up most easily this way—I played the Harlequin."

"You mean—acted like a clown?"

"The Harlequin is much more than a clown! He is a trickster, a troublemaker, a manipulator who brings about confusion but stays aloof from it. The Harlequin is a very compelling image for me.

"So, in Harlequin fashion, I set out to cause trouble.

Your group's game, I reasoned, was already spoiled, so I would hurt nothing by meddling further. How much did the game mean to its participants? Would they leave it for an intriguing, mysterious summons? I typed out the poem—laboriously indeed, since I have never learned to type—and had a copy delivered to everyone in the group except you and Brian. I expected confusion, mistaken identity, farcical misunderstanding, perhaps even a bit of shouting —everything except what happened."

At last he's telling me something, Sally thought. All along, it was his game. I knew it was. "How did you know where people were staying?"

"That was easy enough. A few telephone calls. The only troublesome one was Rolf, but Brian had told me the name of the bistro where Rolf worked in Paris, so I called and asked for his Venice address. By midmorning, the poems were delivered. I was prepared for an amusing afternoon."

Michele rubbed his eyes with thumb and forefinger. "So Rolf, Tom, Francine, and Jean-Pierre received intriguing poems about Medusa. Jean-Pierre was the only one who knew the Medusa was Brian, but all of them would see the Medusa in the Piazza. What would they do? I intended to give them something to do and, at the same time, discover how compelling an impression I had made on Brian himself the night before. I wrote out an urgent message asking Brian to meet me and gave it to him in the Piazza."

"The game is over. Come see me now," Sally said. "It was in Brian's glove."

Michele nodded sadly. "Yes. I drew a map to show the meeting place. He answered my summons and left the Piazza."

Of course he did, Sally thought. Couldn't you make him follow you, if you wanted to? Isn't that your specialty? "I saw him leave, and went after him," she said.

"Yes. How did that happen? Did you see a copy of the poem after all?"

"No. I just recognized Brian and wondered what was going on."

"I myself left the Piazza and waited at the point I'd indicated on the map. It was enough out of the way, I thought, so crowds wouldn't add to what would obviously be a fine scene of confusion. I waited, and Brian didn't arrive."

Sally could hear rain splashing on the balcony outside. Rain seemed to have been falling forever, and she couldn't believe it would ever stop.

Michele said, "I became concerned after a time, although please understand that I never thought anything horrible had happened. I simply didn't want to miss the fun. I came searching, and I found you."

"Bending over Brian's body."

"Yes." He fell silent again, then breathed deeply and said, "So you see, I've wanted to do everything I could to make it right."

Everything except leave it alone. "Couldn't you just tell the police all this?"

He grimaced. "I couldn't. Antonia already thinks I'm completely irresponsible. If I were connected with such a thing, she would never—"

Sally was tired. She stood up. "Okay," she said.

"I thought if I could solve the crime—"

The telephone rang. Michele made an exasperated gesture and got up to answer it. While he was talking, Sally turned and left the room.

AN ALTERCATION

TOM HATED this even worse than he'd thought he would. He had never felt like such a jerk. To make it worse, Ursula kept jostling him and digging his ribs with her elbow, obviously trying to prompt him so he'd follow her plan to the letter. Tom cocked his own elbow and tried to jab back, but he didn't make contact.

Tom and Ursula were standing at Count Zanon's back door. Water poured off the eaves and rattled down the gutter pipes. A young man in a blue smock peered out while an older man with a bandaged head hovered behind him. The two were obviously accustomed to strange sights at odd hours, as neither showed surprise at seeing two salacious nuns on the doorstep.

As Ursula's elbow landed in his ribs again Tom said, "Michele Zanon, *per favore*."

The young man inclined his head politely and said something.

"He is asking what is your name," Ursula hissed to Tom.

Tom said his name.

The young man's jaw sagged, and he stepped back. The older man, on the contrary, leaned forward and spoke in a loud, interrogatory tone.

"He is asking your name again," whispered Ursula, sounding nonplussed.

Unnerved, Tom repeated his name, more loudly than he had intended.

The man with the bandaged head gave an angry, inarticulate roar. He pushed the young man out of the way, reached out and grabbed Tom's wimple and dragged Tom into the room. He shoved Tom into a corner and started to pound his head against the wall.

Tom began to flail. He pushed his assailant, who, still roaring, pushed Tom back. Tom fell against a bench, lost his footing, and bumped painfully to the floor. The man jumped on top of him.

Gasping and struggling, Tom became aware that other things were happening around them. Ursula was screaming. The young man was shouting and trying to pull Tom's assailant away. As the young man pulled on the older one's shirt, Tom managed to loosen the thick fingers from his throat. "Are you crazy?" he yelled furiously. As the man was hauled off him, Tom landed a punch and heard a satisfying click as the man's lower and upper teeth made contact.

"What the hell is going on?" Tom demanded as he staggered to his feet. His mask was askew, and he adjusted it, glaring at the man with the bandaged head, who seemed to have been considerably sobered by Tom's punch. "You want to fight, I'll show you a fight!"

He heard Ursula's voice, high-pitched, speaking rapid Italian. She was in a little side room, on the telephone. She made several vigorous, hysterical-sounding points before slamming the phone back into its wall cradle.

She turned to face the doormen, and delivered another stream of words which left both of them looking sheepish and apprehensive. Then she spoke to Tom. "I have told Michele that his doorman made a vicious, unprovoked attack on you," she said angrily. "He has asked that all of us see him upstairs."

ROLF SUCCEEDS

WITH SWELLING excitement, Rolf felt Sally struggling against him. It was beautiful, beautiful. The hysterical arch of her backbone, the shudders that seemed to come from her center and ripple outward, the pounding blood in her neck. It was as good as he'd hoped.

She was breathing in long, ragged snorts through her nose, because, of course, he'd gagged her first. That was the beauty of having investigated beforehand. He had known already that here in the closet was a rack of magnolia-scented scarves hanging like multicolored medieval banners. He had even chosen the ones he would use— royal blue with golden suns to gag her, cool sea-green chiffon to tie her hands. Now she could only tremble and arch away from him, her eyes staring and wide with the terror he had imagined so often.

Her hair was falling down. A drop of perspiration crept along one of her eyebrows. Rolf watched, fascinated, as it slid to the corner of her eye.

He had thought he would wait until the house was dark and quiet, but he hadn't been able to wait any longer.

When he heard her leave her room and go down the hall, he'd slipped downstairs. Crouched in her closet, he'd left the door open a little, and when she came in, very pensive, and tossed her hat on the bed, he had been watching. He had been ready, completely prepared, when she opened the closet door.

She was trying, clumsily, to kick him. He almost laughed aloud. *Give up, little girl.* Behind the devil mask, his face pulsed with heat. He pushed open the closet door and dragged her with him to the door of the bedroom. Now to get her out of here. He had thought of taking her upstairs, but if they missed her, they'd probably search the whole house. He didn't want to worry about that. Everything was going his way, that much was obvious, so he knew they'd get out.

She continued to pull and writhe. Rolf had another couple of scarves in his pocket, in case he needed to tie her ankles, too, but it would be a lot easier if he could make her walk. He opened the bedroom door a crack. Everything was quiet, but then Sally started to make a small gargling noise. Rolf closed the door softly. he dragged her to the center of the room and slapped her, medium hard, across the face, watching her eyes widen and then redden. "Shut up," he whispered hoarsely, as a couple of tears slid down her cheeks and soaked into the blue silk gag.

When he next opened the door, he heard faraway voices, and a few minutes later an army's worth of footsteps on the stairs. He shrank back and watched as four people, two masked nuns and the two doormen, filed down the hall.

Rolf couldn't believe his good luck. The downstairs door, at least for the moment, was unattended. As soon as the four had disappeared he frog-marched Sally into the hall. The two of them stumbled, practically plummeted, down the marble stairs.

They had reached the ground floor when Rolf heard pounding on the garden door. He stopped still. Now what?

Somebody, or perhaps more than one person, was out there. He was trapped.

He thought fleetingly of the storage rooms, but as quickly discarded the idea. He wanted out. Then he noticed the upended rowboat in the far corner, the oars standing against the wall. This room had two outside doors, after all—one to the garden, and one to the Grand Canal.

Surely somebody would be coming down, but Rolf didn't hear anyone yet. Maybe Count Zanon had had enough company for one evening. The door to the Canal was fastened with a long, heavy bolt. Rolf dragged against it, and it slid easily. The door swung open. Christ, the water was so high it was practically coming inside. He pushed Sally out onto the mossy stone stoop and said, "If you try to get away I'll shove you into the Canal."

Back inside, he dragged the boat to the door. In his highly excited state he thought it weighed nothing. He shoved it, and it slid over the mossy surface and nosed a few inches down and into the Canal. The oars under his arm, Rolf pulled the door shut. He grabbed Sally and shoved her into the boat, then jumped in himself. The boat rocked as he pushed them away from the stoop with his oar. He settled down, fixed the oars in the oarlocks, and began to row.

FRANCINE PIERROT

BREATHING HEAVILY, Francine stood, the bundled-up Pierrot costume in her arms, in a small but well-appointed bedroom. How had this happened? After her long wait she had had not even five minutes' conversation with Michele, and now she was hiding like a thief. She hurled the satin bundle at the bed, where it unfolded loosely. The mask, face down, rocked back and forth. She glared at it until it was still.

Francine had waited downstairs an outrageously long time after Michele and Sally ascended. At last she insisted, using sign language, that the doorman call Michele and ask if she could come up. She had been considerably mollified when he indicated that she could.

Michele, still in his Harlequin garb, had mollified Francine further by being very apologetic, albeit in a harried way. He begged her forgiveness and offered her wine, saying he'd had complicated family matters to attend to.

After that, matters deteriorated abruptly. There were noises from below, and then the telephone rang. Listening to Michele's end of the conversation, Francine could tell that something disturbing had happened. When he hung up he said, "How strange. Your friend Tom and Ursula, an acquaintance of mine, are downstairs, and they've had a terrible fight with Sandro and his son."

Francine jumped to her feet. "Ursula!"

"That's right, you know her, don't you? The two of you were at the Scoundrels' Ball together. Yes, she and Tom—"

Francine could imagine. Ursula, storming into the palazzo in search of Francine, had already injured the doormen. "Oh, God. Don't let her know I'm here," she cried.

Michele looked confused. "But she's coming upstairs now."

"No!" Francine blotted her face. She forced herself to say, "She thinks I'm having an affair with you. She'll make a horrible scene."

Michele looked, for an instant, as if he might laugh. He darted to a chair, picked up a black-and-white bundle, and pushed it into Francine's hands. "Go quickly," he said. "Change into this in one of the bedrooms. Avoid Antonia's, the second on the right, but any of the others will do. Then, if Ursula sees you leaving, you'll be just a friend in costume who came to have a Carnival drink." He led her through the dining room and pointed. Without thinking, Francine fled down the hall and through the nearest door.

So here she was, thwarted once again by Ursula. Tears of rage filled her eyes as she stared at the Pierrot costume. There was nothing to do but take Michele's suggestion and put it on.

The cap would be a problem. Francine would have to braid her frizzy and abundant hair and pin it up. She took comb and pins from her purse, parted her hair in the middle, and gave it an angry yank before she began to braid. After a moment her fingers slowed. She was back in Poitiers, and her mother was saying, "Be still, Francine, or you'll be late for school. What horrible hair you have!"

Francine continued to braid, her fingers leaden. The

palms of her hands stung the way they used to when *Maman* smacked them with the bristly side of the hairbrush. Her face in the mirror was that of a woebegone child.

Her hair secured, she pulled the satin trousers on over her jeans. The legs were far too long, falling in folds around her feet as she pulled in and tied the waist. She slipped the blouse over her head. It reached to her knees, and the sleeves fell past her fingertips. She felt like a little girl trying on her mother's clothes. Anxiety crashed in on her.

Francine wiped her eyes. This was absurd. Making an effort to get hold of herself, she pinned the skullcap over her braids, tied on the mask, rolled up her pants legs as best she could, and left the room.

In her disguise, makeshift as it was, she felt oddly safe. She could hear voices in the salon. In her head, also, she heard Michele's voice: Avoid Antonia's, the second on the right—

That door was standing ajar, and the room was dark.

Francine, it seemed, had had some luck at last. She knew, because she'd seen Sally entering it earlier, that this room was not Antonia's, but Sally's. She had assumed that Sally would be in it, but obviously Sally was elsewhere.

It was a risk, but it was also Francine's opportunity to salvage something from the appalling comedy of errors this evening had become. She had to take that opportunity.

Francine entered the room. She found the light switch, turned it on, and closed the door. She gazed around her at the carved furniture, the marble fireplace, the paintings, the silver-backed brushes on the dressing table, the half-open closet that revealed a row of brilliantly colored clothes.

Francine had an uncomfortable feeling that she might have been mistaken, that the woman in the señorita costume was Antonia, not Sally after all. Then she caught sight of Sally's tapestry handbag lying on a chair. She picked up the bag and began to go through it methodically.

She was briefly elated when she saw the folded paper, but it proved to be only a handwritten copy of the Medusa poem. Food for thought, but not what she was looking for. Francine put down the bag.

The drawers yielded nothing—a jumble of cosmetics, surely Antonia's. Antonia's silk lingerie, plus a little pile of cotton underpants that were just as surely Sally's. Francine went to the closet, feeling pressure mounting inside her. With every minute, the likelihood of Sally's return became greater.

In the closet, she saw the suitcases. Here was the answer. Feverishly, she turned one of them on its side and opened it. It was Brian's. What fantastic luck. Francine plunged her fingers into the side pockets, shook out the neatly folded sweaters and underwear. Totally intent on her task, she heard nothing. Only when Michele's hand touched her shoulder did she realize he had entered the room.

"You won't find what you are looking for here, but I may be able to help you," he said. "Shall we have the talk you wanted?"

MICHELE GETS
READY

I THOUGHT THEY were from you. I suspected you all along," Michele said. He was trying on his Harlequin mask, looking at his reflection in Antonia's dressing table mirror.

Francine sat sullenly on the bed. The four letters she had sent to Brian lay on the dressing table. *Desire is defined as trouble. Fear is a flight; it is a fainting. Slime is the agony of water. To be dead is to be a prey for the living.* She had been found out, and she wasn't going to be able to talk with Michele after all, because he was going out to look for Sally. She was filled with disgust.

"They're quotations from Sartre, aren't they? From *Being and Nothingness?*"

Francine nodded. "You know Sartre extremely well, to have guessed."

Michele positioned his bicorne hat. "I don't know Sartre at all, but I thought there was a literary feeling about them. They sounded threatening, but not like the normal sort of threat. Not like, 'Look out, I'm going to kill you.'"

"They weren't meant to be real threats. I only wanted to

put him off balance, reduce his arrogance." From the first, it had been a laborious, ill-fated effort. Francine had gotten an English translation of *Being and Nothingness* from the library. After days of intense inner debate, she had selected the quotations on the basis of brevity and ominous tone. She had then had to bribe Sophie, her landlady's daughter, with ice cream and nail polish and pieces of cheap jewelry to convince her to copy the quotations and address the envelopes. At the time, she had found it rather satisfying and had enjoyed seeing Brian grow jumpy and preoccupied.

Michele turned toward her, his disguise complete. "Very literary, and a bit passionless and hollow," he said. "I considered also that they might be quotations from Tom's book, which I know no better than *Being and Nothingness*. But Tom didn't react to the line I said to him."

"That's surely the only time Jean-Paul Sartre's work has been confused with Tom's," said Francine.

"So you sent the letters, and then Brian was murdered, and you were in the position of having sent him quasi threats. No wonder you wanted them back." Michele picked up the letters from the dressing table. He unbuttoned a front button of his diamond-patterned Harlequin jacket, tucked the letters inside, and refastened the jacket.

Francine didn't reply.

Michele looked around the room. "You didn't see Sally at all? Or hear her leave?"

"No."

"What has she done? She was so upset she didn't even take her bag with her."

"Michele—"

"Yes?"

"I have to know. What are you going to do?"

He stood in the doorway. "What am I going to do? I'm going to look for Sally." He sketched a wave, and left her.

A
MISUNDERSTANDING
UNRAVELED

TOM SAT in the salon, glowering at Ursula. This enterprise,
all her idea, had been every bit the disaster he had known it
would be. Because of her wild-assed notions, Tom had
been beaten up by a psychotic doorman and embarrassed in
front of Count Zanon. After the four of them came upstairs, the conversation had slipped in and out of Italian—
more in than out—and Tom hadn't completely grasped
what was going on. First, Ursula delivered a tirade. Then,
the man with the bandaged head spoke, haltingly at first
but gathering passion and volume as he went, casting accusatory glances at Tom. At some point Ursula jumped in
again, and the two of them talked, or, more accurately,
shouted, simultaneously for a while. The younger doorman, although initially deferential to his elders, had also
insisted on having his say, and since the other two hadn't
shut up, the duet became a trio. Through it all Count
Zanon listened with a bemused look on his face. When at
last he held his hand up for silence, they had heard the faint
sound of someone pounding on the door below.

The young man started to leave, but Michele stopped

him with a gesture. He turned to Tom. "I must ask you a question. Did you dress as Pierrot this afternoon, come here, announce your name, and savagely beat Sandro? And after you had knocked him unconscious, did you tie him up and gag him and leave him in the storeroom?"

Tom looked at the man with the bandaged head, who he guessed was Sandro. "Of course not!" he said indignantly. "I was never here before. I never saw him before."

Michele nodded. "And if you had, you would hardly return and boldly announce your name to your victim again. No, our Pierrot was someone else."

Michele spoke to Sandro. Sandro, still looking doubtful, came and stood in front of Tom. *"Scusi, Signor,"* he said.

"It's okay," Tom said.

The pounding started again, and both doormen got up. Michele, too, stood. "I'd better see what's going on. Will you wait for me here?"

That had been fifteen minutes or so ago. After they left, Ursula said, "So it was a mistake in identity. Not serious."

"Not serious at all," said Tom sarcastically. "Just a little beating."

"Yes," Ursula said. "And still we know nothing of Francine."

Tom lapsed into hostile silence. At least his notebook, which he could still feel prodding his rib cage, didn't seem to have suffered in the fray. He'd start work tomorrow, for sure.

Michele reentered the room. He had put on his Harlequin mask and hat. "I must leave you. I have been called away urgently," he said.

Tom couldn't believe it. After all the trouble Tom had been through, Michele was taking off. "But why?" he blurted, and then, to cover his consternation, "Did the person at the door have bad news?"

"The person at the door was no longer there when we arrived. No, this is something else. I must go. Forgive me. Ciao."

"Wait!" Tom cried, and Michele, halfway out the door, turned back, "I have to ask you," Tom blundered on. "You know the cops are looking for me. I wondered if you told them about—you know, what you heard—"

"About the bearded man who was ejected from Brian's hotel? The bearded man who is bearded no longer? No, I didn't. I suppose they are looking for you because I told them a man in a Pierrot costume, who gave your name, was here this afternoon. He attacked Sandro, and I believed he had abducted Sally as well."

"Oh," Tom said. As Michele moved away, Tom added, hoarsely, "I cheated, I admit that, but I didn't—"

He stopped talking, because Michele wasn't there any longer.

IN THE ROWBOAT

THE MAN in the devil mask leaned forward and back, forward and back, as they moved over the black water. Sally lay in the bottom of the boat watching. Sometimes they crossed a patch of light, and she could see drops of rain sliding in the creases of his mask, giving an impression of intense effort or intense grief. Mostly, it was dark, and she saw only a dark figure looming up and leaning back, the oars rattling in the oarlocks as he rowed.

She eased herself to a sitting position. Her hair was streaming, and Antonia's shawl, still around her shoulders where Michele had placed it when they left the masked ball, was sodden. She could see out, now, see that they were close to shore. They bobbed past lighted palazzos and dark ones. The water was very high, streaming over the walkways bordering the Canal, slapping at the water gates of the palazzos, shining under the infrequent streetlamps.

They were close to shore, but that was no good to Sally. Tied up as she was, if she jumped in, she would simply sink and drown.

She leaned her head against the side of the boat. The rain actually seemed to be letting up a little. A frigid wind gusted over her and left her quaking.

She hadn't been thinking about being attacked, there in Antonia's room. She had been thinking about Michele, about the story he had just told her. She had been wondering if, even now, he was lying. She hadn't been thinking of protecting herself from a black figure who hurled himself at her when she opened the closet door, whom she had barely glimpsed before she was his prisoner.

She moved her head from side to side. She wanted this gag off. If it were off, everything would be better. She felt the knot pressing into the back of her head. She moved her head from side to side again.

The man in the devil mask loomed forward, then leaned back. Forward, back. Sally moved her head again and felt that the silk knot was soft, loosened with rainwater. She drew her lips in as far as she could and tried, by moving her head, to scrape the knot down.

The first couple of tries, she missed the angle. She pushed at the cloth with her tongue. Was it a little looser? She scraped at the knot again, and this time discovered that she could catch it against the rim of the boat. She did that a couple of times, using gentle pressure, and the scarf fell and settled wetly around her neck.

He hadn't noticed. Now she could scream, but she quickly decided that would be a mistake. She could scream, and somebody might hear her, and even if they did, he could throw her overboard or choke her before she could be saved. She wouldn't scream. She'd work on freeing her hands.

She had only begun to test the strength of the chiffon scarf binding her wrists when they passed a brilliantly illuminated palazzo. Music floated out from it, and the boat was surrounded by music and light. Sally froze and turned her head to one side, hoping he wouldn't look at her. The rhythmic sound of the oars stopped. Reluctantly, she faced him. In that moment, she saw that the man in the devil mask was Rolf.

His eyes gleamed. He leaned toward her, reaching for the gag, and she scrambled backward and said, "No! Don't put it on again! Please!"

She thought he laughed. He leaned back, picked up the oars, and started rowing again.

Michele said Rolf was the mirror-man Sally had seen leaning over Brian's body. Michele said Rolf had killed Brian, thinking Brian was Sally. Maybe he had, and now he was going to try again. Day after day, at the Café du Coin, he had watched her, and she had never understood why.

Sally cleared her throat. "Rolf," she said.

He stopped rowing. He shifted his weight toward her and she cowered back. In his eyes she saw an eerie avidity.

He likes me to be scared, Sally thought. That's what he wants. She straightened her backbone. "I know it's you," she said, trying to make her voice steady and strong.

He began rowing again. Shortly, they came to the entrance of a side canal. Rolf turned the boat, and they glided down the narrow black waterway, so full it was licking over its edges. "Talk to me," Sally said. "If you're going to kill me, tell me why."

They were coming to an arched bridge. As they passed under it, Rolf caught the stone edge of the bridge with his hand and stopped the boat. It was very dark. Faint reflections from the water played on the bridge's underside. Rolf's end of the boat rested at the canal's edge, while Sally's stuck out in the water.

"I wasn't going to kill you. That wasn't the idea," Rolf said.

Sally could have wept with relief that he'd spoken. She worked at the scarf binding her wrists. "What was the idea then?"

"I don't have trouble with women. Not a bit," he said in a boastful tone.

315

She pulled at the chiffon. It was still tight. She set her jaw and pulled again.

"It's not that I have trouble." His voice was louder, querulous.

"I don't imagine you do," said Sally in a soothing tone.

"I didn't mean to hurt her. I told her I wasn't going to."

Sally's wrists felt raw. She stopped twisting them and said, "Her? Are you talking about Brian?"

He guffawed harshly. "Brian? What do you mean?"

"I mean—the Medusa? Is that who you didn't want to hurt?"

"The Medusa? Are you crazy?"

The scarf had slipped down enough so she could pick at the knot with the tops of her fingers. "I just meant—"

Rolf leaned toward her, or she sensed he did. "I thought the Medusa was you," he said.

"No. It was Brian."

"Yeah. That's why the Medusa was strong enough to grab the staff away from me. Because it was Brian and not you."

"The Medusa grabbed the staff?"

"Oh, I said something about 'Changes trusting friends into people alone,' and he grabbed the staff. So he's holding the staff, with the mirror on the end, and I tried to grab it back, and he wrestled it away from me, and then somebody jumped on me from behind and started hitting me. I couldn't see because of that damn mirror-face; all I could see was the mirror on the staff, and it flashed bright and blinded me. It was two against one, and I couldn't see, so I ran."

Sally's hands were free. "You don't know who jumped on you?"

"No. I thought it must have been Brian, and he was hitting me because you and I were fighting. I was really pissed off. A little later I went back to get the staff, and I saw the Medusa in the canal. Then a loony-looking bride saw me from across the canal, and I took off."

Sally wondered whether to tell him she had been a corpse, not a bride, but decided to let it go. "You didn't hit the Medusa with the staff?"

"Shit, no. I didn't get a chance."

After a moment's silence, Sally said, "But why did you come after me?"

"Because of something else. Something else."

He sounded more calm and sane now. Sally wondered if she should risk trying to get away. Maybe she could talk him out of whatever he had in mind. If she couldn't, she'd have to get past him somehow.

She was still trying to decide when a shadowy figure appeared behind Rolf's head. She could just make out that it wore a black bicorn hat and a diamond-patterned costume. It raised a weapon—a wooden baton?—and brought it down on Rolf's skull with a decisive thud. Sally cried out, and the Harlequin hit Rolf again. Rolf fell to his knees, then slumped forward and lay motionless at Sally's feet.

SALLY AND
THE HARLEQUIN

How DID you find me?" Sally said. She was shaking. She cooled her burning wrists with the dripping ruffles of Antonia's skirt.

The Harlequin didn't answer. He put his white-gloved finger to his lips in a hushing gesture. He stepped into the boat, and it rocked and slipped farther beneath the bridge.

Sally lowered her voice, but her sense of release wouldn't let her stop talking. She had an infinite number of things to say. She looked down at the motionless black lump that was Rolf. "I don't know if he was going to kill me. He said what he was doing was connected to something else. Maybe you heard that part?"

Sally hesitated. The Harlequin sat down, but said nothing.

"He didn't kill Brian, either," she went on. "I'm pretty sure I know who did it, now. I'll tell you something. Don't get mad, but for a long time I thought it was probably you." A choking sound escaped from her throat. She rushed on, "You're different from anybody I ever knew. Where I come from, the men—don't take offense at this, but they aren't like you at all."

The Harlequin gave no sign that he had taken offense.

"I wondered a lot about you," Sally said. "You're good at getting people to love you, I can see that. What I can't see is if you care about them at all. Even Antonia. The way you talk about it, it sounds as if you're pretending. And the way you played with Brian and the rest of them . . ."

Her voice trailed off. She wanted to stop this, but at the same time, she needed to go on. They were drifting slowly beneath the bridge. In the light of a street lamp ahead she could see water curling over the sidewalk. "Remember when you and I danced?" she said. "It was almost as if we were one person. I didn't imagine that, did I? You know, the best way I can explain it is to say I felt as though I had power. A lot of power. And you did, too, and we were using it together."

How could she say it? "I felt something strong for you. I don't know what it was, but it's more than I ever felt for Brian."

The Harlequin made no response. Sally bowed her head. "I'm so sorry about Brian. Imagine how he must have hated himself. *The woman whose visage turns others to stone*. The funny thing is, I don't think I even knew him that well, but the minute I saw him in that Medusa costume, I was positive it was Brian, in a way I can't put into words. And it made me so sad."

The Harlequin shifted his weight. The boat rocked. They had passed under the bridge now, and the light rain that continued to fall wet Sally's face. The boat bumped and rubbed against the edge of the canal. All at once the Harlequin was moving toward her, the wooden baton still in his hand. As he raised it to strike, Sally threw herself to one side and felt wet stone slipping beneath her fingers.

ACQUA ALTA

THE BATON smashed solidly, decisively, against the side of the boat, which tipped dangerously as Sally tried to clamber out. The edge of the canal was an inch or two under water and the boat's violent motion washed more water over it. Sally struggled to her knees and flung her upper body onto the swimming pavement. She kicked herself free of the boat, her legs and skirt dragging in the icy water and managed to get a knee onto the edge. An oar cut through the air beside her head and hit the pavement with a shivering blow. Sally dragged herself up onto the pavement and struggled to her feet.

The Harlequin stood in the rocking boat, close enough to jump to shore. She ran, splashing along the walkway, her brain paralyzed with shock. Moments later, she heard him behind her.

Her boots squelching, wet clothes clinging, she stumbled through the twisting streets. He wasn't far behind. He'd surely catch her, light on his feet as he was.

Her breath was short, her side beginning to hurt. As she became more exhausted, she began, insidiously, not to care whether he caught her or not. Everybody seemed to want her dead. Let him kill her, get it over with. Why was she struggling so hard to stay alive, running through this dark, nightmarish labyrinth? Where did she think she was going? She had no friend, no haven, no home.

Sally thought of Otis Miller. She saw Otis Miller, from Eufaula, Alabama, behind the desk at his hotel. Otis liked her. Otis would help her, if she could only find him.

Surprisingly, the Harlequin's steps behind her seemed to be slowing. Sally entered a *campo*. If she were going to find Otis, she had to get her bearings. She glanced around frantically, trying to figure out where she was and which way to go.

Suddenly, a hideous howling cut through the air. All Venice seemed to be howling. Sally froze, at bay before the cacophony, which at first she assumed was directly related to her own troubles.

When she realized it was sirens, she also realized that she had, for a moment or two, stopped running. The Harlequin, perhaps also immobilized by the sudden noise had not yet come into the *campo*. Off to one side was a *sottoportego,* one of the low, covered passages that led from one street to another. That might be a place to catch her breath. She ducked into it and pressed close to the wall.

Almost immediately, he appeared. The sirens continued. The two of them seemed encased in an envelope of noise. Now he wouldn't have the clue of her footsteps to guide him. She edged to the other end of the *sottoportego* and looked out. She had a general idea of where the Piazza was. If she could get there, she knew she could find Otis Miller's hotel.

She slipped out of the passage and started to run again, and, as abruptly as they had begun, the sirens stopped. Venice was dead quiet except for the reverberating thuds of Sally's footsteps—and, almost immediately, the Harlequin's as well.

The way began to look familiar. The square in front of

the San Moisè Church was under water. She splashed across it, and heard the Harlequin splashing behind her.

On the street beside the San Moisè, Sally kept to the narrow swath of pavement above the level of the water. She was close to the Piazza now. Otis Miller's hotel was on the other side. She careened past closed shops displaying shoes, glassware, porcelain masks of Pierrot and Harlequin.

The Piazza was a cold, dark lake. She rushed into it calf-deep before she could stop herself. Opposite her, at the other end, stood the Basilica, ghosts of its domes floating on the water. Mindlessly, she pushed toward it, fighting the water's freezing drag against her legs. She had gone only a few feet before she saw that the Harlequin had outflanked her and was watching her from the arcade of the Procuratie Nuove. She was wading through the deepest part when she could have gone through the shallower water at the top of the steps.

She backed away, but the Harlequin leapt toward her. She heard his breath wheeze as they shoved and grappled.

He lurched against her and lost his footing. As the two of them went down, she felt under her own feet the submerged bottle that had tripped him. They fell with a splash. He was underneath, and she felt the breath go out of him.

Frigid water darkened the diamond patterns on his costume. She pushed down on his neck. His hat slipped off and floated near them, riding the waves of their struggle.

Water washed over the black mask with its prominent brows, flowed into the holes where his eyes stared. She pushed down harder, and his body convulsed and went limp.

She would drag him to the steps. She didn't want him to drown. She had pulled herself to her knees and raised his head when she heard someone calling her name.

SALLY ANSWERS

SALLY SAT on the pavement of the Procuratie Nuove, gazing at the drowned Piazza. A breeze ruffled the waters where a bicorn hat still floated.

"My God, I am so stupid," said Michele.

Sally didn't reply. Despite being wet through, she didn't feel cold. She didn't feel anything.

Jean-Pierre retched and pushed himself up on one elbow. Water ran out of his mouth and splattered on the stones.

"It isn't the same costume at all," Sally said.

"His Harlequin disguise? It's a common one you can buy anywhere. But all of them look very much alike."

Especially when you see what you want to see, Sally thought. So instead of Jean-Pierre, I saw Michele. When you figure that in, it makes sense.

The police would be arriving soon. Michele had hailed a passerby, his shoulders hunched against the early morning cold, and asked him to bring them.

Michele dangled his own Harlequin mask and hat from his fingers. "I was wrong about everything," he said, "I thought I could solve it. I was certain I could."

Sally looked at him. He was the picture of dejection—head bent, eyes downcast, shoulders curved forward gracefully. It was a perfect presentation. "Do you ever do anything but play, Michele?" she asked.

His shoulders lifted in an almost imperceptible shrug. "I don't know."

"You enjoy messing around and stirring things up, but you don't want to take the consequences." The bitterness in her tone came from the knowledge that, even now, if she could dance with him again at a Venetian masked ball, she would do it gladly. "You don't care how much trouble you cause, do you?"

He winced, but his glance held a flicker of defiance. "Be fair, Sally. I wanted to put everything right. I did a bad job of it, but I tried."

"You wanted something else, too," Sally said.

"Yes?"

"You wanted something to do."

He said, almost eagerly, "I needed to fill up my life. It was Carnival. Things should happen at Carnival. If they go on just the same, there's no reason for Carnival at all."

They were silent. Across the way, a group of men arrived and began moving planks and metal stands. "They are putting up platforms for people to walk on during the *acqua alta*," Michele said.

"Is that what the sirens were about?"

"Yes. To warn everyone. By tonight, it will have receded. Until the next one."

The sky was brightening, and the wind picked up.

Jean-Pierre whispered, "Sally." She looked down at him. His pale face was mottled with bruises. "Tell me," he said. She bent to hear him. "Did Brian make love to you again, ever, after he fell in love with me?" he asked.

Sally remembered the night before Brian's death—his breath smelling of wine, his body sliding into hers. She knew only one answer would see Jean-Pierre through what he was going to face. He had killed Brian, and had tried to kill her as well. Still, she gave him what he needed. "No. Never."

Jean-Pierre's face relaxed a little. Sally didn't want to look at him, didn't want to see what love could do. She put her head on her knees. In a few minutes she heard voices and footsteps. The police had arrived.

A RECONCILIATION

YOU HAVE LIED to me at every opportunity," said Ursula.
The look on her face was so ridiculously tragic that Francine wished she would put on the equally ridiculous mask
she held in her hand.

"What have I done to deserve such treatment?" Ursula
continued. She ticked off her points on her fingers. "I have
given you a place to stay. I have translated, copied, and
delivered your silly letter to the police. I have given you
my deepest, most profound—"

Her voice broke, and she took a swallow of Michele's
red wine. They were in the salon of the Zanon palazzo.
Francine stared at the toes of her shoes, which just peeked
out from the white satin folds of the Pierrot trousers.

Ursula's reaction when she found Francine sitting on the
bed in Antonia's bedroom had been utterly predictable.
Fired with suspicion as she was, the Pierrot costume Francine wore hadn't fooled her for an instant. "So here you
are!" she cried. "Dressed up to play funny games with Michele! Is this how a murder investigation is conducted?"

Now, Francine judged that the scene had almost run its course. It was time for her to think of some palliative explanation, so Ursula could forgive her and they could go on.

"Your other lovers turn up at my door, making scenes," Ursula said. "This latest one, poor Tom. You can't imagine how he has suffered. Only *I* can imagine."

Francine looked around. "Yes, Tom was here, wasn't he? Where is he?"

Ursula gave a dismissive wave. "He said he had work to do. He's in the library." She blotted her eyes and went on, "And the other lover, the brutal one. And now Michele—"

Francine finally broke. She threw the Pierrot mask to the floor and said, "I am sick of this! You have whined at me, dogged my footsteps, humiliated me! I can't stand any more! Leave me alone!"

Ursula pulled herself up in an attitude of immense hauteur. "Very well," she said coldly. "And when the police want to know who wrote a lying letter accusing an innocent woman of murder, they will surely be interested in what I have to tell them."

"Tell them! Tell them!" said Francine. "I don't care what you do!"

With exaggerated dignity, Ursula nodded once and left the room. A few minutes later, Francine heard her talking with Tom as the two of them descended.

Francine sat until her fury cooled. She began to wish she hadn't been so hasty with Ursula. When Ursula spoke of telling the police about the anonymous letter, she had sounded sincere. Francine was already in some trouble, she feared, because of the letters she had sent to Brian. If the police learned of this one also, they were likely to be even more annoyed. Francine got up. She wondered if she should approach Ursula tonight or wait until morning.

When she went downstairs, however, a nun wearing a lascivious mask was sitting on a bench in the ground-floor room. The nun was holding a notebook bound in marble-ized paper. Francine forced herself to sound joyful. "So you waited. I'm glad," she said. She put her arms around the nun.

"Yes, I waited," Tom said. He sounded delighted. "I was really looking forward to seeing you tonight."

AFTER CARNIVAL

A FEW DAYS later, when the *acqua alta* had receded and
Carnival was over, Sally walked across Venice from Otis
Miller's hotel to the Zanon palazzo for tea. It was a gray,
wintry day, with a few snowflakes spiraling down. Sally's
parents had bought her a new coat with a fur collar and
new boots and a new dress. Sally hated to think how much
they had spent, but they kept wanting to buy her things.
Sally's hair was coiled in a chignon at the back of her neck,
and she was wearing her mother's gold earrings.

There was frost in the garden, lightly dusting the top of
the wellhead, dulling the ivy's green. Sandro let her in, and
she climbed the stairs to the salon, where Michele was
waiting. The circles under his eyes had deepened, and his
face seemed more lined, but when he said, "Sally! How
adorable you look," she saw that his charm hadn't diminished. He embraced her and said, "I am so glad you came
—so glad you were willing to come."

"I wanted to."

He took her coat and poured tea for her and asked, "Are
you well?"

"I have nightmares. That's about all."

Only one nightmare, really. In it, she was running down a dark corridor toward Michele, and the closer she got to him the more terrified she became.

Michele's face darkened. Then he said, "I suppose you've heard that Jean-Pierre has been able to talk with the police."

She had heard, but something in her quailed at the thought of Jean-Pierre, and she hadn't wanted to listen. She said, "I know a little bit."

"He followed Brian from the Piazza, as all of you did, but Brian evaded everyone except Jean-Pierre. Brian was crouched down, I presume hiding, by the bridge when Rolf happened on him and they had their quarrel. Jean-Pierre pummeled Rolf. After Rolf ran away, Jean-Pierre and Brian fought bitterly, and Jean-Pierre lost control and killed him."

"Jean-Pierre loved Brian so much," Sally said. Her voice almost cracked, and she stopped talking and cleared her throat.

"Jean-Pierre is insane, you know," Michele said. "And yet, everything he did was extremely shrewd. Concocting a Medusa costume, then dressing as Harlequin—"

"All because he blamed me," Sally said. Jean-Pierre had threatened her as Medusa, then dressed as Harlequin to get near her. The thought of his hatred opened up a vast emptiness inside her. "He either followed me or knew where I was the whole time."

Restless, she got up and walked to the bull's-eye glass doors that opened onto the balcony, and stared through them at the distorted Canal. Michele followed her. He put his hand on her shoulder. "We won't talk about it."

She fumbled in her pocket for a tissue and blew her nose. "It's okay." After a minute she said, "Rolf hasn't regained consciousness."

"No. They aren't hopeful that he will."

"So I probably won't ever know what made him come after me."

"Perhaps not." Michele shook his head. "Rolf had a capacity for finding or causing trouble. The pounding on the door that night was the husband of a local woman with whom Rolf had had a brief affair. Under duress, the woman told her husband Rolf had a connection with me, and he got drunk and came here to have it out with me, or Rolf, or anyone. When we didn't answer the door, he went to sleep in the garden shed. Sandro found him the next day."

Sally smiled bleakly. "We all got drawn here, one way or another."

Michele touched her cheek. "Sally, will you ever forgive me for my part in this?"

She had known he would ask. "I haven't gotten it all sorted out," she said. "I can't say yes right now. Part of the reason is, I can't just let this go. It's too important. Something in me doesn't want to make it easy for you. I feel like I owe it to Brian, too, not to say it's all right. I mean, it *isn't* all right."

Her tone had been more vehement than she'd planned. Michele nodded, and compressed his lips. Sally burst out, "I had so many things to tell you! I *told* you, only—"

"Tell me," Michele said.

She shook her head. "I can't. Everything's different."

He put his arms around her, and she rested her face against his shoulder. When she pulled back, she said, "What's going to happen to you?"

He sighed. "The police are taking a lenient view. Antonia is not. This time, I believe she will really divorce me."

"I'm sorry."

"You should know by now that Harlequins are resilient," he said, but his face had a sunken look.

They finished their tea. They talked, and once or twice they laughed. Then Sally said her parents were expecting her, and Michele helped her with her coat, and they said good-bye.

A PUPPET SHOW

JEAN-PIERRE'S decay was complete. He tasted the same rising, rotten tide that had choked Brian. As Brian disinte-
grated, Jean-Pierre felt his own limbs loosen.

Jean-Pierre stood and sat, he answered questions if answers drifted to him, but he was with Brian. If a gray-
haired woman bent over him, her face dreadful with tears,
and called his name and said he was her son, Jean-Pierre
saw her through Brian's eyes, as a stranger. He would
rather be with Brian in this underwater life than be without
him. He would rather be here than be dead, because if he
died, Brian would die, too.

They asked him about the Rio della Madonna. Sometimes, through the tides, he could see the scene performed
in pantomime in a puppet theater he had passed in one of
the *campi*. Children sat in front, giggling as he made his
dejected entrance as Pierrot, the sad clown. Brian, the Medusa, hurled the mirror-staff to the ground and it broke, to
the children's delighted screams.

Pierrot slunk to the Medusa, supplicating, bending deep
and groveling, his every attitude saying, "Please," and "I'll

do anything," and "I can't bear it."

Please, Jean-Pierre almost spoke aloud, as Brian's string pulled the Medusa in expressions of "I'm sick of this," and "Leave me alone," and, worst of all, "No."

The Medusa's back was turned to Pierrot, the snakes shivering in violent rejection. The cringing Pierrot reached for the staff. In the puppet show, this part would be slow —grasping the staff, taking aim, rehearsing once, twice, three times for the blow as the children shrieked to the Medusa to beware. And at last, despite the cries of warning, the Medusa toppled like a toy, and water splashed behind the stage, and the spangled curtain fell despite the childish protests.

MINNESOTA

DEAD LEAVES clung to Rolf's shoes, and the air was damp and chilly. She was already there, waiting. He could see her, a bundled-up figure leaning against a tree. His stomach knotted.

Nobody could see them here, among the trees. The tip of her nose was red with the cold. She was talking, but her words meant nothing to Rolf. How could he possibly listen?

Rolf's hands were around her throat. He could feel her blood pulsing against his thumbs in a way that drove him wild.

Suddenly, her neck writhed out of his hands. He struggled to seize it again, but it twisted beyond his grasp. He wanted to scream, but he couldn't scream, only groan deep inside himself as he reached out.

He was in Minnesota, standing by a narrow, dark green river next to an arched stone bridge. Rolf knelt on the paving stones at the river's edge. He wept with relief that she had escaped.

BACK TO PARIS

Tom stood on the platform, his suitcase and Francine's in front of him. They had ten minutes before the train left, and Francine had decided she wanted some chocolate to eat on the way. He hoped she'd hurry back so he wouldn't have to schlepp the bags on the train by himself. He glanced at the door to the station. No sign of her. He wasn't sure she should be eating chocolate, anyway, considering how plump she was already, but he didn't think their relationship was at a stage where he could say anything.

"Relationship" could be too strong a word. He and Francine had spent a lot of time together during the past few days, including reasonably pleasant interludes in bed, but Tom had to admit that Francine hadn't lived up to his fantasies. Before, she had struck him as a woman who would know how to do a lot of secret and unexpected and delightful things, and she did know some interesting things to do, but it wasn't quite as Tom had pictured it. Tom wondered, too, if her heart were in it. She often seemed distracted, mechanical. Actually, it hadn't been very romantic. The most romantic thing had been that night at the palazzo, when she'd put her arms around him for the first time.

They didn't discuss Ursula, either. Tom hadn't spoken with Ursula since that night, although he suspected Francine had. Tom had seen Ursula once, at the fish market near the Rialto. With her were two slim, olive-skinned, dark-haired young women who might have been twins. One of them carried a wicker shopping basket and the other led a muzzled greyhound on a leash. Ursula, inspecting the fish, sea urchins, and freshly skinned eels with her companions, hadn't noticed Tom.

The past few days hadn't been easy. The worst part, for Tom, had been admitting to the police that he had cheated in the game and gotten himself kicked out of Brian's hotel for snooping around. Tom was glad that Francine, too, had something to confess. She'd sent Brian some quotations out of *Being and Nothingness* that could have been threats.

Francine had better get a move on. Tom took a couple of steps toward the waiting room, then walked back to the suitcases.

Neither Tom nor Francine had been allowed to visit Jean-Pierre. Tom tried to insist, saying it was necessary for his work, but he was given to understand that he couldn't expect any special consideration. Tom was undeterred. He was going to proceed with his book, and it was going to knock all of their socks off. So far, he hadn't written much, but when he got back to Paris he'd have the distance he needed. It would come together in no time.

Jean-Pierre's family had unleashed an army of lawyers. Tom figured he would be locked up in a fancy sanitarium, and that would be that.

Rolf still hadn't regained consciousness. Tom figured Rolf was a goner. Nobody would ever know why he'd attacked Sally. He *had* attacked her, though, and then Jean-Pierre had hit Rolf over the head because Jean-Pierre wanted to kill her instead of letting Rolf do whatever Rolf was doing.

Poor old Sally. Tom had to pity her. She had looked awfully strained, wandering around with the worried-appearing man and woman, so polite, hesitant, and out of place, who turned out to be her mother and father. Tom hadn't seen much of them.

Tom and Francine hadn't seen much of Michele, either. His wife, Antonia, had shown up when the scandal broke, and Tom had glimpsed her with him once. She was chic, blond, and pretty, wrapped in apricot-colored fur and looking pinched around the eyes and mouth. She probably wasn't happy about Michele's part in this mess.

Francine emerged from the station door and walked toward him, carrying a chocolate bar. She said, "Let's get on board," and they wrestled the suitcases into second-class smoking. Tom hefted them onto the overhead shelf. They sat down, and Francine unwrapped the candy bar and began to eat it without offering Tom a bite.

Tom looked out the window, impatient to get moving. Tonight he'd be back with Olga and Stefan. The thought didn't make him feel as leaden as it might've. Olga and Stefan, who'd been kept up-to-date by phone, would want to hear his account of the whole thing in person. Tom thought Stefan would probably be impressed by his book plans. Tom rubbed his chin and realized how infrequently he did that these days. He had decided to keep shaving after all. Now he hardly missed his beard.

Olga and Stefan. He'd see how it went. After all this, he would surely be able to get down to serious work. There was Francine, too. He'd see how it went. Tom settled himself in his seat. In a minute, maybe two, the train would lurch and they would be off.

EPILOGUE

MORE THAN A YEAR later, on a beautiful early-summer day in Paris, Sally was walking down the rue de Varenne on the way home from her job near the Invalides. Bright red geraniums hung lavishly from window boxes. The forbidding heavy iron doors that lined the sidewalks were flung open today, revealing sober, majestic facades and leafy courtyards dappled with sun. Passing one of these open doors, Sally looked into a courtyard and saw Michele.

She had no idea why he would be in Paris. He was standing under a spreading tree, deep in conversation with a man she didn't recognize. He wore a blue business suit with a yellow rosebud in the buttonhole. He didn't glance at her for the few moments she stood watching him before she began walking again.

Sally no longer lived in the apartment she had shared with Brian, but in a tiny flat on a quiet street in Montparnasse. She had not returned to Tallahassee after all, because she had realized it was too late. Her own life had begun. She worked for an American professor in Paris on sabbatical, filing things, proofreading his book, and when the French wasn't too complicated, looking up information he needed. Her French was improving, and she was able to help him more all the time. She was lucky to have the job. The professor and his wife had been kind to her in many ways. She had a few friends, too—mostly Americans, but one or two French people. She and Otis Miller kept in touch faithfully. She never saw Tom or Francine.

Sally was always careful. She thought a day might come, eventually, when she wouldn't want to be careful anymore. Now, she kept walking. It wasn't the time for her to see Michele.

She was living in Paris. Dangerous and extraordinary things had happened to her. She walked down the rue de Varenne through the early-summer afternoon.